Praise for *New York Times* bestselling author
CHRISTINE WARREN

DRIVE ME WILD

"Warren is back with another sexy, sassy romp, focusing this time on the oh-so-sensuous Rafael De Santos. As always, there is a great deal of humor, sizzling sex, and off-the-wall adventure in Warren's Others series, which makes for a truly lively, amusing read."   —*Romantic Times*

"Christine Warren sets the pages ablaze once again with *Drive Me Wild*!"   —*Joyfully Reviewed*

ON THE PROWL

"Christine Warren brings her blend of humor, romance, and thrilling mystery to *On the Prowl*."
                                                                          —*Fresh Fiction*

"Christine Warren has created an incredible, alluring world and then populated it with the most amazing heroes and heroines. Never a disappointment, Christine Warren continues to dazzle our senses with her books of the Oth.......   —*Single Titles*

NOT YOUR ORDINARY FAERIE TALE

"Warren has made a name for herself in the world of paranormal romance. She expertly mixes werewolves, vampires, and faeries to create another winning novel in The Others series. *Not Your Ordinary Faerie Tale* showcases Warren's talents for creating consistent characters with strong voices and placing them in a fantastical world."

—*Romantic Times*

"*Not Your Ordinary Faerie Tale* is a delightful read from the first word to the last. Christine Warren has created two amazing characters, given them an incredible plot, and laced the story with witty conversations, lots of snark, and a hefty portion of danger."

—*Single Titles*

"Christine Warren merges lust, laughter, and intrigue magnificently in her latest installment of The Others. *Not Your Ordinary Faerie Tale* is a fun and fast faerie adventure."

—*Joyfully Reviewed*

BLACK MAGIC WOMAN

"Excitement, passion, mystery, characters who thoroughly captivate, and a satisfying romance make [it] a must-read."

—*Romance Reviews Today*

"Will capture your senses and ensnare your imagination. Another great novel from Christine Warren."
—Single Titles

"Sexy, action-packed romance!" *—Joyfully Reviewed*

PRINCE CHARMING DOESN'T LIVE HERE

"Christine Warren's The Others novels are known for their humorous twists and turns of otherworldly creatures. Like her other Others novels, *Prince Charming Doesn't Live Here* is an excellently delicious story with great characterization."
—Fresh Fiction

BORN TO BE WILD

"Warren packs in lots of action and sexy sizzle."
—Romantic Times BOOKreviews

"Incredible." *—All About Romance*

"Warren takes readers for a wild ride."
—Night Owl Romance

"Another good addition to The Others series."
—Romance Junkies

"[A] sexy, engaging world . . . will leave you begging for more!"
—New York Times bestselling author Cheyenne McCray

BIG BAD WOLF

"In this world . . . there's no shortage of sexy sizzle."
—*Romantic Times BOOKreviews*

"Another hot and spicy novel from a master of paranormal romance." —*Night Owl Romance*

"Ms. Warren gives readers action and danger around each turn, sizzling romance, and humor to lighten each scene. *Big Bad Wolf* is a must-read."
—*Darque Reviews*

YOU'RE SO VEIN

"Filled with supernatural danger, excitement, and sarcastic humor." —*Darque Reviews*

"Five stars. This is an exciting, sexy book."
—*Affaire de Coeur*

"The sparks do fly!"—*Romantic Times BOOKreviews*

ONE BITE WITH A STRANGER

"Christine Warren has masterfully pulled together vampires, shape shifters, demons, and many 'Others' to create a tantalizing world of dark fantasies come to life. Way to go, Warren!" —*Night Owl Romance*

WALK ON THE WILD SIDE

"A seductive tale with strong chemistry, roiling emotions, steamy romance, and supernatural action. The fast-moving plot in *Walk on the Wild Side* will keep the readers' attention riveted through every page, and have them eagerly watching for the next installment." —*Darque Reviews*

HOWL AT THE MOON

"*Howl at the Moon* will tug at a wide range of emotions from beginning to end . . . Engaging banter, a strong emotional connection, and steamy love scenes. This talented author delivers real emotion which results in delightful interactions . . . and the realistic dialogue is stimulating. Christine Warren knows how to write a winner!"
—*Romance Junkies*

Also by Christine Warren

Anthologies

HUNGRY
LIKE A
WOLF

Christine Warren

St. Martin's Paperbacks

NOTE: If you purchased this book without a cover you should be aware that this book is stolen property. It was reported as "unsold and destroyed" to the publisher, and neither the author nor the publisher has received any payment for this "stripped book."

This is a work of fiction. All of the characters, organizations, and events portrayed in this novel are either products of the author's imagination or are used fictitiously.

HUNGRY LIKE A WOLF

Copyright © 2013 by Christine Warren.
Excerpt from *Heart of Stone* copyright © 2013 by Christine Warren.

All rights reserved.

For information address St. Martin's Press, 175 Fifth Avenue, New York, NY 10010.

ISBN: 978-0-312-35725-2

Printed in the United States of America

St. Martin's Paperbacks edition / July 2013

St. Martin's Paperbacks are published by St. Martin's Press, 175 Fifth Avenue, New York, NY 10010.

10 9 8 7 6 5 4 3 2 1

To all the amazing readers who have taken this journey with me, and wandered around in the world of the Others. I wouldn't be a writer today without all of you.
Thank you, from the bottom of my heart.

With special thanks to my editor, Monique Patterson, for discovering my work and deciding to share it with everyone else.
I'll never forget that.

One

Logan Hunter and Rafael De Santos strode up the wide granite steps to the front door of Vircolac's, braced to plunge headfirst into the heart of the enemy camp. Well, Logan was braced. Rafe's step had a suspiciously eager spring to it, and his expression looked more lazily amused than wary. He'd recently defected.

Few people had been more surprised than Logan when Rafe decided to take a mate, especially a human witch. Actually, Rafe might have been slightly more astonished, considering he'd spent most of his adolescent and adult life demonstrating where the expression "tomcatting around" came from. But he had taken a mate, and apparently it didn't matter to Rafe that he was supposed to be one of Logan's closest friends. In matters of marriage and mating, not even friends could be trusted.

"Last week they somehow managed to rig the door of Graham's office to lock from the outside." Logan held open the door for his companion and checked the hallway to be sure none of the perpetrators he was currently griping about lay in ambush. "Then they sent me in there to wait for him. As soon as I stepped inside, the door slammed shut and trapped me in there with Annie. Annie, of all people!"

Rafe grinned at Logan's obvious dismay. "I thought you liked Annie. She is a very attractive woman, after all. And intelligent. I would think she'd make some lucky Lupine a fine mate."

Logan growled. "I grew up with her, man. It would be like sniffing my sister."

"You and your pack mores. It's not like she's actually any blood relation to you."

"That's not the point."

"Right. Because the point is that you probably humiliated a beautiful and sensitive young woman by tearing down the office door just to get away from her. How do you think that made her feel, you insensitive clod?"

Logan scowled. "I didn't tear it down. I just kicked it in. But Annie knew it wasn't about her. She's cool with it. She's not interested in me, either."

"Right, puppy. She just smiled and thanked you for opening the door and told you to have a wonderful day."

Logan paused and remembered. "She told me to shove the door up my ass and shit splinters."

"Precisely. Logan, you need to learn that whether she's a werewolf, a shapeshifter, a witch, or a human, women are women. They all need to be flattered and coddled and made to feel special." Tipping the attendant who took their coats, Rafe led the way down the main hall and toward the club library. "It is a wonder to me that you've ever managed to get a woman to stand still long enough to take her clothes off."

"And that's such a sophisticated observation," the Lupine scoffed. "Don't bother to pretend with me, De Santos. Under that pampered, nancy-boy Casanova image you like to project, you're just as much an animal as I am."

"I might be an animal, my friend, but *I* am not a dog."

"Very funny. And it's *wolf,* Garfield. Not dog."

Rafe smiled a feline smile.

"You can't tell me all those single females didn't drive you crazy." Logan sniffed the air in the hall outside the library. His keen senses caught the faint but unmistakable odors of breast milk, perfume, and female skin, and his body went on high alert. Well, part of it went on high alert, the rest just went tense and frustrated.

Damn it.

Bracing himself, he clenched his jaw involuntarily as he reached out to open the door. "They were after you almost worse than me."

"They meant well."

"I don't care what they mean. I want them to leave me alone."

"Aren't you supposed to be happy about the

idea of finding a mate and settling down with one single female forever and ever and ever? You canines usually seem so taken with the idea."

Rafe slipped ahead of Logan and entered the room. The fire crackling in the hearth at the far wall cast a very becoming glow on the skin of the two women standing beside it. Logan shook his head as he saw his friend's gaze shift and fix on the one who looked like a curly-headed urchin. He was still getting used to that possessive gleam that sparked in Rafe's eyes every time they turned toward Tess Menzies De Santos.

"And you took to it just fine, Morris. But that doesn't mean I don't want to do my own finding, damn it." Logan had lowered his voice, and he looked carefully away from the women at the hearth. "Missy's friends just don't seem to understand that mating is a whole different ball game from just getting married. Maybe if they weren't all so . . . human."

Rafe shrugged. "Regina is not human. And Tess might technically qualify, but she is a cut above the average, you must admit."

"Regina has been Other for less time than it takes me to mark a fire hydrant. And Tess doesn't count. She's a witch. And she's taken."

"Damn right."

Logan heard the possessive note in Rafe's voice and watched the Felix stalk toward his wife. The Lupine fought the simultaneous urges to snicker and roll his eyes. A couple of months ago, Logan would have bet his left canine tooth that Rafe would never settle down with one woman, let alone one who wasn't a shapeshifter. Good thing for him no one had taken him up on that bet, because the marital bliss that followed Rafe and Tess around like a cloud would have meant some seriously tough hunting for Logan.

He still really didn't get it. Not that he had anything against taking a mate—he was Lupine, for God's sake—but he liked for there to be a certain sense of order to his world. And in his world, a Felix did not settle down with one woman and look happy about it. Of course, in the ideal version of his world, the only woman he'd wanted for himself in longer than he cared to think about didn't up and marry his best friend—who was also the pack alpha—either.

Shit.

Tearing his gaze away from the sweet, smiling face on the other side of the room and plugging his nose to the warm, milky scent of new motherhood that wafted from the same direction, Logan turned on his heel without bothering to say hello to the ladies. Damn Graham for getting to Missy first, and damn himself for caring. Graham Winters was like a brother to Logan. For all intents and purposes, the men *were* brothers, and Logan did not poach on his brother's territory. Even if the concept didn't go against every fiber of his loyal body, it also meant risking a fight to the death with an outcome that he honestly couldn't predict.

He swore once more and then again, quietly, because in this house, you never knew who might pick up on it. Some of the folks who frequented this club had sharper ears than he did, and that was kind of a scary thought. He took a firmer hold of his self-control and tried to beat back the restlessness that seemed to roil constantly inside him these days. He had been called to a meeting with his alpha about pack business, and he'd present a businesslike demeanor if it killed him. Graham did not need to know that his beta had the hots for his mate.

Graham kept an office on the first floor of Vircolac in the heart of the action. He said it helped him keep an eye on the happenings at the club, and when your clientele consisted mostly of werefolk, vampires, and other assorted creatures of the night, keeping an eye on things made a heck of a lot of sense. Technically, it should have been Logan's job as head of security, but Graham was the owner and the alpha, and that made him the boss. Logan suppressed the instinct to growl and stuffed back the newly ferocious tide of resentment. He could not let himself go there.

Puppy, you have got to get ahold of yourself. You are not the alpha here, and your best friend is. So quit trying to sniff on his wife and do your damned job.

He let himself into the outer office then paused outside the door of Graham's inner sanctum to take a deep breath. He repeated his new mantra a time or twelve. *Not mine. Not the woman, not the pack. Not mine.*

He took another breath and waited for the hair on his neck to settle back into place before he raised his hand to knock. He ignored the voice in the back of his head that pointed out how the settling was taking longer and longer to happen these days.

"Come on in."

Logan pushed open the door with his game face on. His brown eyes took in the office, empty except for Graham, and he met the other Lupine's gaze for a second before he shifted his own to stare politely over his alpha's shoulder. "Sorry I didn't come earlier today. I was at the gym until after two, and I didn't get your message until I got back."

"Don't worry about it." Graham pushed back in his chair and closed the folder he'd been working on. He waved Logan to a seat. "It was your day off. I didn't expect you to be on call."

Logan settled himself in the leather armchair that faced Graham's desk, but he didn't relax. Oh, he sprawled and stretched out just the way he always had, but relaxation was out of the question. On the inside, he remained coiled and tense, the way he always did these days, and he felt Graham's gaze on him. The sensation made his hackles rise, and he fought back the growl that wanted to rumble low in his chest.

Damn it, this is not happening. You are not challenging your alpha in his own damned home, moron, so shut up and play nice doggie. Now.

He clenched his teeth so hard, he thought he heard the grinding sound echo in the quiet office.

"All right. That's it." Graham leaned back until his chair threatened to tip over. He crossed his arms over his chest. "What the hell is your problem lately?"

"I don't have a problem."

"Right." Graham's eyes narrowed, and Logan looked at the alpha long enough to guess his own were probably sparking with an eerie amber light. "That's why in the past month you've been in four fights, broken three pieces of gym equipment, driven six waitresses to tears, and destroyed the door to my office. Because you don't have a problem."

"Right."

The nasty little voice inside Logan's head was telling him to go ahead, pick a fight. Let him and Graham have it out and finally see who deserved to be alpha over this pack. To hell with the Winters line, to hell with Silverback tradition. To hell with loyalty. Alpha was about strength and ruthlessness and power, and Logan had more than enough of it to make the pack his own.

Logan had to fight the urge to curl his lip and meet the alpha's gaze head-on, no more turning aside, no more avoiding the fight his wolf wanted so desperately to pick. His wolf wanted more, wanted a pack of its own, wanted to lead and rule and run at the front. His wolf knew it had the strength to be alpha on its own, and the role of second-in-command had started to feel more like a muzzle than a medal of honor.

The man in Logan hated that his wolf had begun to erode his relationship with the man he'd always called brother. That side of him, that voice was the one that screamed a denial every time the wolf began to growl and pace and look for a weak spot. Damn it, Graham was his best friend, the closest thing he had to family, closer than any other member of the pack. Logan would die for that man.

But damn it if he didn't really want to kill him right now.

"You know this can't go on forever." The alpha's voice rumbled deep, raising hackles. "Sooner or later, you won't be able to ignore it anymore. What happens then?"

Logan's lip curled, and he wrestled it back into place. "I don't know what you're talking about."

"Don't be an asshole. Don't lie to me, and don't act like I'm not supposed to figure it out. It's not like it's a surprise. I knew it would happen one day, because I know you."

Graham leaned forward and willed his friend to meet his gaze. Their gazes crashed together like two bighorn sheep on the top of a mountain. Logan could almost hear the echo.

"I know you, Logan, and I know what you're going through. We can find a way around it—"

"There's. No. Problem."

Silence descended, stretched thin, and finally snapped with a backlash that stung.

"Fine." Graham's voice indicated things were anything but. He sat back again and picked up a piece of paper, which he tossed across the desk to Logan. "You say you don't have a problem, that's terrific. Because I do."

Logan caught the letter in one hand, but didn't bother to glance at it. He snarled in satisfaction. "Perfect. Who do I get to kill?"

"No one. It's not that kind of problem."

Well, shit. Just when he could have used a little judicious bloodshed.

Suppressing another growl, Logan got up to pace around the office. The restlessness inside made it impossible for him to sit still for long. "Fine. Then what do you want me to do?"

"If you'd read the damned letter, you might have a clue. There's been a death in Connecticut. The White Paw Clan has lost its alpha."

That bit of news actually managed to get Logan's attention. He turned toward Graham with interest. "Ethan Tate is dead?" He paused, letting it sink in. "Challenge?"

Graham shook his head. "Cancer. And apparently he managed to hide it from the pack until the end."

Logan let out a low whistle. That was old-school wolf, and a hell of an accomplishment. In the old days, any sort of illness that might compromise an alpha's ability to lead would have been punished by a swift challenge and the likely death of the sick or wounded Lupine. Knowing that, the toughest alphas of the past would hide any sign of weakness, using whatever means necessary to camouflage their vulnerability and maintain control of their pack. But with an illness like cancer, it was damned difficult. Most Lupines could smell the taint of the disease and would have known immediately. He wondered how the old alpha had done it? Tate had been a tough old bird, but hiding cancer . . . ? That took balls.

"So no one guessed at all? Not even his beta?"

"That's probably one of the things that helped him fool everyone." Graham nodded to the letter in Logan's hand. "The e-mail I got is from his beta, who was also his daughter. She probably didn't want to think her father was ill, so she denied it, and that made it even easier for him to deceive everyone else."

A female beta? Female alphas and betas weren't unheard-of in the Lupine world, but they were few and far between, more like myths and legends than actual people. Boadicea had been a pack alpha, but Logan couldn't think of one more recent than that. The fact was, even if a female Lupine was ten times stronger than the average human male, a male Lupine was twice as strong as that. Females rarely managed to battle their way to the top of the pack structure, and when they did, they even more rarely managed to stay there. A male would always challenge, and males generally won. The old Lupine adage said, "A female alpha is a dead alpha."

Female betas occurred only marginally more often. Usually they won the position not through challenges, but by appointment, and they kept their places with cunning more often than with strength. Tate had obviously installed his daughter as his beta, either before or after learning of his illness. A wolf strong enough to hide cancer would sure as hell be strong enough to ensure no one protested his decision on that front, but with Tate gone, his daughter would now be fair game. Given the traditional Lupine pack structure and its basis in rule through strength, when a pack alpha died, the logical choice to take his place was usually his beta, the next strongest wolf in the pack, but when that wolf was a female . . . Well, all of a sudden the old rules didn't apply anymore.

Again, Logan felt a stirring of genuine interest, interest in something other than another man's mate or a violent coup d'état even he didn't really want to see happen.

"Do you think she can hold the pack together?" he asked.

Graham shrugged. "I have no idea. I haven't visited the White Paw since I first took the reins from my dad. Because they're one of the clans under the Silverback protection, I paid a courtesy visit. But she couldn't have been more than nine or ten at the time. I'm sure she was introduced, since she was Tate's daughter, but I didn't pay her much mind. She could have grown up to be Queen of the Amazons, but even if she did, all it would take is a strong male to bring her down."

Ironically enough, that wasn't a sexist comment. If any of the parties involved had been human it would have constituted cause for a new feminist revolution, but when it came to Lupines, it all boiled down to physiology. Lupine males had evolved to be physiologically stronger than females, by a pretty hefty margin. There was no such thing as a fair fight between the Lupine sexes.

"All right. So what's the situation right now?"

"Tate was supposed to be buried this morning, and according to the daughter, there were already two male pack members making noises about a challenge. One sounds like he's just a cub, but the other one might bear watching. His name is Darin Major, and apparently he bucked for the beta job before Tate appointed his daughter. History's only going to make things messier."

Logan growled a little at the thought of the males calling a young female beta to an alpha challenge. There were just some things a Lupine didn't do. Which was why females rarely became pack alpha or beta. Females mated with alphas and betas; they didn't become them. "You want me to make sure the challengers let her live?"

Graham shook his head. "Noises aren't the

same thing as actual challenges. What I need you to do is go up to the clan center and assess the situation. Tate's already been gone a couple of days, and if they buried him this morning, it may already be a moot point. As soon as he's in the ground, the laws state that it's open season on his job. The pack may already have a new alpha. But if the girl is still alive when you get up there, the situation gets a whole lot more interesting. I won't take the pack away from an alpha that can do the job, no matter what is or isn't between her legs. But if she can't hold her pack, I need to know. White Paw is too close for me to let just any wolf take it over. I need someone stable and trustworthy heading that pack. If it's not a Tate, I want an open challenge, and I'd have to oversee that myself to make sure the pack gets what it needs."

"Is that what the girl asked for? For you to guarantee a clean challenge?"

"Not exactly." Graham paused. "She asked for me to formally acknowledge her succession to alpha."

Logan couldn't help the eyebrow that shot up at that. "Does she think you saying, 'Go for it, princess,' would be enough to keep the challengers away?"

"It might scare off the weaker ones, and it surely couldn't hurt. Having the backing of the regional alpha makes her a strong candidate to lead a local pack," Graham pointed out, not with arrogance, but with the cool acknowledgment of the way the world worked. He was the highest-ranking alpha in the northeastern quadrant of the United States. He was stronger than almost every Lupine Logan had ever met. That was just the way things were.

But you're just as strong, the voice in Logan's hindbrain whispered. *You could rule a region just as well as Winters.*

Logan clenched his jaw and slammed a lid on the voice. Now was not the time. Now Graham was handing him a distraction on a silver platter, and damn if he wouldn't grab that sucker like a lifeline and tow himself all the way back to sanity. Maybe someone else's struggle for rank in her pack would keep him from worrying about his own need to lead.

"For how long?" Logan asked. "Even with your backing, it would take a female version of Genghis Khan to keep the title for more than a few months."

"I know. Hell, every Lupine on earth knows that. True female alphas come along as often as three-headed wolves." Graham shook his head. "I don't want to see a female in alpha challenge, not when it could be prevented. I checked the records. It hasn't happened in almost two hundred years for a damned good reason. The last woman who took a challenge ended up gang-raped and confined to her bed for nearly a month before she could even stand upright again. And she was widely acknowledged as the strongest female in five generations." The snarl that passed over Graham's face at that thought would have scared most people half to death. It just reminded Logan of why he considered this man his brother. "Tate's daughter can't be more than twenty-four or so, and I've never heard anyone but her own father mention her name. The chances that she's strong enough to be alpha are slim to none. She'll be like a rabbit in the lion's den. If I can keep that from happening, I will. Or rather, you will."

"Damn right." Logan growled again and finally glanced down at the printed e-mail in his hand. "Provided someone hasn't killed her already."

"Right. Provided that."

"So, if the girl is still alive, you also want me to make sure she doesn't get into trouble while I scope out who's likely to take Tate's place?"

"Yeah." Graham's grim expression said he didn't hold out much hope. But then again, neither did Logan. "And either way, I want you to keep an eye on the pack until the matter's settled."

Something about Graham's tone made Logan look up and meet the other man's gaze. He felt his mouth quirk in a reluctant smile. "What you want is to get me the hell out of your hair until I calm down, brother."

"There is that." Graham's expression turned rueful. "Look, I don't know how this is all going to play out, brother, but I'm hoping a week or two in the country will give you the space to settle your damned nerves or something. 'Cause you're starting to get on mine."

Logan clenched his teeth, drew a deep breath, and blew it out through his nose. "Hell, I'm starting to get on my own nerves. I don't blame you for making me go stand in the corner."

"It's not like that. You're the one I want handling this for me. Period. That would be true even if you were acting perfectly normal."

"But I'm not."

Graham didn't answer, and Logan flipped him an obscene gesture on his way out the door. Just because Graham was right, didn't mean Logan couldn't call him a dick.

Two

Honor Tate bolted through the front door of her home and straight into the bathroom. There, she proceeded to throw up her breakfast, her lunch, and several of her internal organs. It didn't help. The taste of blood in her mouth was strong and metallic. It should have been familiar. Instead, it was sickening—sweet and sticky—and it coated her tongue in a thick, persistent layer like an oil slick.

She clutched the rim of the toilet bowl and heaved again, so violently she almost missed the sound of footsteps padding across the wooden floor of the big cabin's great room.

"Honor? Honor, are you okay?"

She bit back a moan, her fingers clenching, as another dizzy wave of nausea swept through her. Her cousin's voice sounded as soft and concerned as always, and it was the next to last thing she felt like dealing with right now. She spat into the toilet, trying to rid herself of the taste of blood and bile.

"I'm fine, Joey." As fine as a Lupine could be after chewing off the hand of one of her oldest friends and pretending to enjoy it. "I just wanted to wash off some of this grime."

There was a pause, then she heard a soft question. "Why don't you go upstairs, then? Take a proper shower? I can make you some dinner and bring you up a tray."

The word "dinner" set her stomach racing toward the back of her throat, and she quickly shoved on the faucet full blast to mask the sound of more retching. Trembling violently, she wiped her mouth with the back of her hand and forced her voice to sound steady as a rock and calm as Sunday church. "Well, I was going to finish up delivering this week's wood to the cabins on the lumber road . . ."

She let her voice trail off and crossed her fingers that her tenderhearted cousin Josephine would reply as she hoped.

"Don't be silly. You've done enough today." Joey's voice sounded firm and soothing, and made Honor's shoulders sag in relief. "Michael can finish the deliveries. You should take a shower and relax this evening. Or if you have to, work on the books. But stay in and get some rest. It's been . . . a difficult few days."

Honor stifled a laugh and flushed the toilet, grabbing a neatly folded towel from the bar beside the sink. A difficult few days? Why? Just because her previously healthy, arrogant, indestructible father had died, she had inherited his position as alpha over the White Paw Lupine pack, and had fought three alpha challenges in the same number of days? Pshaw.

She cupped her hand to her mouth and rinsed away the last taste of bile. Then she wet one end of the towel and used it to wipe her pale, chalky face. Damn it, she looked like hell, and that was not the sort of face she could let anyone in the pack see. Not even Joey. If Honor was going to assume the title of alpha, she would need to act like an alpha at all times. Even when she felt more like a sniveling, whimpering puppy.

Even when she felt like crying.

Stuffing down those very dangerous thoughts, she draped the towel around her neck and used one hand to hold it to her face as if she were cleaning up, then reached for the doorknob with the other. One deep breath later, she stepped out into the great room with a false smile and the towel half concealing her face.

Joey stood just beside the door, her hands clasped nervously together, her brow wrinkled in concern. "I'm sorry it was Paul," she said in that soft, come-down-from-the-ledge voice she thought was soothing. "I know how close you two always were."

"Don't be." Honor forced her voice to sound casual as she turned and headed for the stairway. "If it wasn't him, it would have been someone else. That's just the way it goes." As soon as she had her back to Joey, she let the towel drop and reached for the banister instead. She made a point to barely touch it rather than to clutch and lean against it the way she wanted to as she walked up to the second floor. "Go ahead and tell Michael to finish the wood deliveries. I'm going to go take that shower. Send up a tray whenever it's ready."

Her steps remained brisk and measured all the way down the hall to the master suite and did not vary until the door closed securely behind her. Then she leaned back against it, squeezed her eyes shut, and willed herself not to cry. Pallor she could handle with a little makeup, but red, puffy, bloodshot eyes would take a lot more effort to conceal than she felt capable of just now.

"Damn you, Dad."

The curse had somehow become her mantra over the past three days. Damn him for dying, damn him for leaving her his business, his pack, and his problems all in one fell swoop, and damn him again just on general principle. The bastard deserved every extra second he spent in whatever passed for hell these days.

Pushing away from the door, Honor paused for a few seconds, swaying gently with the rush of fatigue and nerves that seemed to plague her constantly now. She could barely remember what it felt like to relax. And to think the fun of leading the pack was just beginning.

Wheeeeeeeeee!

She padded across the floor toward the bathroom, thinking that right now a shower sounded better than sex or chocolate. Or sex involving chocolate. The smell of blood and sweat and soil lingered on her skin and clothes, and she was pretty sure she carried enough small twigs and dried leaves in her hair for a decent fire. She doubted the ability of soap and hot water to make her feel clean, but at least it could get rid of the surface detritus.

Ignoring the cavernous room, looking even bigger now that it had been denuded of all her father's personal possessions and the stamp of his decidedly masculine taste, she pushed into the bath and flipped on the lights. She turned on the shower and let the water heat while she stripped. Her clothes landed in the wastebasket rather than the hamper. She'd never be able to bring herself to wear them again, so why bother scrubbing out the stains?

When she stepped under the stinging spray, she hissed at the scalding temperature and felt her skin immediately heat to a rosy glow. She kept her eyes squeezed shut as the water sluiced off the worst of the blood and dirt, not wanting to see the water turn as pink as her skin as it circled down the drain. The steel fence she had erected to cage in the memories of this afternoon still had a few weak spots, and she couldn't afford to encourage any escaping thoughts.

She lingered in the shower, scrubbing herself from head to toe with a loofah three times before she could stand the feel of her own skin. That's when she opened her eyes and reached for the conditioner. She applied it liberally to the mess of knots and debris that passed for her hair and let the thick liquid ease everything free. When she couldn't feel any more pieces of bark or clumps of mud, she rinsed and applied a generous handful of shampoo. She lathered, rinsed, and even repeated it twice before she could make herself stop. Then she conditioned again and turned off the shower.

Hesitating for a long moment on the bath mat, dripping water onto the porous rectangle, she contemplated grabbing a towel, but found herself heading for the bathtub instead. She still didn't feel really clean, but the shower had done the best it could. Time to give the big Jacuzzi and her least favorite scented bath salts a shot.

She set the tub to fill, grateful for her father's ridiculously large water heater, and wrapped a towel around her hair before dumping two huge handfuls of subtly spicy-floral salts into the tub and turning on the jets. She slipped in before the tub was full, leaning back against its sloped side, and left the water running until she was submerged up to her chin. Eventually, she used her foot to turn off the water and let the rumble of the jets lull her into a half-trance.

That was her first big mistake. As soon as her body began to relax from the pounding streams of water around her, her mind began to wander. And, of course, it went directly to the places she didn't want it to go.

Damn Paul Clarke, anyway. Why had he needed to play the big man with her? Why now, just two days after she'd lowered her only surviving parent into a cold, dark grave? They'd been friends since they were whelped, for God's sake. They'd spent their childhoods playing fetch and chase together, their teen years learning to hunt side by side. They'd even brought down their first deer together. She'd considered him a friend. So why the hell had he chosen today to challenge her for the leadership of the pack they both loved? What the hell had he been thinking?

That he could win.

The thought echoed in her head, mocking her with the simple fact that it was completely true. That was exactly why Paul had challenged her now, when stress clouded her thinking and grief slowed her reaction times. As the beta, second-in-command of her father's pack, and a young Lupine in her prime, Honor should logically have been too much for him to take on. But as an unprepared and insecure new alpha—as a female alpha without any sort of extraordinary power—she had been ripe for a challenge. Three of them, as a matter of fact, so the one coming from Paul never should have surprised her.

But it did. It shocked her to her toes. She hadn't known what to do at first. Not until it became clear that even if she didn't want to take the challenge seriously, that's exactly how he had meant it.

Deadly serious.

He had gone for her throat, and as tough and strong as Honor was, she couldn't underestimate a male Lupine who outweighed her by a good fifty pounds and had several inches on her in reach. Her father had taught her that every challenge needed to be dealt with swiftly and decisively, and he had made sure she knew enough to make her moves count. If she couldn't compete with strength and size, she could use speed and treachery and use them well. Her father had pounded that into her until it became instinct. He had preferred the traditional end to a challenge— death—something Honor hadn't been able to do. She had held back at the last minute and taken Paul's hand instead.

She hadn't wanted to. She'd tried stopping at a pin, as she had with the first challenger, but as soon as she let up, Paul had attacked again. So she'd hamstringed him, thinking if he couldn't walk, he couldn't fight. But still he had come for her, launching himself toward her throat with his good hind leg, and suddenly there hadn't been any other choice. It was his hand or his throat, and Honor had chosen his hand. He wouldn't thank her for it, but at least her conscience would survive for another day.

She laughed at herself, not with humor so much as disbelief. Like she could afford a conscience. That item now counted as a luxury in her life. It would until the challenges stopped, and she knew exactly when that would happen.

When she died.

Or when the Silverback alpha came to Connecticut and formally acknowledged her as the White Paw alpha.

Right. I predict that will happen on the third Tuesday after he also names me High Queen of the Oompa Loompas.

Honor sighed again and reached up to turn the jets to a lower setting, no longer quite in the mood to be battered. At first, she had thought sending that letter to Graham Winters was the solution to her problems. The alpha of Manhattan's legendary Silverback Clan commanded respect from just about every Lupine east of the Mississippi River, and, she suspected, from a few of those out West, too. She had only met him once, when she was nine, but she remembered him vividly. He'd been a handsome young man then, only a decade or so older than her, but worlds apart. He had known his place as alpha and lord over the Northeastern Clans. She'd heard he had a good heart, as well, and recently, rumors of his marriage to a human had circulated into her pack's little corner of Connecticut. They said the regional alpha had a son now, another Winters cub to lead the Silverback Clan into the future.

Good thing *someone*'s future was secure.

Honor made a face and turned the tap with her toes to let more hot water flow into the tub. The temperature had dropped below scalding while she brooded over Paul. If she made a habit of this, she'd need to get a second job just to pay her water bills. The way things looked, Paul wouldn't be the last childhood friend to try their luck against the new, female alpha. Not unless the Silverback Clan finally got around to answering its frickin' e-mail.

She growled.

"Honor? Are you okay in there?"

Argh. What spawn of Hades gave Joey her sense of timing?

"I'm fine," she called out. "Just enjoying a soak."

"Oh." A pause. "I brought you a supper tray. I made venison stew. And biscuits."

Honor's stomach launched a violent protest at the thought of food, reminding her exactly how badly she needed to brush her teeth. "Just leave it near the chair, Jo. I'm almost done in here."

"Okay, then. Is there anything else I can get for you?"

Some warm milk, perhaps?

"Nothing. Thank you."

Grateful for her Lupine hearing that could pick out the sounds of Joey moving around the bedroom even over the roar of the tub jets, Honor listened until she heard retreating footsteps and the sound of the bedroom door opening and closing. Only when she was sure Joey had gone did she sit up in the tub and turn off the jets. Time to brush her teeth and flush that dinner down the toilet so Joey would think she'd eaten.

She dragged herself dripping from the tub and

wrapped herself in a huge towel before padding over to the sink and the comfort of her toothbrush. The cinnamon flavor of the paste improved greatly on the lingering traces of blood and bile in her mouth. She scrubbed for several minutes, making sure to brush her tongue thoroughly before she rinsed out her mouth and reached out to unwind the towel from her hair. The long, dark strands, almost black with the weight of the water, fell down her back in ripples that would dry into semiwild curls. She ran a comb through them quickly then left her hair to dry and headed back into the bedroom.

As she had expected, Joey had turned down the bed, lit a couple of lamps, and touched a match to the fire laid in the hearth. The tray of stew, biscuits, and chilled dark beer sat next to her father's overstuffed armchair. It looked like a room well prepared for the lord-of-the-manor routine, except that she didn't feel a bit like a lord.

But the man staring at her from the door to the hallway certainly looked like he did.

Logan watched the slim, young brunette emerge from the bathroom in a cloud of steam, and placed an immediate stranglehold on his need to pounce. And sniff. And lick. And maybe taste. Even through the perfumy fragrance cloaking her natural scent—bath salts?—she smelled nearly good enough to eat. He inhaled deeply and considered whether or not to try a nibble. Suddenly she turned and noticed him standing in the door, and he revised his plans.

Definitely nibble.

"How did you get in here?"

Logan tore his eyes from the plane of creamy, pale skin rising from the top of the woman's towel and saw the weary suspicion in her gaze. He also made note of the long, fresh scratch across her forehead and the bite mark on her right shoulder. It looked as new as the scratch. Seeing the obvious wounds, he made a surreptitious inspection of the rest of the skin he could see—which was quite a lot, praise be—and noticed a good dozen bruises. Some looked a few days old, others just pale shadows, not yet fully formed. She also had one skinned knee and a slowly bleeding cut on her left shin. This would-be alpha had gone through an interesting couple of days.

"Your housekeeper let me in." He looked her in the eye as he answered her question, curious to see how she would react to the aggressive action. It also helped him ignore the stirring of involuntary interest he had immediately felt in her. She met and held his gaze, her brown eyes steady and serious, but made no other show of force. Maybe alpha, but not stupid with it. "She also offered me dinner but I stopped in town and ate while I got directions up here. You aren't exactly easy to find."

"She's my cousin, not my servant. Now, who the hell are you?"

Logan raised an eyebrow. "Some say they're all servants to the alpha."

She didn't answer.

"My name is Logan Hunter." He watched her face for a reaction. "I'm beta of the Silverback Clan. My alpha has requested that I offer you his condolences on the recent death of your father."

"Beta. Sent to offer his condolences." She blinked; her wide, chocolaty eyes seemed slow to focus, but her expression didn't shift. "Right. Tell your alpha to shove them."

Then she turned her back on him and walked to a closet.

Logan tore his eyes from the point where her towel dipped down far enough to threaten to reveal what looked like a truly luscious bottom. Before Missy, he'd never really been an ass man, but as Graham could tell you, that little human had an ass that could inspire men to poetry. It had inspired Logan to a thing or two over the last few months, but now the image of this stranger's derrière had all but supplanted Missy's from his mind.

The thought caught him by the scruff. Lately, part of Logan's subconscious had compared any female he encountered with the Luna, because he couldn't get the woman out of his head. Just because he knew he couldn't have her didn't stop his wolf from insisting that no other female was worth his trouble. Until now. When he looked at Honor Tate, his finicky beast made not a peep of protest.

Huh.

With all that going on in his head, it took Logan a few extra seconds to register what she had said.

Shove them?

"Excuse me?" he ventured.

"You heard me. Tell him he can shove his condolences up his ass with a pogo stick. I don't want them, and I didn't ask for them."

Logan watched as she pulled some things from a drawer inside the closet and tried to keep his mind off the possibility of that towel coming loose and landing on the floor. And of him coming loose and landing on top of her.

"He knows that. He doesn't offer you sympathy because you asked for it. It's just the right thing to do."

"No, the right thing to do would have been to come here himself instead of sending his lackey. And to have agreed to my very sensible request for a formal recognition of my new position as alpha of this pack. Since he has done neither, he can go take his pogo stick and have a little moment of privacy with his thoughts."

She began pulling on clothes with that peculiar talent women have for dressing without undressing first. She pulled a pair of loose cotton pants on under the towel and topped them with a tank top that she managed to don without displaying one additional millimeter of skin.

Logan bit back the wave of disappointment

and shoved his hands into his pockets while he attempted to wrestle his attention back to the question at hand. "The Silverback alpha hasn't made up his mind about whether he's going to agree to that request or not. That's why I'm here. Before he makes a decision, he wants to hear an outside opinion of the workings of the White Paw Clan."

"The White Paw Clan works just fine," she growled, turning to face him and tossing aside the towel. "You can tell Graham Winters I said that. And you can tell him that if he will not honor the request of his fellow alpha, then he and his pack members are not welcome in our territory."

Logan heard the fierceness in her tone and scowled. "That sounds like a hasty decision. Breaking ties between the clans won't benefit either one of them. And in your current situation, frankly, it can only make your position in the pack even more precarious. Your people are not going to like hearing that you bu-fued three hundred years of cooperation between our clans in a fit of pique."

He hadn't expected her to move so quickly, and only instinct kept him from jerking backward when he blinked and found her about three inches from the end of his nose, snarling up at him with a fierceness that surprised him.

And aroused him.

"This. Is. Not. *Pique*." The low rumble in her chest told him she meant every word she spoke.

"And I am not the one who 'bu-fued' anything between our clans. That would be your alpha, the one who has denied our request in our time of need."

Logan did not back down; it wasn't in his nature—the only creature on earth he backed down from was Graham, and even that was a struggle these days—but he willed his hackles not to rise to the bait she presented. He could make her regret taking this attitude with him, but he was here on a diplomatic mission and pinning and mating the alpha of another pack with no warning, no invitation, and no permission stretched the bounds of allowable behavior. Actually, it was out of bounds. But it would have been satisfying.

"If you would listen more carefully to my words, you wouldn't need to make an ass of yourself by making groundless accusations and hurling unnecessary insults." He spoke through clenched teeth until he managed to force his jaw to relax enough for normal speech. "Graham Winters has denied you nothing. What he has done is to send me to observe the situation in your pack and conclude exactly what decision he can make that will result in a positive long-term outcome for both our packs. Graham has no horse in this race; he doesn't personally give a shit who leads this pack, but as the alpha of this region, he most definitely does give a shit that whoever leads is qualified to do it. The most important thing to him at the moment is preserving the peace we currently

enjoy in this part of the country, and he's not going to let *anyone* jeopardize it."

She sneered at him, her tempting pink lip curling up to expose her white canines. "Right. And
what exactly do you plan to conclude then, Mr.
Hunter? How long will you hang around here
pretending to mull things over before you run
back to Papa Wolf and tell him no female could
ever be qualified to lead a pack as well as a male?"

"I won't be pretending anything, Ms. Tate."
He tried not to make it a growl, but a man could
only do so much. "I'm here to do a job, and I intend to do it, not just go through the motions or
phone it in. I don't know about you, but I've got
better things to do with my time than play games
like that. I was sent here to check out the situation, so that's what I'll be doing, and if it takes
me a day or a week or a fucking year and a half,
then that's how long it takes. This isn't something I can rush, Ms. Tate, and neither can you.
When we last spoke, the alpha and I figured it
would take at least a week or more before any
conclusions could be drawn."

She laughed then, though the sound had not a
trace of humor that Logan could detect. "Right.
In a week or more, I won't need your alpha's en-
dorsement, Mr. Hunter. Because I will already
have been forced to cripple every adult male in
my pack. So don't you tell me about waiting for
a royal blessing from his majesty, the King of In-
decision."

* * *

Honor turned her back on him then, but not before she saw his nostrils flare and his lip curl at the insult. She really couldn't have cared less. Her day had already been for shit; this just topped the cake. She had been counting on Graham Winters, and now she'd found out her problem wasn't even important enough to get his personal attention. He'd sent a worker bee instead. Well, fuck him. She'd been dealing for this long, she could deal a while longer. As long as it took.

She stalked back toward her closet, determined to don a pair of fuzzy slippers, find a bottle of Valium, and dose herself into oblivion at least until morning. She didn't want to hear one more thing about Lupines, packs, alphas, challenges, or even the remotest connection to reality for at least eight hours. After that she'd go back to coping, but damn it, she needed a break.

It was a lovely thought, but it didn't last much past the foot of the bed. She got about that far before she sensed his movement. She spun around just in time to avoid being tackled to the carpet, but not fast enough to prevent his getting a good grip on her upper arm. She felt his fingers digging into her skin, nearly bruising her, and she instinctively bared her teeth.

"I just took off one man's hand, Silverback. I don't have a problem with taking another."

"And I don't have a problem with putting you in your place, White Paw." She saw his golden eyes snapping and felt her stomach knot at the knowledge that he spoke the truth. "I came here as an impartial observer, but if you want to make this personal between us, feel free. No one dismisses me but my alpha. Understand?"

She growled at him. "Oh, I understand perfectly well, *beta*." She spat the title like a curse. "But you need to understand that no one gives me orders in my own territory. I don't care how big, bad, and wolfie you might think you are. *I* am alpha here, and I don't take insults lightly."

"You might be alpha of this pack, but you still answer to the Silverback Clan. Don't forget that."

"I *respect* the Silverback Clan, beta. I *answer* to no one."

Their gazes clashed for a long moment, a heavy silence weighted with rapid pulses and the sharp smell of temper. Neither of them blinked. Then the Silverback beta's hand slid from her arm to the back of her neck, and he hauled her forward, mouth descending on hers for a rough, violent kiss.

It lasted no more than a handful of seconds, but it seared her senses with lips, tongue, teeth, and hunger. She tasted the thick, spicy flavor of him, smelled the musky, woodsy scent that clung to his skin, and felt the sharp edge of his strong, white teeth. When he pulled back, she blinked up at him, silent.

"We'll see, honey. We'll see what happens once I get around to asking the right question."

Then he turned on his heel and strode out of her bedroom, closing the door softly behind him.

Honor stared at the white wooden panels for a long time before her knees unlocked enough for her to sink to the bed, where she sat for a while longer, trembling.

Three

Damn him and the horse he rode in on.

Honor lay in her father's huge sleigh bed and stared at the ceiling in frustration. The clock on the bedside table gave off an eerie green glow announcing three A.M. and Honor's fifth unsuccessful hour of attempted sleep. She blamed it all on her unexpected visitor from Manhattan.

Next, she planned to blame the instability in the Middle East on him as well.

She really could kill him for . . . well, for nothing that was actually his fault. But far be it from her to buck the long-standing and honorable tradition of killing the messenger. In reality, her father was the one to blame, but he was inconveniently dead, and therefore a much less satisfying target than the arrogant, sexy beta from the Silverback Clan.

Sexy?

Shit.

Honor groaned and rolled onto her side. The second to last thing she needed in her life was to develop a mad crush on any man, let alone the beta of another pack sent to evaluate her leadership capabilities in the first week of her rule. Because no matter how politely Logan Hunter had phrased it, that was exactly why he'd come to this remote corner of northwestern Connecticut to mingle with the White Paw Clan.

He'd come to grade her like a teacher on report card day, and Honor didn't like it one bit. She didn't like it because no alpha's earned position in a pack should ever be called into question, especially not in any way so transparent to subordinate pack members. She doubly didn't like it because she really wasn't all that confident she would be given a passing grade.

She didn't doubt her ability to lead the pack, to make decisions that would benefit them as a whole and help ease them into the twenty-first century in a way her father had never been willing to attempt. She didn't doubt her ability to hold her own among the international council of packs, where decisions affecting Lupine society as a whole were discussed and debated and voted upon once every five years. Honor didn't even doubt her ability to win any alpha challenge that presented itself to her. Lord knew she'd won three since the moment her father had drawn his last breath, and she knew in that sick place in her gut that'd she'd face even more; but she also knew the wolves in her pack. She knew their strengths and weaknesses, and unless a new, stronger wolf tried to come in from outside the pack, she didn't fear for her position. No, Honor didn't doubt for

a second that she had the ability to become as
confident and capable an alpha as the White Paw
Clan had ever seen.

What she doubted was her desire.

"I was happier being beta."

She whispered the words to the ceiling and
heard the truth of them ringing all the way down
into her soul. It felt like a sin to speak them, but
the good kind of sin; one of the ones involving
lust and gluttony and sloth, like staying in bed on
a Sunday morning to make love and sleep and
nibble on decadent pieces of dark, rich chocolate.
Possibly all at the same damned time. She knew
that if any of her pack could hear her words,
they'd assume she'd lost her mind. Hell, if any
nonsubmissive wolf in the whole damned world
could hear, they'd think the same damned thing.
Dominant wolves always wanted to lead. Period.
The end. Happily ever after, and all those old
clichés.

So, maybe Honor wasn't so dominant after all?

She thought about that, mulled it over, tested
out the taste and feel of it while the sounds of
weighted tree branches settling and night critters
scurrying drifted in through her open window.

It was a more complicated question than it
seemed, but then, among Lupines, dominance was
a complicated issue. No matter what their furry
instincts might tell them at times, Lupines were
not wolves. Not entirely. They could take the shape
of wolves, they shared some physical, some psy-

chological, and even some emotional character-
istics with wolves, but they had their human
sides, too. They might have the instincts to rip
out the throats of any people who angered them,
but they had the ability to reason through why
that might not be a good idea. They might understand that one of the best ways to get to know
someone was to take a good whiff of their scent,
but they still knew better than to greet newcomers
by sticking their noses into other people's crotches.

Like wolves, but not wolves; like humans, but
not humans.

Among wolves, packs really amounted to little
more than families, and in those families, the
oldest—and therefore most often the strongest—
male led the way. It was, if not simple, then at
least a fairly straightforward and logical method
of organization among animals, but when you
factored in the human side of a Lupine's nature,
any thoughts of logic and straightforwardness
flew right out the nearest window.

Lupine packs were definitely not family groups.
They contained families, but because of their integration into wider human society, they needed to
become more than that. Instead, wolf shapeshift-
ers grouped in territorial packs, with all of the
Lupines in a designated geographical area falling
under the authority of the alpha of that area. In
the beginning, it had probably started as a security measure, allowing all the Lupines in a community to keep an eye on each other and protect

each other against threats from hunters, witch hunters, werewolf hunters, and the like. Over the centuries, it had become a political measure, maintained in order to keep the peace among groups of Lupines with no relationship to each other, to temper their natural instincts to get to the top of the food chain. Lupine alphas spent less time making sure everyone in the pack was fed and more time making sure they didn't eat each other, to be blunt, something that required managing not only wolfish instincts, but human egos, emotions, and psychodramas. Frankly, Honor would rather lead an actual wolf pack any day of the week. At least wolves didn't lie to each other.

Honor rolled onto her side and punched her pillow into shape, ignoring the twinge in her aching knuckles. With her Lupine metabolism, such a small discomfort would be gone by morning, but it was the only one of her problems that would be. When the sun rose, she might feel physically better, but she'd still be the reluctant alpha of an endangered pack, with a meddlesome stranger breathing down her neck and half of her childhood friends gunning for her blood. Her only real choice was what to do about it.

If she honestly didn't want to be alpha, should she just step down? Just give her place to Paul or Darin or one of the other males who hadn't hesitated to tell her that a female would never be fit to rule them? Honor's very soul rebelled at the idea. First, because she'd be damned if she'd let any male tell her what a female was or wasn't capable of doing. An alpha might need strength to lead a pack, but she also needed intelligence, cunning, an open mind, and an eye on the future. Testicles, as far as she could tell, counted as entirely optional.

Secondly, she truly did believe she would make a better alpha than any of them ever could. Her father had raised her to be just that. He had taught her not only about the pack and how its members related to each other, but also about the business that kept it financially afloat. She'd learned to do all that at her father's side; no one else had that training or that experience.

Honor's personal relationship with her father had been rocky and even tumultuous at times, but their working relationship had functioned as if it had been designed by a Swiss watchmaker. Ethan Tate had given the orders, and Honor had seen them fulfilled. She had guarded his back, his pack, and his privacy, and she'd done a damned good job of it, too. She had helped keep the White Paw Clan running smoothly and fluidly, but she'd still had time for her own pursuits. She had been on call twenty-four hours, true, but in a well-managed pack, those calls had come rarely.

Over the years, Honor had taken up kayaking and snorkeling. She had studied Native-American and Lupine mythology and taught herself how to throw pots. She had earned a degree in business administration with a minor in environmental management and spent most of her spare time in the studio, spinning her wheel and stoking the fires in the brick kiln she had built with her own hands. In other words, before her father had died, Honor had been a normal woman with a life of her own. Now she began to understand that as alpha, the pack would become her life.

She didn't want that. Her sense of duty to the pack ran just as deep as any Lupine's, but the need to serve it did not consume her. She had the willingness to give, but not the willingness to give up that which the position of alpha required.

Why then was she fighting to stay alpha of the White Paw Clan?

Good question, and one she had begun asking herself almost hourly.

Gods knew it wasn't for the glory of it. Honor snorted at the thought. There was very little glory these days in being alpha of any clan, and even less in one of the small, subordinate clans like this one. Being the Silverback alpha might float Graham Winters's boat, but the Silverback was the overpack to the entire Northeast. All the packs from Maine to D.C. said their pleases and thank-yous to the Silverback. The White Paw Clan had less than a hundred and fifty members, and that generous estimate included the pups and the elders. There wasn't a whole hell of a lot of glory to be found in "ruling" a group the size of the local high school's graduating class when most of them could run their own lives just fine without any interference from her.

To be honest, the only answer that had come to her had been that she wanted to lead the clan by default. Hardly a rousing answer, but a truthful one. It wasn't that Honor wanted to lead the pack; it was that she didn't want anyone else to do it.

She didn't think it was a power trip. After all, given the lack of glory, one could rightly assume that the power of the position didn't exactly shake the earth. So, not a dog-in-the-manger routine. She just honestly didn't see how any member of the pack could make a decent White Paw alpha.

It hurt her to think it, actually. She hated thinking so badly of her family and friends, the group of people she'd grown up with, that she knew and loved. Or at least tolerated out of a sense of familial loyalty. She wanted to believe every one of those people had the strength and intelligence and fortitude to lead the pack into prosperity, but the sad truth told her none of them did.

If there was anyone, it might have been Paul. Paul was smart. At least, she'd always thought so, before he decided to challenge her earlier that afternoon. He had a good head on his shoulders, and a sense of humor that had seen him out of more than one scrape in his life. But he also had a temper that could get out of hand if he wasn't careful, and for all his considerable intelligence, the man couldn't devise a long-term strategy if it came with illustrated instructions. He could barely manage to plan what his next meal would be, and often didn't even bother with that. The pack just couldn't afford that sort of leader. This was a critical time for them, and if they didn't have an alpha who could lead the pack in a new direction, Honor felt certain they would stagnate themselves into extinction.

Stagnation wouldn't be the way they got to extinction under Darin Major, the other most vocal of Honor's detractors. Darin would herd the pack toward oblivion while running behind them with a whip just to keep them moving. The man was arrogant, chauvinistic, cruel, selfish, and no more intelligent than your average dung beetle. With him, leading the pack was all about setting himself up as king of his own little universe. He wanted the power and the glory, and he could care less about what it cost the pack. The only place he would lead the White Paw was straight to hell.

The pack needed a leader with vision. Someone who could see the future and lead them to it. And failing that, they needed someone who would at least keep them from regressing into the past or standing stock-still as the world progressed around them. Honor didn't delude herself into thinking she knew best for every member of the clan, or even that she knew best for the clan as a whole, but she thought she had a good idea of what would be worst.

The pack desperately needed to move forward. They needed to learn how to survive in an increasingly urban world. Their little compound in the forests of Connecticut provided them with a momentary oasis, but every day, developers moved a little bit closer to their retreat, and every day, they got one step closer to the sprawling metropolis of Manhattan, less than a hundred and fifty miles to the south. If the White Paw didn't learn how to function in the society of the modern human city, they could kiss their lives and their sanity good-bye. Progress would not be stopping for them.

Honor wanted to see her pack move from a culture of reclusion to one of integration. She wanted pack members to become computer geeks and businesswomen and police officers and engineers. And if the pack continued to wallow in its stagnation, none of those things would ever happen. The world wouldn't just pass them by; it would bulldoze over them and plow them under.

Now if only she could manage to convince the rest of her pack of this. And quickly, before Mr. Snooper-Sexy decided to support another Lupine's bid for her job.

The recollection of Logan Hunter made Honor groan. He was the absolute last thing she needed in her life. Perhaps tied with a frontal lobotomy and Chinese foot binding. All three promised to cause her intense pain, considerable inconvenience, and no few worries while accomplishing nothing useful.

In fact, while she was having fun with analogies, the man reminded her of French fries, one of her biggest weaknesses. Like the junk food, the Silverback offered no nutritional value and promised to do little more than weigh her down and leave her hungry for more a few hours later. And also like French fries, her craving for him came out of nowhere and refused to be pushed from her mind no matter how hard she struggled.

Damn him.

Honor kicked off the light cotton blanket, suddenly way too hot to tolerate even the minimal covering. Unlike some of the Lupines she knew, Honor didn't just keep a blanket on her bed, she even used it on occasion; but not tonight. Not while she was obsessing over a sexy stranger, and definitely not three days before she was due to go into heat.

Of all the rotten luck. Her father couldn't have died immediately after her heat when her hormones would settle down and make her life and her interactions with every male on the planet a hell of a lot easier. No, he had to time it so that her alpha challenges were just as likely to turn into attempted rapes as attempted murders.

Gee, thanks, Dad.

To add insult to the injury of her past few days, she'd been forced to start using the scented bath salts, which gave off a fragrance way too heavy for her sensitive nose, to try and mask the beginning of the changes to her body chemistry that any Lupine worth his salt would have known indicated her approaching heat.

And while she was at it, she thought she'd throw in a few menstrual cramps and a case of boils. That sounded like fun.

Right. Sitting up in the bed, Honor ran her hands over her face and groaned. She figured she could either sit here till dawn and brood, or she could get up, go downstairs and make up for the dinner she'd never eaten. Now that the taste of blood had finally faded from her mouth, her Lupine metabolism had reared its head to let her know just how wildly it disagreed with the notion of her skipping a meal.

She swung her feet over the edge of the bed and onto the floor, ignoring the chill of the boards. Her stomach overruled her soles. She paused long enough to pull on the pajamas she'd never intended to sleep in and made her way down the hallway to the stairs.

The house sat silent around her. It always seemed silent since Ethan's death, but especially at night. With just her and Joey there now, silence almost came with a guarantee. Joey barely made noise when shouting at the top of her lungs, and Honor only seemed to get into the house just long enough to fall unconscious for three or four hours a night. Since she didn't snore, that meant things stayed pretty quiet.

She heard little more than the sound of her own breathing and the rattling of the bare tree branches in the yard as she made her way through the house. The glow of moonlight silvered the floor in front of the windows, making it look almost as cool as it felt against her bare feet. She ignored the chill as she headed for the kitchen. If she was lucky, Joey had left a snack or two in the fridge. A half calf or twelve would go down fairly smoothly right about now.

If she hadn't been so hungry and so tired, she probably would have heard the soft sound of breathing coming from inside the kitchen. She knew she would have noticed the smell—that musky, woodsy smell she'd detected earlier in her father's bedroom when she'd emerged from her bath.

The smell of the stranger.

But she didn't notice a thing, not until she turned on the overhead kitchen lights and found her eyes focusing on the half-naked male form standing beside the center island.

"Care for a snack?"

Logan wanted to make a snack out of her.

He stifled the urge to bare his teeth and inhale deeply, since it wasn't precisely the polite thing to do, but damn, he wanted to. There was something about her scent, hidden under the too heavy perfume of whatever she'd added to her bath . . . something indefinable and elusive.

Either that, or he had a cold.

"What are you doing here?"

Okay, not exactly the hey-sailor-buy-me-a-drink he'd been hoping for, but he figured that might be pushing things a tad.

"I got hungry. The diner in town's not bad, but their idea of all you can eat and mine aren't precisely the same." He held up a chunk of the sirloin he'd been munching. "Your housekeeper told me to help myself."

"She's my cousin. And she should have told you to help yourself to the opposite side of the front door."

He watched her cross her arms over her chest, figuring it gave him the perfect excuse to stare at her breasts without being caught staring at her breasts. How was that for smooth?

"Ironically enough, she decided to go with the whole polite thing. She put me in a guest room overlooking the woods. Private bath. Pretty homey."

"Really, and did she leave a mint on your pillow?"

"Chocolate. I had it before I came downstairs."

She rolled her eyes and stalked past him toward the refrigerator. "I'm surprised you didn't just call up for room service."

Logan seized the opportunity to reevaluate the ass he'd been so struck by earlier. He almost choked on the beef. Lord, but it looked even better than the last time he'd seen it.

He quickly finished swallowing and shook his head in amazement. He still didn't quite get why he found this woman so compelling. She pretty much defined "not his type." Dark-haired and dark-eyed, she should have had dusky, tanned, or olive skin. Instead, her complexion looked pale and milky and perfect, especially in the silver light of the waxing moon that had illuminated the kitchen before she'd turned on the lights.

She'd looked like a shadow as she slipped through the dark house. Her form, slender and tallish, seemed almost too delicate to be Lupine. He was used to women of his species being sturdy and athletic, but this girl looked as if a good strong handshake might do her an injury. Her cousin had certainly seemed convinced that Honor could hold her own as alpha, but Logan found himself even more skeptical after meeting her. Somehow, he could not picture this woman facing an alpha challenge, let alone winning one. Or three, as Joey had told him. Just this week. It boggled his mind.

Of course, part of that might have had something to do with the fact that he could picture a whole lot more appealing things to do with her than fight, once he got his hands on her.

She slapped a plastic container down on the island and peeled off the lid, reaching inside for a bite-sized piece of pork. "So what time are you leaving in the morning?"

The pointed question made him smile. He had to give her points for effort. "About a week from next Tuesday, I figure. If everything goes smoothly."

"Perhaps I'm not making myself clear, but you really aren't welcome here. I want you gone. Now."

"No, I actually think that's pretty clear. The problem is that what you want really isn't the issue. For the past three hundred years, the White Paw Clan has been swearing fealty to the Silverback alpha. That makes your clan his responsibility, and from where Graham Winters stands, there are two things that could happen here." He ignored her glare and stole a piece of her pork, more to keep his hands occupied with something other than her sweet curves than because he was still hungry. "Either way, the White Paw alpha will need to renew that vow of fealty at the next Silverback howl. The only remaining question is whether the White Paw alpha will be you, or someone else."

He watched her while he spoke, so he saw the muscles in her jaw clench and her eyes narrow when he made that statement. He tried to ignore the way the spark in her gaze made his jeans fit a little too tightly.

"I am the White Paw alpha. And I will remain the White Paw alpha for a very long time to come."

"That's what I'm here to determine. Maybe you will hold the title, maybe you won't. The Silverback is not so much concerned with who keeps your pack as with the knowledge that the pack is well kept."

He could almost see her hackles rise. "I. Will. Hold. My. Pack. Did you get that? Or do I need to use smaller words?"

Logan clenched his teeth to hold back the

growl he could feel reverberating in his chest. His wolf didn't like to be challenged. It reacted instinctively to her aggressive tone. "You need to watch your mouth."

"Make me."

She knew almost before the words formed on her tongue that saying them would be a mistake, but they launched themselves into the quiet room before she could stop them. They hung between her and the sexy stranger like the ripe scent of heat, and she couldn't take them back. She felt the words pulse between them for all of three rapid heartbeats before she made her fateful mistake.

She blinked.

He was on her before her eyelids completed their upswing, launching himself over the island in a leap at least four feet high from a standing start. She had the vague impression of muscles tensing and shifting under tight denim, the image of tanned skin and dark hair moving toward her, and as fast as her reflexes were, she couldn't outrun him. He caught her just as she turned her back on him in an instinctual flight response. Even her subconscious mind knew she had pushed him as far as his limits would allow, but her subconscious wasn't fast enough.

He carried her to the tile floor, one hand outstretched to catch their weight as they tumbled to the cold, hard surface. She tried to flip them, but he had surprise and brute male strength on his side. He pinned her almost immediately, both hands above her head, legs parted around his granite-hard thighs. She felt helpless, and decided she didn't much like the unfamiliar feeling.

She repeated that thought to herself like a mantra while she tried to ignore the way her body softened instinctively beneath him. She didn't need to be thinking about the rapid pulse beating in her chest or the restless heat pooling between her legs. She knew perfectly well that he was aware of both, and she didn't have a chance of escaping him if she let her stupid hormones control her.

The air stirred around them as he lowered his head to her throat and sniffed. He drew breath like a starving man drew sustenance, as if he could take in her essence as it floated in the air around her. The act made her shiver, and he growled, low and rough, above her.

"I'd be happy to watch it for you," he rumbled, pressing his body down over hers, not enough to crush her, but enough to remind her who had the upper hand. "I can keep very . . ." He paused to nip her lips. "Close." Lick. "Track."

Then his mouth closed over hers, and he feasted.

She wanted to hate it, waited for the rough surge of rage that had consumed her the last time any Lupine had dared to touch her uninvited. She braced herself for disgust and outrage and fury to come to her aid, but all she got was melting and hunger and greed. She wanted to devour him as surely as he devoured her.

She cursed her body for its betrayal, her hands that clenched into fists instead of sprouting claws to tear him to shreds. The thighs that spread and knees that lifted to cradle him closer. The lips that softened and parted under his, clinging and encouraging. Goddamn it, but her life would have been so much easier if this man had repulsed her. Even just a little. A mild sort of nausea whenever she got too close to him. Was that too much to ask?

Apparently.

Instead of feeling her stomach roll, she felt her body shiver when his tongue tangled with hers. She tugged at it, let her teeth scrape the surface, and struggled in vain to suppress the moan building in her throat. It boiled out of her, a muted sound swallowed in the fever of their kiss. Still, even muffled it seemed to excite him. He answered with a growl of his own and shifted his grip on her wrists until he pinned both of her hands with one of his own. She could have broken the hold if she'd tried, but she was too busy trying to remember how to breathe when his newly freed palm closed over her breast and squeezed.

When she gasped in reaction, she breathed in the air he expelled on a satisfied grunt. It carried the taste of him even deeper inside her, the rich, warm taste of heat and spice and passion. She wanted more of it, wanted it filling her up and making her blind to everything else in the world.

The luxury of the thought went to her head almost as fast as he did.

Then he went for her skin even faster, and she forgot such a thing as the world even existed. He caught the center of her tank top in his fist and yanked, and the garment shredded in his grasp. He threw away the tatters with an impatient motion, then paused for a breathless moment to stare down at her. His gaze fixed on her breasts, nipples already tight and beaded in arousal, and she could almost see his mouth watering. His scent intensified, drowning her in the heady fragrance, and she knew hers must be doing the same to him. Not only was she at least as aroused as he was, but her heat was now only forty-eight hours away.

If he knew, though, he was already too far gone to process the information rationally. All he seemed to know now was hunger and urgency. He pulled her hands, forcing her to straighten her arms more, the action lifting her breasts higher until he could lean down and set his mouth to one tightly beaded peak.

Honor screamed.

She didn't mean to. In fact, she'd have given her left incisor if she could have caught the sound before it emerged, but no such luck. It tore from her throat, low and raw and hoarse, like an animal's cry. He heard and answered, not with a matching sound, but by taking her nipple between his teeth and tugging. Then his mouth closed over the entire peak and began to draw on her. The hot, wet suction sent her body bowing beneath him, bending in a taut arch in response to the unbearable pleasure of the sensation.

He growled a low, tense encouragement, and she felt his hand shift from her breast where it had toyed with her other nipple down over the smooth expanse of skin of her belly. She felt a nail catch in the soft fabric of her pajama pants before it slid beneath. His palm glided over the softness of her stomach to tangle in the damp curls at the apex of her thighs. One long finger dipped, parting her slick folds and finding the center of her pleasure.

Again she screamed. This time the sound of her frustration shook the entire house, but she couldn't have cared less. She began to fight him in earnest, not to escape his touch but in her fever to do some touching of her own. She ached for the feel of his slick skin under her fingers, and she intended to have it. Rearing up, she turned her head and sank her teeth deep into his bicep, the nearest bit of his flesh she could reach. He yanked his mouth from her breast and snarled down at her. She met his gaze fiercely.

"Want. More."

His eyes narrowed at her hoarsely panted demand, but his expression only turned more predatory. He didn't seem to object. Instead, he slowly pulled his hand from between her legs, letting it stroke every individual nerve ending it could reach along the way. The entire length slid along her clit, making her buck and shudder and curse him. Then his nail caught it in a wicked flick, and she yelped.

He flashed her a feral grin, raising his glistening fingers to his mouth before he growled, "So do I."

Honor watched as he licked her moisture from his hand. She saw the way his eyes narrowed as he tasted her, saw the knowledge light them, and she swore.

"Heat."

She had rolled out of his grasp before the word cleared his lips. Seeing the flare of dominance and possession in his eyes poured a bucketful of icy cold common sense all over her enflamed skin. Damn it, she should have known all the bath salts in the world couldn't disguise the flavor of her heat from a mature male Lupine. He'd known the minute he lifted his fingers to his lips that the new White Paw alpha was just hours from the start of her heat cycle. It was irresistible to any male Lupine, but to one with as many dominance tendencies as her Silverback visitor, it was like the proverbial red flag in front of the bull. She might as well have tattooed "Come and get me, big boy" across her forehead.

"Here," he snarled, even as she sprang to her feet and looked for a clear path to the door. "Come. Here."

She growled in response, baring her teeth at him, body coiling in preparation for flight. If she could make it around him and out of the kitchen, she might have a chance of outrunning him. If not, then she could definitely lose him in the woods. He wasn't familiar with them like she was, and there were ways she could mask her scent at least well enough to confuse him.

"Now."

She shook her head and crouched. She wished she still had her tank top on, or that she dared to take the seconds it would cost her to shift to her wolf form. Running bare breasted through the woods at three-thirty in the morning hadn't made her top ten list this year, but it looked just about inevitable.

"Here."

She opened her mouth to defy him again, but she never got the chance. Before she could speak, Joey stepped into the room, wide-eyed with concern. "Honor? What's going on here? Is everything all right?"

Honor nearly burst out laughing. She might have, if the tension weren't thick enough to choke the sound out of her, and if she weren't keeping her gaze glued to Logan's face in anticipation of his next move.

"Get out."

Logan barked the order as if he had every right, but what pissed Honor off was that Joey actually started to obey.

"I didn't say leave, Joey. And you still take your orders from me. Don't you."

It wasn't a question, and Honor didn't bother to look in Joey's direction to gauge her answer. She refused to so much as blink. She didn't trust the Silverback visitor not to use the slip to his advantage.

Logan snarled. "You'll take them from me."

"I'll take them from no one." All the days of tension and struggle and uncertainty suddenly overwhelmed Honor, and she struck out where she could. At Logan. "I am the White Paw alpha. Not you. Not Winters. No one but me. And the alpha does. Not. Answer."

They stared at each other, teeth bared, eyes narrowed. Honor could feel the skin between her shoulder blades shift and tighten, raising the hackles she didn't actually have in her human form. She'd bet Logan could feel the same subtle crawling beneath his skin. She almost said a prayer of gratitude for it, since if they'd been in their were or wolf forms, they'd likely have already been locked together, either ripping out each other's throats, or mating furiously on the kitchen tile. Which one it would have been was entirely up for debate.

"Can I get anyone anything? A cup of tea? Or I could make cocoa . . ."

Honor snorted. If the tension had been any less thick, she might have laughed. Instead, she straightened her spine and reached out a hand to her cousin, never taking her eyes off Logan's. "No. We're done. Give me your robe."

Joey didn't hesitate, but untied the thick, terry-cloth robe she wore and shrugged out of it, laying it over Honor's outstretched arm. She shivered a little in the thin cotton nightgown she wore, but she didn't say a word.

Honor pulled the robe on and belted it closed, concealing her bare breasts from the two people in the room she felt really didn't need to be seeing them right now. "I'm going to bed. Because the White Paw Clan is an honorable one, I won't ask you to leave tonight, Mr. Hunter, but I expect your bags to be packed in the morning."

Then she did what she never would have done if Joey hadn't been there. She turned her back on Logan Hunter and walked out of the room.

Four

Like he needed this to get any more complicated.

Logan rounded the corner into the kitchen still brooding over the incident the previous night. Developing a severe case of the hots for the alpha he had come here to evaluate did not sit well on his shoulders. Doing the evaluation promised to be complex enough as it was. He didn't need the added complication of a constant erection. Nor did it help much to find out that the alpha he had the hots for, the one he was here to evaluate, tasted like she'd be hitting her heat on the night of the next full moon.

Could you say, "Shit hitting the fan," maybe?

"Good morning, Mr. Hunter. Can I get you some breakfast before you leave?"

Logan glanced in the direction of the question and saw Honor's cousin, the small, quiet one who had interrupted them last night, backed up into a corner where two sides of counter converged. She held a pair of tongs before her like a weapon and shifted nervously when his gaze fixed on her.

"I'm making bacon, but there's some sausage as well, and plenty of eggs. Steak, too, if you prefer."

Logan could practically see the nerves vibrating beneath the woman's skin. He almost expected to see her nose twitch, because to his mind, Joey Tate looked more like a scared little rabbit then a grown Lupine. If he hadn't already been told she and Honor were cousins, he never would have guessed the relationship. Where Honor had creamy skin and hair the color of dark chocolate, her cousin appeared almost colorless, the pale skin giving way to hazel eyes of muddied gray and hair the color of a field mouse, a brown so ashen it looked almost silvery where the light hit it. Given the way she currently eyed him as if expecting him to demand her entrails on his breakfast plate, she appeared not to have inherited any of her cousin's strength or passion, either.

"What makes you think I'm leaving?" he asked, pulling a chair out from the small table and taking a seat.

She shifted again, her eyes darting nervously about the room. "Well, Honor said. She said Greg would be taking you into town as soon as you finished eating. How do you like your eggs?"

"Sunny side up. With bacon. But I'm not leaving today."

"But Honor said—"

"Honor is mistaken."

Joey didn't say anything else, just placed a mug of steaming coffee on the table in front of him and turned back to her frying pan, but he could feel the way she kept shooting him suspicious glances while he ate. Needless to say, he didn't linger over the meal.

He took the last slice of bacon with him, munching as he left the house and followed Joey's nervously worded directions about where to find her cousin.

She'll be down at the stone yard. That's where the Howls happen. She and some of the men will make sure everything is secure and safe for the pack. But I don't think she'll be expecting to see you.

Logan disagreed. He knew that if Honor Tate had half the intelligence he credited her with, surprise would not be her first response to seeing him again.

And he should have been less surprised when a voice called out behind him.

"Morning!"

The greeting came from the direction of the gravel road that Joey had mentioned led to some of the pack's communal structures—a dining hall, an informal rec center, and the like. Logan turned to see a man approach wearing battered fatigue pants and a plaid flannel shirt. He looked like the illegitimate offspring of G.I. Joe and Paul Bunyan, but he was smiling widely and extending his hand as he strode to a stop.

"You must be the Silverback I heard was in town," the man said, gripping his hand just a little too firmly, his smile broad and toothy. "Thought

I'd take a minute to welcome you to the territory. Name's Darin Major. Pleased to meet you."

Logan had never been one to back down from a dominance challenge, but neither did he have any interest in macho pissing contests. He shook the man's hand with his usual grip, but he met his gaze straight and square until Major's smile dimmed a watt or two.

"Logan Hunter." He nodded and withdrew his hand without breaking the eye contact. That would be the White Paw's job. "But you didn't have to go out of your way to play Welcome Wagon for me. I've already been greeted by your alpha. She's been gracious enough to put me up at her house while I'm here."

And it seemed to have strained her grace to the limit, but Logan didn't mention that. Instead, he watched Major's smile wilt like an unwelcome erection and the expression in his green eyes shift from calculating to resentful.

"This pack happens to be between alphas at the moment," Major said, hooking his hands into his pockets and shifting his gaze to Logan's left ear. "The alpha died a few days ago—from disease, not a challenge—so we're what you might call in transition until the matter sorts itself out."

Logan had noticed the change in Major's sight line. It was subtle, but significant. The weaker wolf couldn't hold a more dominant Lupine's gaze any longer, but he had tried to save face by looking just to the side in an attempt to fake the eye contact.

Logan wasn't fooled. He also wasn't impressed. He remembered Graham mentioning the name Darin Major in their initial meeting as one of the male pack members who might pose a challenge to Honor. From what he'd seen so far, he'd bet Honor could take him. Major wasn't alpha material.

Not to mention that the scent of him rubbed Logan the wrong way. His instincts clearly told him that Major wasn't worth the time it would take to kick his ass, but they also told him not to turn his back on the wolf anytime soon. His scent smelled of treachery.

Logan smiled coolly. "Come on, Major, we both know there's no such thing as a pack without an alpha, not even during a 'period of transition.' Nature might abhor a vacuum, but a Lupine pack hates it even worse. You might not like having Honor Tate as your alpha, but that doesn't mean that's not exactly what she is. And you know the way things work. Whoever claims the title of alpha holds it until someone stronger takes it away."

The last of the White Paw male's genial good-ol'-boy persona faded away in a snarl of resentment.

"No female is fit to run a Lupine pack. At least, not this pack," Major spat, "and you know it, too, or you wouldn't be here, Silverback. If your alpha had any confidence in that bitch's leadership, he'd have thrown his support behind her with a formal acknowledgment, not sent some lackey to scope out the lay of the land."

Logan met the sneer with a hard look. "How do you know that's not exactly what I'm here to do? Maybe I *am* the formal acknowledgment of Graham Winters's support."

"And maybe cats make great pets for werewolves. An acknowledgment takes fifteen minutes timed for the start of a pack Howl, not a full suitcase that shows up four days before the event. The Silverback alpha knows the bitch can't lead, and you're the proof."

Eyes narrowed, Logan leaned forward and curled his lip in warning. "I'd be careful about putting words in Graham Winters's mouth if I were you. Almost as careful as I'd be about putting them in mine."

Major backed up a step and glared, but the object of the expression seemed to be Logan's shoulder so the visitor remained unaffected.

"The bitch can call herself alpha until her lips turn blue," Major growled, "but when the pack gets together and sees how weak she really is, she'll be singing a different tune. Just you wait."

The Lupine spun and stalked away, leaving Logan gazing after him until the trees swallowed him up.

"So much for pack solidarity," he muttered, and turned back to the direction he'd been headed when Major had stopped him. Now he was even more anxious to lay his eyes on Honor Tate again. He wanted to see if his impressions of her from the night before held up, because the woman he remembered could have handed Major his own testicles in a fair fight. If Major was her biggest threat, maybe he really would be acknowledging her claim and heading home sooner than he'd expected.

He followed the trail that Joey had indicated through the woods. The scent of the pine trees and the crisp chill of winter air lessened a little of the tension inside him. The terrain was certainly a far cry from his home hunting grounds on the streets of Manhattan. Usually he didn't mind the city. He'd lived there for as long as he could remember, so it felt comfortable and familiar to him. Like home. But there was something about the forest, the crunch of packed snow beneath his boots, the tang of pine and soil in the air. The smell of game and the rich sounds of a living ecosystem all around called to his primal instincts.

He snorted to himself and ducked beneath a low-slung branch. Primal instincts? If he wasn't careful, he'd be scratching behind his ears in public any minute.

The path wound through the woods long enough for him to stretch his legs, but he wasn't worried about getting lost. He could smell the years of Lupines winding through the trees, concentrated on the path ahead of him. It guided him more surely than signposts. Every pack had its own scent, and he thought he was beginning to recognize that of the White Paw, but he didn't particularly care. The only scent he cared about was rich and earthy and still bore the faint trace of flowers.

Sweet pea, he thought. And clover. Delicate blossoms under the masking jasmine and ginger of last night's bath. But even the scent of flowers couldn't hide the trace of her approaching heat. Now that he had tasted her, he knew what that trace of spice to her scent had signified, and it made the fit of his jeans tighten uncomfortably.

He swore under his breath and kept walking. Speaking of complications he didn't need, this had to be the biggest. Adjudicating the right of an alpha to lead his—or, in this case, her—pack was a touchy subject to begin with. Not many people appreciated an outsider settling pack business, as Darin Major had so kindly pointed out. Heaven knew Logan would have bitten the face off anyone who tried it with the Silverback Clan. Yet here he stood, ready to do it to the White Paw. He didn't blame Honor for being a bit miffed with him.

From the little bit of information he'd managed to pry out of her cousin—and from the tenor of Major's recent greeting—Honor's brief tenure as alpha had not been a peaceful one. At the pack meeting she'd called to announce her father's death, she'd received her first challenge from a young male who thought a female beta could be overlooked, but a female alpha should be overstepped.

Honor taught him the error of his ways, fairly

bloodlessly, by accepting the alpha challenge and pinning him by the throat in less than five minutes of combat. She had thought a swift display of strength would cement her position and demonstrate to the pack that she intended to keep the title that had come to her. No such luck.

Two days later, the second challenger had stepped forward. According to Joey, Honor had almost welcomed it. The Lupine who called her leadership into question was a bad apple in the pack. Less intelligent than he was brawny, Chet had needed to be taken down a peg or two, and if Honor had to be the one to do it, so be it.

The fight hadn't been a quick one. While Honor had been fighting to the surrender, Chet had been fighting to the death. They had wrestled across the pack's ceremonial grounds, the stone yard, for almost two hours before Honor had admitted to herself that Chet would not surrender unless forced. She had applied that force to his hind legs, slicing through his hamstrings with razor-sharp teeth and leaving him alive, but crippled. The injuries would heal, though not quickly, and Chet would remember the bite of both an alpha and humiliation for a long time to come.

The final challenge had apparently been the worst for Honor, and it was the one about which Joey had said the least. It had occurred just the night before, only a few hours prior to Logan's arrival on White Paw lands. The challenger, he gathered, had been one of Honor's childhood friends, and his bid for alpha had shocked her. Even more shocking to her had been Paul's insistence on turning their challenge into a death match.

She hadn't killed him, Logan knew. Joey hadn't given him any specifics, but it sounded as if Honor had again gone for a crippling wound instead of taking her challenger's life. It didn't speak well for her in terms of her ability to lead the pack. Logan admired compassion from a theoretical point of view, but he knew it had little place in the hierarchy of a Lupine pack.

For all the veneer of civilization their human forms lent them, at their core, a Lupine pack functioned in much the same way as a wolf pack. The strongest led, the others followed, and the weakest either made themselves useful, or they didn't live to see another winter. To humans it sounded brutal; to Lupines it was the way things worked. They didn't make the rules out of cruelty. They simply knew that the survival of the pack was more important than the survival of any one pack member, and a hell of a lot more important than manners.

Given the three challenges Honor had had, Logan wondered why Major hadn't followed— or even preceded—any of them with a challenge of his own. He clearly thought he would make a better alpha than a female, no matter how wrong he might be, so what was he waiting for? Did he think the others would wear her down and make her more vulnerable, or did he have some other sort of scheme in mind? Logan's curiosity had been piqued.

He made no effort to silence his footsteps as he strode toward the stone yard, and he wasn't surprised to break through the tree line into the clearing to find Honor and two teenaged males staring at him.

Honor thrust the tip of her shovel into the dirt at her feet and pointed toward the west. "Town is that way."

"I'll keep that in mind." He smiled pleasantly and walked toward her and the fire pit she and the teens looked to be repairing. "For when I'm ready to leave."

"You're ready now."

"Not true. You're ready for me to leave, but me? I prefer to stay a while." He turned toward the two boys who watched the interplay avidly. "You guys might want to go now."

Both boys turned to look at Honor, who scowled but nodded curtly. "Go. Head up to the offices and tell Mike I want you to go along when he looks at that pipe work we want to replace in cabin twelve. I can finish here."

This time the boys nodded and moved off, heading back along the same path Logan had used. At least the young ones knew enough to take orders only from their alpha. But teenaged boys were one thing. He still wasn't sure about her qualifications for leading the entire pack. Just because the one challenger he'd met was a puffed-up windbag didn't mean every adult male in the pack would be the same. There could still be a serious claimant to the title waiting in the background.

As soon as the sound of the boys' footsteps had faded from their sharp ears, Honor turned on Logan with a snarl. "What the hell are you still doing on my land? I thought I made myself pretty damned clear last night. I want you gone."

"Oh, you were clear. And so was I." He met her gaze squarely, not bowing to anyone else's alpha. "I'm not leaving until I finish the job I was sent to do. That means I'm not leaving until I see for myself whether or not you have what it takes to run this pack."

She threw down her shovel and planted her hands on her hips. "Who the hell are you to tell me if I have what it takes? I grew up in this pack, and I've been its beta since I was fifteen years old. I know the way things work around here a hell of a lot better than you do, so who the hell do you think you are to give me orders?"

"I'm the man who intends to see them carried out."

She laughed at him. Literally threw her head back and laughed, but when her eyes met his again, the look in them had very little to do with humor. "You go right on thinking that, city boy, and I'll tell you what my father told me. 'A White Paw leads the White Paw, and everyone else can go fuck themselves.' You can make any damned decision you want, and you can go carry your news to your boss back in New York. But I am telling you right now, what you two think won't make one bit of difference to this pack. We do things the way we do them, and to hell with you both."

Logan smiled, which was the only way he could think of to keep from snarling. Not that he disagreed with what she was saying, because it made sense—although in the end it wouldn't make any difference to his decision or Graham's—but he did have to exercise every iota of self-control he possessed not to jump her where she stood. In the heat of her anger, her scent had intensified. It trailed across the space between them and teased his senses. The spicy note seemed even stronger today, confirmation of how close she was to her heat. He wanted to lick that fragrance from her skin and nibble his way up the insides of her thighs until he could feast on her, unimpeded.

Shit. Why the hell had he decided to wear button-fly jeans?

Dragging his mind off his crotch for a good five seconds, he imagined his feet nailed to the ground beneath him. And if that didn't work, he'd have to try real nails. "I understand your feelings, Honor, but they don't change the fact that I am not leaving until my job here is done."

"Just what sort of job do you think you get to do on our land, city boy?"

The crunch of snow underfoot had both Honor and Logan turning instinctively toward the path to the main house even before the first words were spoken. Out of the corner of his eye, Logan could see the annoyance that tightened Honor's features, but he kept most of his attention centered on the two men who entered the stone yard.

The one who had spoken stood an inch or two less than six feet tall, but he had the stocky, beefy look of a brawler and wore an expression just short of challenging on his bearded face. His clean-shaven friend was a little taller, but less muscular, and his face wore an impassive mask belied by the way his pale eyes darted around the clearing, cataloging every detail. Logan didn't even bother to stiffen at their insulting entrance, but neither did he take his eyes off them. He hadn't gotten to be beta without watching his back.

"Bill. Dave. I thought you two were working on fences today." Honor's tight tone and rigid expression made the male Lupines glance her way, but their gazes turned just as quickly back to Logan. The low rumble in her chest indicated the female alpha didn't like that much.

"We are," the burly one drawled, hooking his thumbs in the front pockets of his blue jeans. "But just before we headed out, we ran into Darin, and he told us there was some stranger come sniffing around the pack. We hadn't heard nothing about it from you, so me and Dave figured we might come take a look."

Huh. Major worked fast. And appeared not to be the only male in this pack with more testosterone than brains.

"Really. You figured."

Logan might not have known Honor Tate for very long, but even he knew enough to recognize that her total lack of inflection boded ill for her pack mates. The question was, how would she handle them? *Could* she handle them?

He stood his ground, his hands hanging loose at his sides. If Honor couldn't deal with the situation, Logan had no doubt that he could. He had even less doubt that if he felt it necessary to step in, the female would make him pay, one way or another.

But she wouldn't be doing it as alpha of the White Paw clan. An alpha that weak couldn't be allowed to stand.

"What's your name, city?" the burly one asked, jerking his chin up and narrowing his eyes at Logan.

And that was about as close to a challenge as Logan had ever let slip past him, but before he could express his generosity, Honor shouldered him aside and planted herself in front of her obnoxious pack mates.

"His name is none of your business, Billy. And neither is what he might be doing here. So you 'figured' wrong."

Her voice had deepened to a growling register that tightened Logan's pants, not that she was paying any attention to him or his fly. Or would have appreciated the gesture if she had been. Her dark eyes had begun to glint with feral flecks of gold, and he could almost see her alpha energy seeping from her pores. He doubted the other men had missed it, either, but they weren't backing down, not just yet. That wasn't a good sign for Honor's desire to keep her spot at the top of the pack.

"You know as well as we do that we got a right to defend our territory when a strange wolf come into it—"

"You don't know shit, William Petrey. That right belongs to the alpha, and last time I looked, you were nowhere near being the alpha of this pack."

Bill's eyes narrowed, and he crossed his thick arms over his chest, mumbling, "Female ain't all that near it, either."

Uh-oh. Those were fighting words.

Under Logan's watchful eye, Honor shifted her weight onto the balls of her feet and began to stretch. Or rather, her body began to stretch, growing a couple of inches taller, muscles beginning to thicken and layer on top of each other. It wasn't quite a change, since her features remained human, and she didn't seem to be sprouting any fur that he could see, but her wolf was definitely rising to the surface, and he could feel the air thicken with the almost magical wash of energy.

Honor's lip curled in a snarl, revealing long,

white canine fangs that looked more than capable of rearranging her pack mate's vocal chords. From the inside out. "Would you care to repeat that, William?"

The force of an alpha's authority began to press down on the atmosphere in the clearing, making both Bill and Dave fidget in distress. Logan could feel it like a weight in the air, but he withstood it easily, maybe because Honor wasn't his alpha, and maybe because she just wasn't alpha enough. Wasn't that what he'd come here to decide?

Bill, though, had started to look uncomfortable. His mouth tightened and his chin dipped, and he broke his gaze away from Honor's, fixing it instead on the ground near her feet. Dave had already stepped back and dropped to one knee. Bill stood his ground, but he said nothing.

Honor moved in a blur of aggressive intensity. One moment she stood just in front of Logan, and when his lids rose from a blink she had reached her challenger and wrapped a dainty, clawed hand around her pack mate's throat.

"If you have something to say to me, say it," she snarled, pressing close until Logan was sure Bill felt the heat of her breath on his face. Thin rivulets of blood trickled down the sides of the White Paw's throat where her claws bit into his skin. "If you question my authority to lead this pack, then challenge me. Otherwise, keep your mouth shut and your muzzle out of things that don't concern you."

She punctuated the question with a rough shake of the throat she continued to grip. The rest of the man's body followed along like the hand of a metronome. He had gone limp in her grasp, finally surrendering. His head dropped to the side, his gaze fixed firmly on the ground, and he bared his throat in submission to his alpha.

Honor accepted the victory with something less than enthusiasm in evidence. Logan could see her fingers flex in the flesh of her subordinate, could see new drops of blood well around her claws, and could hear the tenor of her rumbling growl. She sounded not satisfied but angry. Frustrated. As if she wanted to exact retribution from the Lupine who had defied her. Logan couldn't let that happen. A cruel alpha would be just as unacceptable to the Silverbacks as a weak one. An alpha had to lead a pack with power and strength, mental as well as physical. A leader who ruled with fear could only foster instability in the pack, which was exactly what he'd come here to prevent.

An instant before he stepped forward, Honor released her grip and sent her erstwhile challenger crumpling to the ground at her feet.

"Get back to working fences," she spat, clenching her fists at her sides and taking a measured step backward. "Next time you hear something you think concerns the security of the pack, you check with me. Understand?"

Both men nodded and scrambled hastily to their feet.

"*Go.*"

The men went.

Logan watched while the female alpha struggled to tamp down the wild aggression surging through her. Her entire body vibrated with that feral energy, and he was curious to see her contain it. The mark of an alpha often showed itself not in how he or she controlled others, but in how they controlled themselves.

She took a long, deep breath, and when she blew it out, her body had stilled. Well, all except for her hands. Her fingers still betrayed a fine tremor; at least until she clenched her fists and turned to face him. The golden light of the wolf still shone in her dark eyes, but her face was a mask of hard, cool marble.

"Enjoy the show?" she demanded.

He brushed aside the note of challenge in her tone, chalking it up to the aftermath of adrenaline. "That's not quite the word I'd use, but it was interesting. I'll say that."

Her lip curled at the edge. "I'm surprised you didn't take notes so you could report back to your boss on my obvious incompetence."

"I've got a pretty good memory."

"I'm less worried about your memory than your powers of deductive reasoning. You might be stupid enough to figure that one idiot with too much testosterone and not enough work to do constitutes evidence of my incompetence."

"I never called you incompetent."

"Then you're admitting I can run this pack perfectly well without the interference of the Silverback alpha."

"Nice try, but you're not getting rid of me before this weekend. I won't be making any final determinations before then."

He saw the flash of annoyance flicker across her expression, but then, she didn't exactly do much to disguise it. He figured she didn't care if he knew he was pissing her off. She'd certainly told him enough times already.

"Whatever," she growled, reaching for the shovel she had dropped when Bill and Dave had decided to ask for their asskicking. "At this point, I couldn't give a shit. Like I said, it doesn't make much difference what you decide. This is my pack, and the Silverback will put someone else in charge of it over my dead body."

Logan's wolf snarled at the idea of this woman lying in a pool of her own blood, a victim of her own stubbornness and another wolf's teeth. "That is what I'm here to prevent. No one wants this to end with your death, Honor, least of all me or Graham."

She snorted, but didn't even bother to contradict him. Instead, she resumed her work on the huge fire pit, using the shovel to lever stones back into position along the edges and her hands to restack the ones that had fallen. The barrier they comprised was necessary to contain the flames of the enormous bonfire customary during a rural

Howl. The Manhattan pack had long since been forced to abandon the tradition. Fires that size weren't just illegal in Central Park; they were also pretty hard to miss and tended to attract the attention of humans at the most inopportune moments.

"Honor, look—"

She cut him off, straightening to glare at him and burying the blade of the shovel into the packed earth with an angry thrust. "No. You know what? I've already looked, and I sure as hell don't like what I see. We've each laid our cards on the table. I have no intention of surrendering my pack to anyone, least of all someone appointed to the job by a wolf who can't even be bothered to pay us a visit himself. That's my hand. And you? You're wedded to your little role of judge and jury and alpha's errand boy, and you have no intention of doing the right thing and running back to your boss to tell him that the White Paw Clan is doing just fine without him. That's your hand."

He opened his mouth, but the little she wolf refused to let him get a word in edgewise. He couldn't remember the last time anyone had taken that tone with him, all bossy and pissy and arrogant. Not even Graham did such a good job of goading his wolf as this bundle of anger and oncoming heat. His eyes narrowed as her emotions intensified her scent.

"So, fine. We both know where we stand, and

as far as I can see, continuing to bitch at each other isn't likely to change either of our minds. Why waste the energy? Especially when I've got a thousand and one more important things to do in order to keep this pack running. And that's exactly what I'm going to do. I'm getting back to work. I wish like hell that you'd get your ass out of my territory, but since I don't see that happening any time before Sunday, I'm not going to bother worrying about it. All I ask is that you stay out of my way. Go do what you have to do, talk to whatever members of the pack you want to talk to, watch whatever you want to watch, but just stay the hell out of my way. All right?"

She skewered him with one last glare, wrenched the shovel out of the dirt, and turned her back to him. She actually *turned her back*. It was like waving a red flag in front of a bull, only red was the color he pictured turning her ass, and the bull was the wolf inside him who figured spanking her could wait until he'd pinned her down and mated her a time or two. Or twenty.

His nostrils flared and he inhaled deeply. With every breath he took, he could feel the full moon drawing closer and smell her heat building. The fragrance filled his head like a mist, making his thoughts foggy and his dick hard. Goddess help them both.

"No."

He barely understood himself. The denial came out as more of a growl than a word, a rumble pulled from a throat more inclined to form Lupine howls than human words. His wolf wanted out, and only the force of his will kept his change at bay. He liked to think that if he had been a weaker male, he'd already be sprouting fur. That was the effect this woman had on him.

"Well, that's just sad for you, then." She dropped the shovel and bent down to shift a particularly large stone. "Too bad I don't give a shit. Now go away and leave me the fuck alone."

"No."

He shifted his weight to the balls of his feet. Saliva pooled in his mouth as his beast imagined the taste of her; his palms itched as he pictured the feel of her smooth skin under his hands. His control hung by a thread, and with every insulting word she uttered, it was as if she sawed at that thread with a tiny, diamond-edged knife. A few more strokes, and not even the Moon herself could stop him.

"Okay, you know what? I give up. I didn't think it was possible, but you really are dumber than you look." Honor threw up her hands and all but howled at him. "What part of 'get the hell away from me' do you not understand?"

Logan was on her before she got it out, the thread a distant, severed memory. "The part about 'away,' " he growled, and closed his mouth over hers.

Five

Oh, shit. Not again.

Yes, please, thank you.

Honor couldn't seem to make up her mind. Or rather, her hormones. Was Logan Hunter the best thing she'd ever tasted and the one thing she needed more than her next breath, or did she need to kill him and leave his carcass for scavengers to denude the flesh from his bones?

While she pondered, he gave a little roll of his hips against hers and threatened to turn the tide of the whole debate. Not to mention the planet.

Hell, it threatened, promised, and carried out. One minute Honor was contemplating how his head would look posed on a spike in the flower beds next to the front door, and the next, she clung to him like a honeysuckle vine, arms and legs twined around him as she tried to get as close as she possibly could to the source of her arousal.

Damn heat. Why Lupine women couldn't have a normal female menstrual cycle, Honor had never understood. No, she had to go through a monthly bout of nearly uncontrollable lust and a frantic desire to mate every single time she ovulated. How was that right?

Logan didn't seem to mind. His arms closed around her and hitched her higher against him, until her legs wound around his waist and his hips could grind directly between her legs. That felt good for all of seven milliseconds before Honor wanted more. She gritted her teeth against the urge to sink them into his flesh—something a male Lupine usually took as an invitation—and concentrated on remembering to breathe. That lasted five milliseconds. At that point, she gave up on good sense and reached for his shirt collar, grabbing hold and wrenching her hands apart until his buttons popped open and scattered about the floor of the clearing.

Three milliseconds later, she felt the impact of her back hitting the rough bark of a tree trunk and a distinct draft as her T-shirt tore down the middle and fell to hang limply off her elbows. If the man kept this up, she'd have to live permanently in her wolf form for lack of clothes.

That didn't seem so bad, though, not when he was nibbling a path from her mouth, down her throat, to her breasts. She felt the little stings of his teeth against her skin, followed by the heat of his tongue laving the wounds, and the pressure of his mouth as he sucked her skin against his teeth. She'd look like a hickey map of the Milky Way by nightfall, and she couldn't have cared

less. All she cared about was getting her hands
on him and easing the burning ache between her
legs.

Her hands clenched the material of his shirt,
and she shoved it off his shoulders and arms, tugging furiously until it gave up and fluttered to the
ground beside them. Then her hands were on
him, exploring the smooth expanse of muscle and
skin, the furring of hair across his chest, the tight,
flat discs of his nipples. She wanted to taste him,
but he was too bloody far away, so she memo-
rized his textures as if she were blind and he was
her very own form of Braille. When her hands
slipped below the waistband of his jeans and her
nails scraped intricate patterns in the skin at the
small of his back, he roared and shifted his weight
to the side, tearing open the fly of her own jeans
until he could slip his hand inside and plunge two
long fingers deep into her slick heat.

"Logan!"

Her cry sounded choked and harsh to her own
ears, but it was the most she could manage when
her world was exploding behind her eyes like sum-
mertime fireworks. She tilted her hips to take him
deeper and then moaned in frustration when he
pressed knuckle deep inside her. It wasn't enough.

"More. Now."

He didn't answer, but the rough rumble in his
chest sounded like approval to her. Shaking with
need, she reached between them for the button

on his jeans and popped it open, only to encounter another one. Her eyes widened incredulously.

"Button flies?"

He growled in frustration and used his free hand to yank open the next button. "I know. Never again."

The third and fourth buttons gave easily, practically leaping out of their holes to avoid their owner's ire. As soon as the stiff denim parted, his cock sprang free and Honor all but wept in relief. Her hand curled around it, stroking down the length and back again. He felt amazing, hot and thick and achingly hard, and she needed him inside her. Now.

Giving up the last of her restraint, she ducked her head forward and sank her teeth into Logan's shoulder, directly over the spot where she'd bitten him last night in the kitchen. Holding on, she released her grip on his cock only long enough to unzip her own jeans all the way. The rasping sound seemed to echo around them, then her jeans fell away under his hands and her legs were winding back around his waist. She reached for him again, but he was there before her, guiding himself to her liquid entrance. He paused briefly, his hot gaze capturing hers, before he tightened his hands on her hips and plunged deep.

Her cry, all hoarse triumph and blatant challenge, rang through the clear air around them. Logan grunted and leaned into her more heavily, pinning her to the rough tree trunk as he began thrusting inside her.

Honor squirmed to get closer, ignoring the scrapes and patches of raw skin the rough tree bark left on her back. Her awareness encompassed no more than him. Logan. The man against her, around her, inside her. The man who felt like home, whose body had been made to fill hers.

She thrust back at him, frantic to take him, all of him. His cock stretched her wide, filled her to the heart, and still she wanted more. She braced her hands against his shoulders and pushed, trying to get the leverage to increase the force of his thrusts. He growled a warning and pushed her hard against the tree. She snarled in his ear, but before she could bite, he shifted. His hands snaked down between them and spread her thighs even wider. He hooked his elbows behind her knees and pressed her legs up and back, and she felt his next thrust in the back of her throat.

God, he felt incredible inside her. Hot and thick and hard and so perfect her head spun with it. She felt the truth pounding at her in time with his movements, but she shoved it back in fear. She did not need or want this right now. Sure, her life sucked these days, but it sucked on her terms. If she gave in and accepted the truth she could feel haunting her, her terms would cease to exist. She knew it as surely as she knew her own name. The only terms Logan Hunter intended to play by were his own, and Honor knew that giving in would cost her more than she was willing to pay.

She could feel his muscles tensing beneath her clutching hands. She felt the slickness of sweat and of blood where her nails had bitten deep and carved furrows in his broad back. He began to thrust harder, if that were possible, to quicken his motions until he moved with blurring speed and force and Honor had to abandon her efforts to keep up. She simply held on for dear life. Higher he drove them, and faster, until Honor could feel the tension twist between her hip bones like a tightened rubber band, ready to snap.

She forced her eyes open and met his gaze. His eyes looked hot and wild, glowing a feral gold with hunger and instinct. She knew what he was about to do, and she couldn't let it happen. Her body tensed, the first wave of orgasm gathering inside her, preparing to break. Logan growled in response to her body's instinctive tightening and his hands bit deeply into her hips, leaving bruises where tanned fingers gripped creamy flesh. He shifted abruptly and forced her hips to tilt upward until the base of his cock rubbed against her clit as he thrust, and Honor broke.

The climax seized her by the scruff of her neck and shook her like a disobedient cub. Her body clenched around him, milking his cock in hot, slick motions, dragging him into ecstasy behind her.

She felt the moment of his explosion and twisted

her-torso to the side, raising one arm to deflect his bite, catching it on the muscular flesh of her bicep, rather than on the shoulder where he'd been aiming. She heard his muffled roar, but his jaw had already clenched shut around her arm and he couldn't pull away. He mouthed the skin as his body emptied itself inside her, a growl rumbling low in his throat. Honor hung there, pinned between the tree and his shuddering body for endless minutes until his tension eased.

He raised his head to glare at her, brown eyes still glowing an amber gold with the aftermath of his climax. "You shouldn't have done that."

"You shouldn't have tried to mark me." She shivered, suddenly aware that they were all but naked outside in the stone yard in the middle of winter. Never mind that steam billowed off them in a hazy fog; she wanted her clothes.

"You are mine." Logan shook her, staring into her eyes as if he could will her to agree with him.

"I don't belong to anyone. Least of all you. I bear no man's mark, and I intend to keep it that way."

He snorted. "What are you? The Virgin Alpha? I hate to break it to you, sweetheart, but your name isn't Elizabeth."

"It doesn't need to be." She shoved hard at his shoulders, and he grunted, but didn't release her. "Let me go and get the hell off my property. We've said everything we need to say, and I need to go take a frickin' shower."

His jaw snapped shut, loud enough for Honor to hear the click. When he spoke from between clenched teeth, it sounded as if it came from a wolf's throat, not a human larynx. "Not yet. I'm not done. You will be my mate, Honor. No matter what I have to do to convince you."

He carried her to the floor of the clearing and went ahead with the convincing. All Honor could do was moan.

"This doesn't change anything, you know."

Logan sighed and stretched, shifting his weight partially off Honor's limp body and onto the rough ground. "I never thought it had."

He might have hoped, but he hadn't really let himself believe any different. In the twelve hours or so that he'd known Honor Tate, he'd come to realize she could teach stubborn to Missy Winters.

Logan winced at the reminder of his own pack and why he'd come to Connecticut in the first place. It unfortunately hadn't been to roll around the forest floor with the mouthwatering alpha of the White Paw Clan, but to decide if she had what it took to lead her pack. Something about which he hadn't yet made up his mind.

"Just so we're clear." She pushed him off her, forcing him to roll onto his back so she could sit up and brush the bits of leaves and dirt from her skin. "Now when are you leaving?"

"Sometime next week. Just like I told you."

She turned to him with narrowed eyes, an

expression entirely different from the one she'd worn about ten minutes ago.

"Wrong answer. Try again."

Logan shook his head. "Honor, I've been here for barely twelve hours and I've already seen you have to take down one male and had another all but introduce himself to me as alpha in your place. Do you honestly think—"

"What are you talking about?"

"I'm just trying to point out that—"

She growled, low and vicious. "*What. Member.* Of this pack claimed my title to an outsider?"

Logan tightened his lips. "On my way here, a male stopped me. He didn't tell me he was alpha, but he wanted to welcome me to the territory and clearly would have been happy for me to draw my own conclusions."

"*Who.*"

She wasn't even pretending it was a question.

"Darin Major."

The tension popped like a balloon, huffed out on a bark of a laugh, and Honor returned her attention to searching for her clothes. "Darin. I thought I was going to have a problem for a minute."

"You don't think a male member of your pack assuming your position before outsiders is a problem?"

"No, I just don't think Darin is a problem." She met his gaze briefly. "Trust me, I know all about Darin and his delusions of grandeur. I can handle him. Even if he were to challenge me, I can take him. He's not a threat."

"The question isn't just whether or not you can take him. Don't you think your regional alpha would be a little bit concerned if the alpha of this pack couldn't go a week without someone challenging for the position? Graham wants stability."

"And I'll provide it. In fact, why don't you go tell your boss that right now? If you get on the road before noon, you can beat most of the traffic back to New York."

Logan groaned and covered his eyes with his forearm. "Look, I think we've come to a Mexican standoff." He shifted to look at her and tried desperately not to get distracted by the sight of her bare breasts and the marks he'd made on them, most of which were already fading. "You're not going to change your mind about having me here, and I'm not going to change my mind about staying. So I have a proposal for you."

"Does it involve you catching the next green light back to the city?"

"No. And that's not just because I have lousy luck with traffic signals, either." He saw her looking around for the remains of her T-shirt and felt a twinge of conscience. He handed her his mostly intact, if buttonless, shirt and watched her shrug into it. "I intend to stay until I find out what I came here to find out."

"It doesn't matter what you say. This pack is

not going to change, and I'm not going to give it up and make a graceful exit no matter what you think your job is or what you decide is best for us." She tied the ends of the shirt into a knot below her breasts and reached for her jeans. "You're wasting your time."

All of a sudden he realized she'd never been wearing a bra and his body responded in a pretty predictable fashion. He drew one knee up to his chest and rested his forearm across it. In spite of the pleasurable interlude they had just shared, he still wasn't sure if it was safe to leave any of his body parts sticking out and vulnerable around this testy female.

"It's my time to waste, but I don't think that's what I'll be doing, anyway. But here's what I'm thinking." He waited until she fastened her jeans and turned to him with an impatient expression. "The full moon is in three days." Along with the peak of her heat, but he wasn't thinking about that, and he certainly wasn't going to mention it. "It will be the first Howl since your father's death. It would be a perfect opportunity for me to see the dynamics of the pack and to get the answers to the Silverback alpha's questions. If you can put up with me for another seventy-two hours, I'll leave after that without a fuss."

"Why? Give me a good reason. I have every right to order a nonmember out of pack territory. I don't have to let you stay."

"You do if you want to avoid a clan war."

He saw her pause, saw his words sink in and make her think. He kept his gaze level, but unthreatening. He needed her to know he meant what he said, but he didn't want to come across as any more hard-nosed or unyielding than he had to. He walked a delicate tightrope, but his balance had always been good.

"Winters would really take it as far as a war? That's insane. This pack isn't big enough to make a difference to him. It shouldn't matter to the Silverback who leads the White Paw, so long as they aren't intending to lead it into his business. And trust me, I'm not. So why is this suddenly a life-or-death situation?"

"The White Paw pay fealty to the Silverback. It's his job to care."

"That's bullshit. Even if it's true, it's bullshit. It's his job to make sure my pack doesn't pick a fight with his, reveal ourselves to the local human population, or otherwise compromise the safety of the larger Lupine community. Anything more than that is just someone with too much time on his hands and an overgrown side of busybody." Honor's gaze searched his expression for a minute, then rolled her eyes. "And even if you agreed with me, you're too loyal to say so. Right. Well, I just don't need this crap. Not now. Not here. Not a fucking chance."

Logan shrugged. "You've got it anyway. Now what are you going to do about it?"

She slammed her feet into battered hiking boots

with a snarled curse. "Right now, I'm going back
to the house to change, and then I'm going back to
work. Some of us have real jobs where we have
to be constructive and accomplish things."

He suppressed a smile at that dig. She was cute
when she was mad.

And she'd probably rip his intestines out
through his nostrils if he mentioned that fact.

"Gotcha. I think I'm going to go get a shirt at
least, and then maybe take a look around. See if I
can meet some of the pack. You know, basically
stick my nose in where it doesn't belong. See you
at dinner?"

Logan watched her stalk off back toward the
house and grinned a wolfish grin. He hadn't come
here expecting to find his mate, but damned if it
didn't appear that was exactly what he'd done.
He wondered what she'd say when he informed
her they'd be getting married and having cubs
together. If he knew her at all, he guessed what
she'd say didn't bear repeating. But what the
hell? Logan Hunter loved a challenge. And this
one looked to be a doozy.

By the time Logan gathered and donned what
was left of his clothes—namely his blue jeans, his
boots, and one sock—and made his way back to
the main house, Honor was long gone. He hadn't
really expected anything different, but some
days, he just couldn't quell that involuntary burst
of optimism.

He jogged up to his room, which he'd learned was across the hall and down three doors from Honor's, and grabbed a change of clothes. It took a second to brush himself free of the debris he'd picked up from the ground in the stone yard, but he figured it was better to take a moment now than spend half the day fighting with a twig in his trousers.

He was still buttoning up a new shirt as he made his way downstairs and into the kitchen. All his exercise from this morning had made him hungry, even if it was still technically an hour or so till lunch. He didn't find Joey in the kitchen as he'd expected, but he did find a brief note on the counter explaining the timing of meals, the contents of the refrigerator, and that he was free to help himself to anything that wasn't on the neatly printed menu beside the note. He took Honor's cousin at her word and foraged in the fridge, emerging with half a rabbit and a full duck breast, cooked beautifully rare.

Sitting at the small kitchen table, he made short work of his snack before he wiped the grease off his hands with a dishtowel and pulled out his cell phone. He noted gratefully that he still got a pretty good signal out here in the woods and dialed Graham's direct line at Vircolac.

"Vircolac," a perky feminine voice announced. "We bring good things back to life."

Logan snorted out a laugh. "What, is that a new ad slogan?"

"It's still in testing. The first focus group yielded mixed results. How are you, Logan? Arrived safely in the wild, untamed north?"

"Missy, I'm only a hundred and fifteen miles outside of Manhattan, and the last yeti from these parts became a stockbroker back in eighty-seven. But I'm fine. Thanks."

"Spoilsport." She sounded remarkably unfazed by the correction. "How are things going so far? Did the new alpha make a good first impression?"

Logan's mind instantly conjured up the sight of Honor silhouetted in the bathroom doorway the instant before she had noticed him. The light and steam behind her had outlined her in lush detail, emphasizing the soft curves of her breasts, those long legs, and the luscious flare of her hips. He felt his body stirring at the memory and cleared his throat. No need to tell the Luna just how impressed certain parts of him had really been. "I'm reserving judgment."

Missy snorted. "Just like a man. I assume you called to talk to my mate, not to me, right?"

The question caught Logan unawares. Not because the answer wasn't yes, but because he realized that for the first time since he'd originally met Missy Roper Winters, he really would rather talk to her husband than to her. The epiphany almost knocked him over. Missy hadn't caused the erection he could feel straining against his jeans—zip front, this time—as they talked; Honor had.

He'd been fine until his mind had conjured up that image of the lithe brunette poised in the bathroom door wearing nothing more than a towel. And when he let his mind wander along its favorite path, he imagined Honor's pale, creamy skin and dark, curling hair, not Missy's blond mop and curvy figure. It amazed him.

"Logan?"

The quiet question shook him out of his meditation. "Right. Sorry, Miss. Yeah, I do need to talk to Graham. Is he around?"

"Sure. He was just showing Ava the door. She stopped over to see Roarke, and Graham never rests easy until he's seen her taxi pull away. I imagine he'll be back any second."

Logan could hardly blame Graham. Of all Missy's close friends, Ava Markham inspired the greatest sense of fear and awe. An unrepentant matchmaker, she'd tried her hand at setting up just about everyone she knew at one time or another. Now, her erstwhile victims spent most of their time praying for the day when someone would turn the tables on her. "Right. Should I call back?"

"No, don't worry about it. Here he is now."

He heard a shuffling sound as the receiver was passed from one hand to the other, then a rough growl replaced Missy's light, feminine voice in his ear. "What's up?"

Logan felt his eyebrow arching. "Nice to talk to you, too. I'm fine, thanks. Didn't sleep that well last night, but somehow I'm not feeling all that many ill effects. Must be the water up here."

"Can it, Hunter. It's been a lousy day."

"I heard. Ava paid a visit, huh? Having the place fumigated?"

"Not yet. Maybe when Missy takes Roarke to the park later. So what's the news?"

"I'm here."

Pause.

"That's it? That's the news?"

"Rome wasn't built in a day."

"Yeah, but they could at least say, 'We're here and we put down some rocks,' right?"

"Okay. I'm here, and I've met Tate's daughter."

Another pause.

"And?"

"There's not much else to tell. I've only been here"—he glanced at his watch—"fifteen hours, and most people around here were asleep for a good eight or nine of those."

He and Honor hadn't been asleep, but he saw no need to bog the conversation down with details.

"Yeah, but you've had time to form a first impression, haven't you?"

Logan paused, reluctant to say anything. On the one hand, he didn't want to hurt Honor's chance to prove herself, but on the other, he couldn't lie to his alpha. "Yeah. She's pretty together, considering what she's just been through. I think she has potential."

"Potential or ability?"

"It's really too soon to make that kind of call."

"What about the pack? Have they settled in to the idea of having a female alpha, especially such a young one?"

"I'm going to start talking to them once I'm off with you. So far I've only met a couple of them, and I doubt that's much to go by."

"It's a start. What did they have to say?"

Logan gritted his teeth for a second before answering. "There have been three challenges since she took the title Alpha."

"Really? Well, she's alive, so I guess that means she can handle herself in a fight. How is she taking the deaths?"

"I don't think her father's death has had a chance to sink in yet. She's been too busy keeping things running to shed any tears over him."

"Understandable. But what about the challenge deaths? Is she holding up after those?"

Shit. He knew this answer was not one his friend was going to like, so he hesitated for a second.

"There haven't been any deaths," he finally admitted.

Again, Graham paused. "What does that mean? If there were challenges . . ."

"She chose to end them without slaying her opponents. The first showed her his throat, and the other two she crippled. But she hasn't killed anyone."

There was a moment of silence.

Not the reverent kind, but the are-you-fucking-kidding-me kind.

"And you still think she has the potential to lead that pack?" Graham asked carefully.

"I think it's possible. She's strong enough. Two of those challenges came from grown men, and she defeated both of them, death or no. She's also damned smart from what I can tell. True, she's got a bit of a feminine notion of mercy, but I believe she would do what needed to be done if it came to that kind of situation."

"She doesn't believe an alpha challenge is that kind of situation?"

Logan felt the need to defend her, which was weird enough in itself, but coupled with the fact that his hackles were going up in response to his alpha, it crossed the line into surreal. "She did what she had to do, and she walked away from the challenges a clear winner. The last one was her closest childhood friend. Imagine how you would feel if you were faced with a choice to let me live or die. How easy would that death stroke be for you?"

"Whoa. We're not talking about you and me, brother. We're talking about Ethan Tate's daughter. Aren't we?"

Logan forced down his growl. "Yes. We are. And I think we need to give her the benefit of the doubt. The first Howl since Ethan's death will be this weekend. Three days from now. The whole pack will be gathered, and according to Pack Law, any outstanding challenges will have to be answered then or held till the next Clans Moot."

"Which is still three more years away. And it's scheduled to be hosted in Silverback territory this time. So she and her clan will have to come here." He was silent for a moment, and Logan could almost hear him thinking. "I won't say I'm not concerned over what you've told me, but I trust your judgment. Stay through the Howl. If you think she's capable of leading the pack after what you see then, I'll accept your word and leave her in power until the next Clans Moot. Then I'll take a look for myself and make a final decision."

Oh, right. Honor would just love that little plan. That just meant that his own carefully thought-out plan would be to not tell Honor a word about it.

"Agreed."

"Good. Now get back to work. I'm thinking about trying to give Missy a new baby for her birthday."

Logan rolled his eyes at the shriek he heard just before the phone disconnected. He flipped the cell phone closed and shoved it into his pocket. Let Graham have fun with his little blond mate. Logan had a darker fish to fry.

Six

The meaty, spicy scent of chili hit Honor the minute she stepped into the meeting hall and clashed immediately with the sick knot of tension that had been twisting around in her stomach all afternoon. Only a mighty act of will—or perhaps sheer cursed stubbornness—kept her from spinning on her heel and racing to the nearest tree trunk to lose what little contents her stomach might have on offer. Damn her father, and damn Logan Hunter. Between the two of them, she hadn't been able to go a day without nausea in close to a week.

As if she didn't have enough to worry about.

Fortunately, all of the recent practice Honor had gotten in recently at keeping her thoughts and feelings (and recently consumed meals) to herself kicked in and reminded her to clench her teeth, take short, shallow breaths, and fake it with authority. With that plan in place, she managed to nod and exchange greetings with the gathered pack members as she made her way to the alpha's dining table at the rear center of the huge room. In pride of place, the table sat apart from the long rows that stretched the length of the hall, allowing the alpha to see and be seen by every other Lupine in the room. Ethan Tate had graced its center chair like a modern, furry Genghis Khan surveying his Mongol hoards. To Honor, it held about as much appeal as an executioner's electric chair. In her mind, she'd taken to calling it Sparky in a morbid attempt at humor. The way she saw it, the title fit—it was the ultimate hot seat.

Of course, that didn't stop her from making her way steadily toward it, nor would it stop her from planting her ass in it and keeping it there while she shared the pack's traditional communal Wednesday-night meal. Her father had designated it as the alpha's seat, so as the new alpha, that was where Honor would sit. Everyone expected it of her.

She felt the eyes on her as she settled into the carved wooden chair and pretended to ignore them, which was easier said than done when you considered that more than two thirds of the pack tended to show up at these twice-weekly group meals. For as long as Honor could remember, the alpha had hosted the pack on Wednesday and Sunday nights in the enormous barnlike meeting hall with the attached industrial kitchen at the back. When she'd been a child, Honor's Aunt Marie had been the head cook, whipping up mammoth pots of chili or stew, or roasting entire deer and cows on spits outside the back door. These days, Joey had taken over, of course. She was her mother's daughter, after all, and feeding anyone who stood still long enough seemed to be her calling in life. That and reorganizing Honor's T-shirts according to some system Honor had yet to figure out but seemed to always get wrong.

"Tonight is the last of the bison," Joey said as she set a heaping bowl of fiery red chili and an open bottle of beer in front of her cousin. "Sunday we'll turn three sheep into stew, but hopefully after the Howl there will be enough clear heads around here to bring down some deer and leave them whole enough to share. Everyone has been asking for venison."

Wrenching her attention back to the present, Honor threw the other woman a smile. "Thanks, Joey. The way you roast it, I'm sure they have been. You let me know if you don't get what you need, though. I'll make sure we bring you a buck or two."

Joey nodded, drying her hands on her apron, but making no move to head back to the kitchen. Feeling awkward, Honor reached for her spoon and stirred her chili. She really didn't feel much like eating at the moment, but she didn't want to insult her cousin. Usually, Joey was so busy at the big meals that she didn't have time to stay around and chat.

"How have things been going with the beta from the city?" her cousin asked after a moment, and Honor reflected that the answer to that question had more to do with the death of her appetite than she would care to admit.

She lifted a spoonful of food to her lips and blew on it. As if she had the faintest intention of eating anything. "Fine."

"He's been asking a lot of questions. The girls mentioned it to me." Joey nodded toward the kitchen doorway where half a dozen women bustled around finishing dishing out tonight's dinner and cleaning up from its preparation. "Most of us haven't been exactly sure what to tell him."

Tell him to go fuck himself.

"I've noticed that myself," a deep voice drawled, and Honor had to exercise a considerable amount of strength not to plant her face in her bowl in a reckless attempt at drowning by chili. If she offed herself that way, at least it would take care of her inner wolf. Her approaching heat had the furry little slut panting and howling every time Logan Hunter got within ten feet of her.

"M-Mr. Hunter," Joey stuttered, her color leaching away and returning just as quickly in a flash of bright red embarrassment. "I didn't notice you come in."

Logan smiled his charming smile. "I'm not surprised. There's quite a crowd in here, but I'm pretty certain that can be explained by the amazing scents I've been smelling for the last couple of hours. Someone around here evidently knows their way around a kitchen."

"Oh, it's just chili. Would you like me to get

you a bowl? I meant it when I said in the note that I'd be happy to fix you something back at the house if you'd rather not eat with everyone else."

"Note?" Honor growled, wondering when her cousin and their uninvited guest had gotten cozy enough with each other to start exchanging notes.

"Your cousin thoughtfully left me a note in the kitchen up at the house letting me know that most of the pack usually eats here at the hall on Wednesday nights." Logan offered the explanation easily, almost as easily as he slid into the chair next to Honor and reached across her for the heaping basket of corn bread and garlic toast. "And, thank you, Joey, I'd love a bowl. If it tastes half as good as it smells, I could probably be persuaded to beg for one."

Honor's wolf snarled at the flirtatious tone and the way Logan smiled at her cousin, which made Honor want to punch herself. Despite their mistake of this afternoon and her horny animal instincts, it was none of Honor's business who the visitor flirted with. In fact, she should thank Joey for taking the annoyance off her hands. She certainly shouldn't be growling possessively over the man, even if he had tried to mate her just a few hours before. That had been about nothing more than her intensifying heat pheromones and the heat of a particularly passionate moment. She hadn't taken it seriously, so there was no reason she should expect him to do so. Besides which, she currently needed a mate slightly less than she needed a full frontal lobotomy.

A spoonful of chili shoveled into her own mouth concealed her instinctive growl.

"Coming right up." Joey offered a blush-pink smile of her own and bounded off to the kitchen. Honor choked down more chili.

"Sweet kid, your cousin," Logan commented, breaking off a chunk of corn bread and raising it to his mouth. "Friendly, too. She's been real helpful since I got here."

Honor's wolf snarled viciously. Possessively. Honor smacked her down, and mustered a passable smirk. "Yeah, well, she's still unmated, and with the lack of selection around here, it's easy for a girl to lower her standards."

"Of course, she doesn't make my dick hard every time I look at her, so I guess it's a good thing she wasn't the one I got naked with a few hours ago, huh?"

This time, Honor choked *on* more chili. Her gaze flew to his face and narrowed on the gleeful spark in his eyes. The bastard enjoyed throwing her off balance. She wondered how much he'd enjoy it when she threw him out a window. What was she supposed to say to something like that? She wasn't an idiot, and she knew that in the time he'd been posing his muzzle into her business— Goddess, had it only been one day!—she likely hadn't made a great impression, at least not in terms of rationality and a cool head for command. Maybe pissing her off was part of his strategy to prove her unfit to lead her pack? Whatever his motive, he seemed to get a real charge out of yanking her tail, and she'd had enough of giving him the satisfaction.

Ignoring him, she set down her spoon and took a swallow of cold beer. It cut through the spicy burn of the chili but did little to cool the heat of the bitch inside her. It whined every time she inhaled and got a whiff of Logan's musky scent, prompting Honor to wonder how difficult it would be to get her hands on some ketamine. The horse tranquilizer sounded about right at the moment, provided it would actually do the job and knock her out. With her Lupine metabolism, drugs tended to burn off faster than they were administered. She couldn't even get a good drunk on without resorting to multiple bottles of the hard stuff. Sometimes, there was no justice.

"How are you feeling, Honor?" He leaned closer, his voice rumbling against her ear in an insidious tickle of heat and smoke. "You ran away before I got a chance to look you over. You're not . . . hurting, are you?"

The question must have been directed straight between her thighs, because that was the only part of her to answer, and she wasn't about to mention the ache she felt there. Not when it had nothing to do with injury and everything to do with renewed hunger. If she could call it renewed.

If she were being honest, she'd have to admit it had never really gone away to begin with. Her wolf whispered evilly that it would take days and days of privacy before that need had a hope of being assuaged.

She forced the bitch to step back and gathered her sanity for a withering glare. "You might think of yourself as the Big Bad Wolf, Hunter, but I'm no Little Red. You can't hurt me with a little ordinary sex, so don't flatter yourself."

His dark eyes lit with gold, then narrowed. His voice dropped. "'Ordinary'?"

She shrugged. "What would you call it?"

He growled his response through clenched teeth. "If you hadn't been such a slippery little devil, I'd have called it claiming my mate."

"You'd have been wrong."

Honor was so done with this discussion. Bracing her hands on the top of the table, she shoved to her feet. Well, she tried to. A very large and very heavy hand on her shoulder kept her in place.

She growled. "When I say, 'Move it, or lose it,' understand very clearly that I *will* bite your hand off at the wrist. It wouldn't be the first time I've done it. This week, even."

"You aren't going anywhere until we've gotten a few things clear between us. *Mate.*"

"I am *not* your mate."

He ignored her bared teeth and laughed, but the sound held little amusement. "Deny it all you like, sweetheart, but you and I both know the truth. You think I wouldn't have known the first minute I scented you? You think I'm a fool?"

"You really want me to answer that?"

"I want you to stop behaving like a brat and admit the truth about a few things. No matter what you keep telling yourself, I didn't come here to ruin your life, and I don't have to be your enemy. Why can't you let me help you?"

It was Honor's turn to laugh at that.

"Help me." She studied the expression of grim determination on his face and shook her head. Maybe he actually believed what he was saying, but someone needed to set the man straight. Apparently, that had just gotten added to her little to-do list. "I already told you how you can help me, Hunter. You can go back to New York, back to Graham Winters and tell him that the White Paw Clan has an alpha and it needs nothing from him but that he acknowledge the change in leadership and then leave us the hell alone. That's the only help I need from you, or from the Silverbacks. Is that straight enough for you?"

"We've had this discussion before, Honor, at least twice now. Do you really want to have it again?"

"If it means I'll finally get through that thick male skull of yours, we can have it three more times tonight and seven times tomorrow."

A muscle ticked above his cheekbone. "And I thought Missy was stubborn," he muttered.

Honor beat back her wolf's displeasure at

hearing him speak another female's name. She really did need him to understand the situation, so maybe it was time to lay it all out for him, to spread every single ugly card in her hand on the table and see if he still wanted to place his bets.

Leaning forward, she caught his gaze and held it, watching the gold lights of his angry wolf play across his brown, human irises. "Look, Hunter, maybe you really do think you're here to help me. I don't know if you're honestly that stupid, but just for a second consider what it is that you think your presence here is going to solve. You're going to walk around my pack for a couple of days and then decide if you think I'm fit to lead it, right? Well, let me ask you something. If you only have two choices—I'm fit or I'm unfit—what do you think is going to happen here?"

She didn't give him time to answer. "Let me tell you. I know this pack a lot better than you do, so I think you can give me some credit for an educated guess. I've been beta of this pack since I was fifteen. For well over ten years, I've been the one supporting the previous alpha and handling both the problems too small to bother him with, and the ones he just didn't want to *be* bothered with, and let me tell you; Ethan Tate may have been my father, but he wasn't a man to go easy on someone just because they shared his name. He treated me just the same as he treated any subordinate member of this pack, and I had to *prove* myself to him to earn my position beside him. He didn't go easy on me and he trained me to be able to lead this pack in his absence, whether that was when he went away for the weekend, or when he dropped dead from cancer. Me. Just me. No one else in this pack has the training or experience that I do, so who else do you think is a better choice to lead it?"

Honor saw his expression tighten and fought back the urge to smack him upside the head. She'd had a lot of years to come to the understanding that some men needed to have the truth beaten into them with a blunt object. She'd hoped Logan was smarter than that.

"Being an alpha is about a lot more than just making sure no one runs amok through the local human population, or convincing young males not to kill each other over some female's first heat," he argued.

"Oh, really? How nice of you to tell me that. Because as a young female pack beta, I didn't ever have to fight a grown male to make him submit to my dominant position in the pack. And I've never stood at my father's side while he negotiated a territory dispute with the Riverside Clan to the north of our territory. And I've never had to help figure out if the businesses my dad ran were going to provide enough meat to feed the males, females, and cubs in the pack who couldn't find jobs out here in Northeast Bumblefuck to sufficiently feed themselves. Thanks so much for pointing out all the other jobs that I've been doing or helping to do here for . . . oh . . . *my entire life.*"

"Do you need a napkin, *sweetheart*? I think you drooled some sarcasm onto your chin."

"Fuck you."

His hand slid from her shoulder to her wrist and gripped firmly. "Been there, done that. And trust me, mate, we'll get to it again real soon."

She saw the promise in his eyes and really wished her brain would talk some sense into her other parts and let them know that this was the time to be angry and disdainful and offended, not horny.

"Look, I'm not trying to dismiss what you've accomplished in the past, or the status you've held in this pack as its beta," he said, obviously struggling to keep his tone reasonable. "But the fact that you saw your father run this pack for your whole life should tell you that stepping from beta to alpha isn't like moving up a year in high school. Not every beta is cut out to be alpha. You don't get there just by being stronger or more experienced than everyone else. You have to be *the* strongest. Wolves don't become alpha; they're born that way."

"You think I don't know that?" She waved her free hand at the rows and rows of pack members ranged about the room in front of them. The ones currently pretending they weren't straining to listen to the conversation between their leader and the strange Lupine who had invaded their territory. "You said you were going to take a look around and talk to the members of my pack before you made a decision about me. You go right ahead and do that. You go try to find someone in this pack you think can lead it better than I can. Then you come back and tell me what you find. Or let me save you the trouble. If you're looking for a male among the White Paw who you think can be a better alpha than I can, you won't find him. This is my pack, Hunter. I know my pack."

"Stop acting like I'm just looking for an excuse to unseat you," he hissed, never bothering to look at anyone else. "Yes, that could happen, but I didn't come here with my mind made up. There are any number of ways this could go, Honor. If you'd climb down off your pile of righteous indignation, maybe you could see that."

Wow, was he really that naïve? She shook her head. "No, this is a true or false question, Hunter, so there are only two possible answers.

"Option one: you take your time looking around, poking your nose into my business and feeling out all the members of my pack, and it finally sinks in that I was right and this was all just a big waste of time. You'll decide that I am the alpha of my pack, and you'll go back to New York and tell your boss exactly what I told you in the beginning: Honor Tate holds the White Paw Clan. True."

He growled at that, and the deep rumble tickled the hairs at the back of her neck. "If you think I'm going anywhere without my mate, you're operating under some serious delusions, Honor Tate. You can't get rid of me that easily. You can't get rid of me at all."

"Which brings us to answer number two." She wanted to believe him. Hell, part of her did believe him. Her wolf knew Logan wasn't lying when he said he was her mate. Her nose wasn't broken. She could smell the truth for herself. What she couldn't do was see any possible way in which the two of them could end up with a happily ever after. Some things just weren't meant to be, and she'd given up on happy a long, long time ago.

"Two A goes like this," she continued, shoving back a pang of grief she had no right to feel. "You decide I'm not fit to be alpha of this pack. If that happens, you undermine everything I've spent the last decade of my life establishing. You tell the males in my pack that you think one of them can challenge me and win, which means they will likely all challenge me. One at a time, I can defeat any male in this pack. I've already done it with two of the strongest, and I'm not going to back down from any of the rest. But, if they all come after me at once, there's no way I can win. Even if they come at me one after the other in honorable challenges, eventually I'll exhaust myself, and one of them will be able to get through my guard. Either way, I'm dead, so the White Paw Clan really would get itself a new alpha. I just wish I'd be around to tell you I told you so when that new alpha leads the pack down the road to hell within the first three months. Maybe I'll get lucky and be able to haunt you."

She saw the roar building up behind his expression and raised a hand. She needed to make him understand what she was saying. She didn't have time for knee-jerk denials or macho possessive-mate bullshit. This was too important.

"Two B is the one where I don't die, but listen for a second and then tell me if you really think it's a better choice. Listen carefully."

She leaned in close, so close she could see tiny pinpricks of silver in the brown of his eyes where the gold had not completely taken over. Even as she watched, they disappeared, his wolf steadily eroding his control and rising to the surface.

"This is the one where you get your wish." She twisted the arm he still grasped until her own fingers could curl around his wrist, clasping him in return until his eyes flared an even brighter gold. "In this one, I admit you're my mate. In fact, I proclaim it in front of my whole pack. Anyone who steps up to challenge me is forced to realize that they can't try to harm me without my mate stepping in to defend me. Since I would only agree to call a male my mate if he supported me in everything I do, I'd still be alpha of this pack, because even though you had called me unfit, your presence at my side would keep me in the position simply because no one would be willing to challenge both of us together. Which would make you, as the mate of a female alpha, not the beta of the Silverback Clan, but the White Paw Clan's Sol."

She paused and watched the truth begin to dawn on this stubborn, arrogant man. Her lips quirked in a bitter half smile.

"So that's false, Hunter. Now which one is it going to be?"

Seven

Sol.

Male mate to the female alpha.

The title had every one of Logan's instincts rebelling in an instant. How could she ever imagine he would accept a position as any pack's Sol? Unlike the Luna of a pack—the mate of a male alpha—the Sol lacked any power or authority. Sure, he was allowed and expected to defend his mate against a direct physical threat; he was still Lupine after all. Outside of that, though, he had no place in the clan's hierarchy. He was not considered his mate's beta, he wasn't an elder, or even a storyteller or lorekeeper, since those were positions requiring age in the first case, and specialized knowledge and training in the others. He'd be the Lupine equivalent of a boy toy, with no power and no identity outside that of his mate.

He'd sooner suffer some sort of comic book–style radiation mishap and wind up a cat. At least then he could pretend to have a little dignity.

His mate's soft snort brought him back to reality.

"Yeah. That's what I thought you'd say." Honor

eased her wrist from his lax grip and pushed back her chair. "There's only one easy way out of this, Hunter, and that's to name me alpha and then get on with your life. In the city. Keep that in mind while you go around asking questions. Sometimes there aren't any good answers."

This time he didn't try to interfere when she thrust to her feet and addressed the crowd.

"White Paws." Her voice rang out in the large room, quieting the conversations and drawing all eyes her way. Their way. He saw plenty of curious glances darting toward him, but they all eventually settled on Honor. "I have an announcement to make. I'm sure some of you have already noticed that we have an unfamiliar male in our territory. His name is Logan Hunter, and he's come here from the Silverbacks to acknowledge the passing of our old alpha and witness our transition into the future."

Whispers and murmurs swept down the tables, but no one raised a voice or a question. Logan, though, could feel their curiosity and the tension of uncertainty. This was an isolated pack, unused to entertaining visitors. They had also been through quite an upheaval lately. And he was only here to cause more.

"I have granted Hunter permission to stay among us until Sunday and to witness our gathering on Saturday's full moon. I expect each and every member of this pack to treat him with the courtesy due to anyone visiting under my authority.

If an individual behaves otherwise, I will deal with them appropriately."

She swept the room with a cool stare. No one said a word.

Finally, she nodded. "Good. Now enjoy your dessert. Smells like pie."

Without another word, she strode across the hall and out the wide double doors, leaving her dinner mostly untouched and Logan still slightly stunned. What the hell was he supposed to do now?

"Here, son. Have some pie. It's apple."

Logan blinked down at the dessert plate that appeared in front of him, pushing aside his bowl of cold chili. Raising his eyes, he watched as an unfamiliar older male pulled a chair up opposite him and settled down with his own slice of pie.

The man raised overgrown gray eyebrows and jerked his chin. "Go on. Dig in."

Slowly, Logan reached for his fork.

"For Pete's sake, I didn't poison it. I think you'd have to worry about that more if Honor had delivered it. Me, I got no grudge against you at the moment. And if I did, I'd sure find a way to show you that didn't involve poison and the waste of a perfectly good piece of pie."

The scowl was what finally won Logan over, perversely enough. It reminded him a little of Honor. He'd seen precious few other expressions on the woman's face since his arrival, so he'd become something of an expert.

"I'm Logan Hunter," he offered, extending his hand to the elder.

"Yeah, I heard." The Lupine shook hands briefly, then went straight back to his dessert. "Name's MacDuff. Hamish."

"Nice to meet you." Logan chewed a bite of flaky crust, crisp apples, and cinnamon-laced sugar. He grunted in appreciation. "Thanks for the pie. This is good."

"Ain't it, though? One thing about Josephine is, she's a damn fine hand in the kitchen. Too bad she doesn't spend more time there."

By "Josephine," Logan assumed MacDuff referred to Honor's cousin Joey. She had introduced herself that way when Logan first arrived, and as far as he could tell, she seemed to spend most of her time doing domestic chores. Of course, there could be another female in the pack with the same name.

He decided to be cautious. "Josephine?"

MacDuff grunted, scraping up the last crumbs of pie with the edge of his fork. "Josephine Tate. Honor's first cousin. Girl can cook like nobody's business. If you ask me, she ought to spend more time at it, and less at watching what everyone else is doing. Takes after her mother that way, if you ask me."

The old man pushed aside his plate with a sigh, and Logan observed him with renewed interest. He looked to be in his late sixties, at least—easily one of the pack elders. That could make him a

valuable source of information, if he proved willing to share.

Logan finished his pie and slid the plate to the
side to join the chili bowl. "Let's say I did ask
you, MacDuff. What exactly would you tell me?"

The Lupine's hazel-blue eyes glinted with appreciation, as if he'd been waiting for just that
question. "I'd tell you that Josephine isn't half as
big a problem for you as Honor is, son. And, I'd
tell you that in spite of that story she just tried to
spoon-feed us, I've been around in the world
long enough to know that you didn't just come
to tell her the Silverback Clan says 'hello.' I know
it's not exactly Manhattan around here, but you
could probably figure out we've got mailboxes
and telephones, and Internet service, same as
you, if that's all you boys had to say."

"We probably could."

"Which means that you were sent here because Graham Winters isn't exactly sure whether
he approves of the White Paw Clan having a female alpha."

MacDuff delivered his summary of the situation, then sat back in his chair, folded his arms
across his stocky chest, and waited for Logan to
make the next move. The younger Lupine had to
admire the man's ability to cut right to the heart
of the matter.

"And let's say that's true. What would your
reaction be?"

"Hell, say it or not, we both know it's true,

son. No need to dance around it. I'm not saying the rest of the pack see it, but you might not want to lump me in with the rest of the pack."

"Why not? Because you're older than the rest of them?"

"Barney Andrews is closing in on me pretty fast. He turned sixty-eight last month. This ain't just about me being an elder. The years tell me a thing or two about how packs operate, but that's not what tells me about how our girl is going to react if you try to hand this pack over to someone else."

"No one said that's what's going to happen," Logan explained, for what felt like the hundredth time in the past twenty-four hours.

MacDuff snorted. "You can't fool me, son, and I don't imagine you got away with fooling my niece, either."

"Niece?"

"Yup. Sadie, Honor's mama, was my little sister. That makes me 'Uncle Hamish.'"

"And you didn't think to mention that when you told me how Honor and Josephine are related?"

"Wasn't talking about me back then. Josephine is Joseph Tate's daughter. Joseph mated with one of Jim Pritcher's daughters. The girl is no blood relation to me. Joseph and Marie died before either girl even started school, and the Pritchers brought up Josephine. Honor, of course, stayed with Ethan, not that he paid her much mind.

Sadie died giving birth to Honor, and Ethan didn't make much secret of the fact that he'd have grieved less if Honor had been born a son. When Joseph died, it was another blow. Joe was Ethan's beta, and everyone assumed he'd take over when Ethan kicked the bucket."

"What about you? Why weren't you in line for the job?"

"I'm not a Tate." Hamish's lip curled. "My brother-in-law was big on family. Plus, I'm no submissive wolf, but I don't have the drive it takes to lead a pack. Never have. I'm not much for politics, and most of the time, I'd rather keep to myself. Loners don't rise too far in a pack, you know."

Logan digested that information, trying to put together the pieces of a puzzle still made up mostly of blank space. "Honor said she became her father's beta when she was fifteen."

"Yup."

"So who took over after Ethan's brother died?"

The old man's bushy brows pulled together. "Why? You think that might be someone you can look to as alpha instead of Honor?"

"I never said that." But apparently, no one in this pack was ready to give him the benefit of the doubt when it came to the decision he still had to make. "Obviously, if Honor took his place, either she's stronger than he was, he left the pack, or he's dead. I just want to know which it is."

"He's dead. Got drunk and fell through the ice on the lake about fifteen years ago."

Just when Honor had become the beta. "So Ethan appointed Honor in his place."

MacDuff guffawed. There was just no other word for the belly laugh that surged from his mouth on a gust of breath. "Hell, no! That right there tells me you never met Ethan Tate before he died and brought you here. Might as well have written it out for me." He dropped his hands to his knees and leaned into the table. "Ethan Tate was just about the biggest bastard the Goddess ever whelped, Hunter. He never gave anything to anybody without making sure they went through hell to get it. He tried naming three young males to the beta spot before Honor. She had to hand each and every one of them their asses, and do it while her father watched, before she could claim that position. And even then, he made her go a round with him before he gave in. Whipped the ass of his own daughter on the pack's ceremonial ground. If she weren't so fast, he'd have killed her, too. The fact that she survived longer than any of the boys she'd beaten is the only thing that saved her."

Logan tried to picture the scene. He couldn't imagine any father treating his own young that way. Even when a son unseated his own father for the alpha position, it was usually more of a show than a real battle. Graham and his father had nearly laughed themselves silly at their ceremonial challenge. The elder Winters had been more than ready to hand over his position, but most important, he had loved his son.

How had Ethan Tate felt about Honor? If that was how he demonstrated it, Logan hated to even speculate.

"So, you're trying to tell me that Honor has already paid her dues, and I need to just rubber-stamp her turn as alpha. Is that what the pie was about? Usually when someone is trying to tell me what to do, they find threats more effective than desserts."

"No, the pie was because you looked so sour when Honor walked out on you, I thought you could use sweetening up." MacDuff laughed. "I'm not threatening you, Hunter, or telling you how to do your job. I don't know you, but you strike me as the sort of man that even if I tried, you'd still go ahead and do things exactly the way you intended all along. I don't believe in wasting my breath that way. I imagine you plan to take the next couple of days to check this pack out for yourself. You'll probably talk to the females and the pups to see what they think of the new alpha, and then you'll likely go check out each of our males in the prime age group and see whether you believe any of them looks like he'd make a better alpha than my niece."

It was like having someone read Logan the contents of his own day planner. That was exactly what he planned to do between now and the Howl. It was the logical course of action. So why did Hamish MacDuff manage to make it sound like such a mindless exercise in futility?

"You seem to know just what I have planned, MacDuff," he managed, carefully keeping his voice level and lacking in snarl. "Would you also like to tell me what I'm going to find?"

"What? And spoil all your fun?" The elder laughed and rose from his chair. "Wouldn't dream of it, Hunter. You'll find what you find, after all. I don't claim to be a mind reader, but I do know a thing or two about being a young, unmated male, and I do know my niece. Which means I also know that it looks like it's going to be a long, chilly night for you, son. You might want to raid the linen closet at the top of the stairs for an extra blanket before bed. Seems to me, you're going to need it."

Eight

The winter sunlight reflected off the snow shortly after dawn the following morning and pierced straight through Logan's closed eyelids. Cursing the end of a night of precious little sleep, he snarled and threw back his purloined blanket. Damn Hamish MacDuff, anyway. It was like the man was some sort of prophet of doom who had cursed Logan with the long, lonely night of his prediction. A night spent without his cranky, contrary erstwhile mate.

The bastard.

Swinging his legs over the side of the bed, Logan sat up and scrubbed his hands over his face. He really had slept for shit, and the hours of tossing and turning—after quite a long and exhausting search of the grounds around the meeting hall and the main house for the elusive Honor Tate—had left him with a piss-poor attitude and the nagging shadow of a headache behind his brow. Nice way to start the morning, right?

Good thing he had plenty to do. Maybe concentrating on his job and sticking to his plan to interview members of the pack today would keep his mind sufficiently occupied. Otherwise, he predicted he would see himself spending every waking minute obsessing over his mate.

Cursing, he stumbled into the shower and cranked the water up high and hot. The pounding stream washed away the remaining fog of sleep, but it did little to turn his mind in another direction. He had mate brain, and for the first time, he felt a surge of sympathy for all the friends and pack mates he had harassed over the years for turning into salivating idiots the moment they scented the female that fate had picked out for them. Unfortunately, he now knew exactly how they felt. The part that astonished him was how different the experience was from what he'd expected.

Mating had taken him by surprise.

Oh, he supposed that was how it always worked. After all, among his kind, men and women didn't meet at a bar or a party or off an Internet site, date for a while, and gradually develop feelings for each other. He knew that was what humans expected, but he was Lupine. He'd always known that one day he'd be at a bar or a party or meeting another Lupine in person for the first time, her scent would hit him, and he would recognize his mate. That was just the way it happened, but he'd be damned if he'd expected it to happen here.

First off, he'd still been hung up on Missy, or so he'd thought. He wanted to laugh about it now, but just a couple of days ago, he hadn't been able to imagine any woman smelling as good to him as Missy Winters. Every time he'd caught the honey-and-vanilla scent of her, he'd felt his dick twitch, and when she'd started to scent of warm milk as well, he'd thought he'd go out of his mind. Intellectually, he'd known she couldn't be his mate because she'd already mated with Graham, and he didn't believe the Goddess could be so cruel as to make the one perfect woman for him belong to another male, not when Lupines mated once and remained mated to the same partner for life. The Moon would never curse him like that; but he'd still wondered. He'd still thought Missy smelled better than any woman on earth.

Until he'd gotten close enough to Honor Tate to detect the true scent of her beneath those cloying bath salts. Now, he realized that she must have used the fragrance in her bath to camouflage the smell of her heat. It might have worked with the members of her pack, especially if she didn't allow anyone close enough to scent her skin directly, but they hadn't been able to fool her mate. He'd recognized her through the distraction, sweet pea and clover spiced with the exotic musk of her coming heat. Just the memory of it affected him in a way the biggest snoutful of Missy's scent never had. Honor's fragrance was like a drug for him, addicting him, making him crave another breath, another taste, another chance to feel her smooth skin and taut curves pressing hard against him.

Goddamn it! If he didn't get ahold of himself, he was going to come right here in the shower, without so much as the pump of his own fist around his cock. That was how his mate affected him, and it went so far beyond what he'd felt for his friend's mate, he finally understood why she had disappeared from his mind so quickly after his arrival in Connecticut. She had never been right for him at all. The only woman he could ever be content with was Honor Tate, but how in the name of the blue Moon was he supposed to make that happen?

The only things haunting him more persistently than Honor's scent were her words from the previous evening. The picture she had painted of their future was starkly engraved on his mind. She had predicted that the only possible outcomes of his presence in her territory were their permanent separation, her death, or a life of intolerable indignity for him. How was he supposed to make that kind of choice? Every one of his instincts told him he couldn't live without her. Even though he hadn't bitten her—nor she him—to formalize their mate bond, he already knew it would send him over the edge to lose her. If she died, he would kill every single Lupine who had touched her, and every single Lupine who had stood aside and let it happen. He would wipe out the entire White Paw Clan, if that was what it took to avenge her, so the idea of him just turning his back and trotting merrily back to New York without her didn't even merit consideration. No way was he going anywhere without his mate.

But could he honestly stay here and pretend that every moment as a powerless pack mascot didn't twist a double-edged knife through his gut? Logan accepted being Graham's beta because he loved his pack mate like a brother, and even then, there were times when it grated to defer to the other Lupine. If he were relegated to the role of Honor's Sol, how long would it be before he resented the very thought of her? He knew his strengths and his weaknesses, and his dominance tendencies, in this case, ranked at the top of both lists.

So, what was he going to do? Cut off his left hand, or his right? Because that was what the choices felt like to him. Either way, he'd walk away from this situation half a man. Which half did he want to lose first?

Logan twisted the water off with a sharp jerk of his hand and reached for a towel. Unless he wanted to turn the dial all the way to cold, the shower had done him as much good as it was able. Hadn't his plan for the day been *not* to obsess over Honor Tate? Time to suit action to words.

Leaping to a decision now wouldn't do him any good. He didn't have enough information to know if Honor's assessment of the situation was the right one. Maybe all his choices *did* suck like a brand-new vacuum, but if there was another

option, any option that would allow him to have
Honor and keep his pride, the only way to find it
was to look. He'd start by looking into the pack,
and go from there. Two birds, one stone.

And one very determined Lupine male.

Honor couldn't remember a more exhausting day
in her life. Who knew eluding one determined
Lupine could take so much out of a girl?

After that incident in the stone yard yesterday,
she'd devoted her entire afternoon to being wherever Logan Hunter was not. Well, there had been
that forty-five minutes she'd spent leaning up
against a tree, trying to remember how her legs
worked, immediately after stalking away from
him. But she wasn't counting that. Or the way it
had taken a good two hours for the pleasant ache
between her legs to fade to the point where she
wasn't constantly having to press them together
to ease the fluttering there.

She wasn't counting that, either.

No, what she counted were the hours she'd
spent running errands in town that could have
waited another week but that kept her off the
pack's property until it was time for supper. The
meal itself, she was trying hard to forget. Neither
the reaction of her inner wolf every time she got
close to Logan Hunter, nor the hard truths she'd
slapped him down with before running away
from him—again—counted among her finer moments. She'd headed straight from the meeting

hall to the house and up to her bedroom, but it had taken all of thirty seconds after she'd gotten there for her to realize it wouldn't take her mate half that long to find her if that was where she stayed. She had thrown a toothbrush and a change of clothes into a duffel and retreated to the remotest empty cabin on the property—one she was almost certain no one would have thought to mention to their guest that it even existed. There she had spent a long, cold, restless night trying to persuade herself that maybe her hormones were lying to her and Logan Hunter wasn't really the mate fate had destined for her.

When that had failed, she'd switched to persuading herself that while he might be her mate, she had survived without him for twenty-four years before now, and she could survive another fifty after he left. No problem.

That had failed, too.

Which pretty much left her right where she'd started—alone, angry, and trapped between a rock and a hard Lupine. Gee, would the fun ever start?

Her secret hideout had protected her from Logan for the night, but the chilly cabin and the lack of sleep had left her feeling stiff and cranky when she finally managed to drag herself into the office for a day of paperwork and monotony. Yes, she was hiding behind a desk, but only because she didn't think anyone had showed Logan her office yet, and when they eventually did, at least she'd have gotten in a few hours with the coffeemaker before he found her. That might be enough to get her through their next confrontation.

That, plus a whip, a chair, and a tranquilizer gun.

Sighing, Honor banished her nemesis from her mind and forced herself to concentrate on the monotony of the responsibilities she'd inherited from her father. She needed to send several boys back to the stone yard to finish off the fire pit that she'd abandoned after the Incident yesterday (her mind seemed determined to refer to their sexual escapades in capital letters, and frankly, Honor couldn't really find a reasonable argument against it).

Settling into her father's chair with her third cup of coffee, Honor dragged out Ethan's dog-eared old appointment calendar. He'd been meticulous about his business, and every scheduled task and due invoice had been neatly noted in the pages of the calendar.

Honor looked over the notes for this week and grimaced. The chores and bills weren't onerous by any means, but she just didn't want to deal with them, especially not since she'd already taken care of everything that could possibly be handled away from the pack's grounds. The business had been her father's passion, not hers, and the cabins they rented to pack members and vacationing Others, along with the commercial properties in town, struck her more as a burden than a vocation. If she had her druthers, she'd be spending her time at a pottery wheel, or hiking through the woods, not cooped up behind a computer. It was just one more sign to her that the life she'd ended up with was not the life she would have chosen for herself.

She looked around the office to be sure no one lurked in the corners, waiting to demand a moment of her time; and she knew it was ridiculous, but she still took the precaution of closing the door and pulling down the shades before she gave in to her desire to lay her head down on the cool wooden surface and close her eyes.

What had she gotten herself into, and why the hell was she now exerting every last ounce of her considerable will and rapidly depleting energy to secure for herself a position she had never even wanted?

Intellectually, she had known this day was coming, the day when she would have to take over the pack, but she'd had no idea it would be this soon. She had thought she had years yet, maybe a decade or two, before she'd have to think of a way to tell her father she didn't want to take his place when he died. But before she could get the words out, he'd been gone, leaving her with a mass of problems and no conceivable way out of them. He had trapped her in the surest way possible, with her own desire to please him.

Maybe if she had ever succeeded in doing that, she wouldn't despise herself for what the attempt had stolen from her.

When she'd been a child, all the way up through her teenaged years, Honor had longed to please her demanding father. She'd done everything she could to get his attention. She'd tried being the obedient daughter, but he barely noticed. Then she'd tried being the top student in her classes, but that failed as well. Nothing had made any impact on Ethan Tate, not when she excelled and not when she rebelled. Nothing had seemed to make any difference to him until she'd begun to move up in the pack.

Her first challenge had been more of a lark than anything intentional. She'd refused to follow the orders of a slightly older male pack member—not surprising since he'd been trying to order her to let him grope her newly developed breasts—and had been faced with the decision to either challenge him for his rank or follow his orders. Honor had gone with the challenge. She had won, leaving the fight slightly bloody, but satisfied that the boy she'd beaten wouldn't be giving her any more grief anytime soon.

That first challenge had earned her barely a passing glance, but the next one had merited a raised eyebrow. The next, a pat on the back. By the time she'd won her first challenge against an adult pack member, the day after her fourteenth birthday, she had found the path to her father's approval—straight through his ego. Every time she won a rank challenge, it reflected well on her father and on the line of Lupines from whom she and he were descended. That was the only act he respected and so Honor had fought the battle over and over until finally it had won her a place at his side, but it had never won her his love.

Honestly, she wasn't even sure anymore whether he'd ever had any to give her. She'd known from her earliest memories that he would have preferred if she'd been a boy—the son he'd always wanted. She had even wondered for a while—especially when he'd tried to appoint other young males to take her uncle's place as beta after the accident that had killed both Joseph and his mate, Marie— whether he might literally try to replace her by adopting a young male pack member as his foster son, but she needn't have worried. Ethan Tate had had too much stubborn pride in his name and his heritage to take that route. "Tates rule the White Paw," he had told her so many times she occasionally heard the words in her sleep. In Ethan's mind, anything else was unthinkable.

That was the real reason why he'd eventually given in and accepted her challenge wins as proof of her ability to be his beta. Only she knew how close he had come to killing her instead. Only she knew that when he'd had her wolf bloodied and pinned to the ground of the challenge circle, she had prevented him from ripping out her throat by telepathically reminding him that if he killed her, she would never be able to have pups; and if she never had pups, there would be no chance that a grandson of his blood would be born to carry on Ethan's legacy.

She had learned at fifteen that the only value she had to her father was as a means of ensuring his immortality. She'd never forgotten the lesson, but her greatest regret was that she'd never mustered up the nerve to tell him to take his pack and shove it. Until his dying day, she'd remained at his side, ruling the White Paw Clan as if she relished each moment.

It hadn't taken her very long as beta before she realized how unhappy the title made her. While she now received her father's attention, and even his grudging approval, there was none of the affection she had craved. Maybe if her elevation in the hierarchy had earned her what she'd struggled for so long to achieve, it would have made a difference in the way she viewed the job, but as it was, she had no love for the chores that accompanied the position. She took no joy in settling disputes between rivals, nor in enforcing the laws of her father's rule. Obviously, she had the ability to do the job and had gained the respect of the pack, but she got no pleasure from it. She didn't relish the power of her station, just lived with it.

Not that she wanted to be omega by any means. She couldn't imagine being the lowest rung in the pack hierarchy, nor even being lost in the middle with the majority of members. She didn't want to drop in rank, she just wanted to not have so much of the responsibility that went with being in charge. And that really wasn't one of her options. So now look at her. Probably the world's only reluctant alpha, and who was currently engaged in an entrenched battle for her position.

Honor groaned and raised her head from the desk just far enough to prop it up in her hands. Viewed through clear eyes, her future stretched before her like a trap. The longer she spent here, doing the things that made her unhappy, the tougher it would be to ever get herself out of it. The more the pack accepted her, the less chance she had to leave. The harder she fought to prove herself to her followers, to Logan Hunter, and to the Silverback Clan, the deeper she dug her own grave. If she won the battle with her mate, the man she had argued with so passionately to acknowledge her claim and leave her in peace, she condemned herself to a life she hated with every fiber of her being.

So here she was, stuck in a place she didn't want to be, doing something she didn't want to do, and telling everyone who tried to talk her out of it to take a flying leap. Not to mention maiming anyone who tried to force her out of the martyrdom she'd stepped into. Sure, that was sane.

If things had been different, the easiest way out would have been to just lose a challenge. It happened to most Lupines at some point. She could throw a rank challenge and let one of the members of her pack take over her position as leader of the White Paw Clan. The plan had a few disadvantages, though, chief among them, the inability to control whether or not her opponent would let her live after the challenge. Traditionally, alpha challenges ended in death, and just because she had been lenient with her challengers did not mean that anyone else would offer her the same option. The second problem had to do with the fact that she could see no current member of the pack who was capable of taking on the role of alpha with any success. No one else had any experience or even enough good common sense to make a decent showing. Just look at who had challenged her so far—a whelp, a wuss, and a would-have-been friend. None of them had had the strength to beat her, and none of the ones still making noises did, either. Like Darin Major. Hell, his main claim to fame was that he ranked as the biggest asshole between here and Bangor. He talked a good game, but the word "blowhard" had been invented to describe him. The only thing Honor would have to worry about from him would be the very real chance that he would try to cheat his way to a challenge victory. Since she'd be expecting it, though, not even that would get him the win. She'd still take him down, and for the first time, she might just be able to stomach the thought of ripping the throat out of her challenger. Darin really was just that offensive.

She sighed and tried to figure out a way to reframe the idea that she led a pack full of nonentities without making herself sound like the world's biggest snob, and there really wasn't one. It wasn't that she believed every single one of her pack members was an idiot, just that none of them would be able to step into her shoes without disrupting the life of the pack to a fairly significant degree. While Honor had been trained for her current position since the age of fifteen, no one else had. It might be a harsh truth, but it was still the truth.

Honor had a vision. She had plans for how she wanted to see the pack join the twenty-first century. She wanted to see them integrating with the modern world, becoming familiar with technology and engineering and science and all the fields that made humans such a threat to the continued survival of the human species. Only by understanding how the human world worked could the Lupines hope to survive the ever-growing encroachment into their territory, but so few pack members had even begun to comprehend that. Most of them had gone reactionary and preached a policy of isolation, cutting the Lupine world completely off from the human one. They saw it as the only way to preserve their culture. Honor saw it as suicide.

The more isolated they became, the more people would choose to isolate them. And that's the sort of thing that led to witch trials and hangings and stonings and such things. Honor would prefer that the stonings did not happen, so the Lupines would need to learn to live with the humans and to accept that sometimes change became necessary. Already, their races were beginning to mingle, and she had heard rumors that the bigwigs across the country (especially the Council of Others in Manhattan) had begun to discuss plans for revealing the existence of their kind to the human world. It posed a big risk, but Honor saw the necessity behind it. It now felt almost inevitable, so why not work to ensure it happened on Lupine terms?

Honor just couldn't risk allowing a new alpha to regress and take the pack with them. It wasn't an option. If she had to fight to the death, turn her back on her mate, and go to war with the Silverback Clan to save her pack from a future of chaos and destruction, that was the only thing she could do. Her very genetic fiber had been programmed to leave her no other option. In spite of everything, she was still her father's daughter.

The final reason why she couldn't bring herself to lose any of her challenges didn't exactly qualify as noble, but it was honest. Her pride wouldn't allow it. Period. End of story. After all these years of proving herself to her father and the world, she simply couldn't fathom the idea of losing a fight. It went against every fiber of her being. She fought to win, and to lose would not only be to lose her position—and potentially her life—it would be to lose face in front of the entire pack, in front of the entire Lupine world. If she did that, how would she ever be able to look at herself in the mirror again?

She couldn't. Therefore, she couldn't lose the battle.

"Welcome back to square one," she muttered under her breath.

She also couldn't afford the distraction presented by her Silverback guest.

Somewhere, she figured, the gods must be laughing at her. She couldn't think of how she might have pissed them off, but that was the only possible explanation for why this was happening to her now. Why else throw a mating into the middle of the most complicated period of her life? Could they find worse timing? Not only did she not have the time for a mate, or the energy to dedicate to one, but how the hell was she supposed to stop fighting to save her pack so she could show her belly to the new dog sniffing around her?

How was she supposed to reconcile the fact that her predestined mate was also the one person who could destroy not just her, but her pack as well?

This just was not going to work. She knew that. It didn't matter that the man made her heart race and her blood heat and her body clench. It didn't matter that he left her with rapid breath and damp panties. She couldn't have a mate right now, and she especially couldn't have him.

The really inconvenient part, though, was that she didn't think Logan had read that memo. He seemed determined to take what he wanted, when he wanted it, and damn the consequences. It was a pretty predictable Lupine response, especially coming from a man as dominant as Logan Hunter, but that didn't make it any easier to deal with, given their circumstances. Honor had a hard enough time keeping her own raging hormones under control, without having to deal with the source of those hormones doing his damnedest to incite further raging. It just wasn't going to work.

Yeah, and if she kept telling that to herself often enough, she just might end up brain-damaged enough to believe it.

Swearing, Honor flipped her calendar open and began leafing through the pages once more. Time to stop brooding and concentrate on some real work. She got as far as opening to the proper page before a loud knock on her door called her attention.

"Come in," she snarled.

She looked up to see a tousled brown head poking through the slightly open door. It wore Max's puppy-dog expression and just below it dangled a bag containing the local bakery's chocolate frosted doughnuts. "Is it safe?"

Honor checked the side of her mouth for drool. "It might be. Provided you throw those doughnuts in first."

Theobromine be damned. She wanted those chocolate doughnuts. Besides, the amount of chocolate an adult werewolf would have to eat to get a bellyache from the toxic chemical defied comprehension. It defied Honor's comprehension, at least. Chocolate was one of her biggest vices.

She caught the bag as it sailed toward her head

and had swallowed half of the first doughnut before Max even managed to park his butt in the chair in front of her desk. She'd skipped lunch again to avoid running into Logan and skipping meals was not a good idea for a Lupine.

"So," Max said, lounging back in his chair, one ankle crossed negligently over the other knee, "what's up with the Silverback dude?"

Honor bit into doughnut number two and felt her eyes narrow. She barely forced herself to chew before she replied. "What do you mean, 'What's up'? He's here because his alpha sent him here. You were at dinner last night. You heard what I said."

"Well, duh, but despite all rumors to the contrary, I am not, in fact, either a clueless pup or a babbling idiot. You told everyone that he came to pay his respects at the passing of the alpha, but if that was all this was about, why would he be poking his nose into everyone's business and asking questions about how the pack operates? What's he trying to find out? And don't tell me he's on vacation, or something. That would hold about as much water as calling it a courtesy visit. Dude is damned sure asking way too many questions for courtesy."

The younger werewolf met Honor's gaze with raised eyebrows, his foot bouncing up and down where it dangled off the edge of his knee. At twenty, Max had energy to burn and yet was in that awkward stage between adult, when he would take his final place in the pack hierarchy, and child, when he could run around the territory free of responsibilities. She would need to find a constructive way to use all that energy, especially since her instincts told her that she was looking at a very high-ranking future wolf, potentially even her next beta. But right now, other priorities occupied her mind.

"Asking questions?" Her stomach clenched. She had known that was what Logan must be planning, but it still galled her to hear about him doing it. "Asking who? And what does he want to know?"

"It's not polite to answer a question with a question."

"It isn't when you do it but I'm the alpha. I don't have to be polite."

"That is so not fair."

"Deal." She snagged a third doughnut and used it to punctuate her point. "Now tell me. Where is the Silverback poking his nose, and what has he been asking about?"

"Everywhere and lots of things." The sneakered foot bounced, and Honor chewed in an attempt to keep her mouth too occupied to betray the true extent of her interest. "He's talked to a good sampling of the present pack. Elders, males, females. He even visited Molly Stevens's day care and talked to some of the little ones. Whatever he wants to know, he wants a pretty diverse perspective on it."

"Have you asked any of the people he talked to what he wanted?"

"Well. No."

"So, in other words, you have no idea what I'm asking you."

"You could say that."

"I just did."

"True. But you could also say that you just didn't ask the right question."

Honor growled. "Max . . ."

"Hey, all I'm saying is, I don't know exactly what he's been asking people about, but I do know that there are some rumors flying around that something big is going to be happening at the Howl this weekend." He leaned forward in his chair, blue eyes glowing. "Something bigger than an alpha declaration and a challenge or two."

That made Honor pause. "What does that mean? What's bigger? And just what challenges are you talking about?"

"Don't try to distract me, Honor. We both know exactly what males in this pack are still dumb enough to want to challenge you to be alpha. You won't change the subject with that. And if I knew what was bigger than the asskickings you'll be handing out on Saturday, I'd know what the Silverback was asking people about. Which I clearly don't."

"Don't be smart with me, Maxwell Clarke."

He held up his hands. "I'm not being smart, Honor. I promise. I mean, I'm just as curious as you are. If something big is going down, it would sure be nice to be prepared for it."

She scowled and leaned back in her chair, mumbling, "You're telling me."

"Then I guess it would be pretty useless for me to ask if you had any theories about what that all means?"

She just looked at him.

"Right. That's what I thought."

Max opened his mouth to speak, but before he got the chance to utter a single additional syllable, the door to Honor's office slammed open and a clearly belligerent man shoved his way inside. He flew to Honor's desk, slapped his meaty hands down on the surface, and inhaled deeply.

"I want to know if it's true, you little slut." His growl was deep and menacing and Honor didn't even blink. "Half the pack is talking about it, but I want to hear it from you. Did you really let that stranger paw you like a bitch in heat? He hasn't even been here for forty-eight hours, and you let him touch what's mine?"

One eyebrow arched up, and when she spoke, Honor knew she could have added several inches to the polar ice caps with her tone of voice. She'd practiced often enough. "Yours? I must be having trouble with my hearing, because I am certain that there is nothing in this room that belongs to you, Darin Major. And the next time you call me a bitch, by the way, I will lunch on your liver. Now would you care to rephrase?"

"You heard me fine the first time, and I meant what I said. I heard three different people today say you let that Silverback cur bend you over like a cheap whore. They're laughing about it. And now I'm going to picture that in my head every time I look at you. When the call to mate the alpha comes, you're going to be mine, and I'm going to wipe that image from my head by replacing it with the sight of you on your knees in front of *me*."

Honor raised her left hand, curled into a fist with the back of her hand facing Max and Darin. Coolly and very quietly she ticked off her points on her fingers as she replied. "One, let me repeat, nothing in this room can be called yours, least of all me. Two, what I do and with whom I do it is not, and never shall be, any of your goddamned business. Three, there will be no alpha mating at the next Howl, because I do not choose to mate right now, and I'll be damned to hell and back before I let some antiquated, misogynistic, *dumbassed* excuse for a tradition dictate who I have to screw." She ignored the protest between her legs and continued. "And four, remove your hands from my desk before I remove them from you.

Understand?"

Nine

Silence fell between them, brief, tense, and marked by the meeting of two gazes, one brown and chill, one green and maddened. But it ended abruptly when the door to the office opened again and another male voice rang out in the now crowded room.

"If I were you, I would do what the lady says, Major. Somehow I doubt she's joking."

Honor never broke her stare with Darin, but her jaw shifted and clenched. "The next one to walk into my office without knocking will find himself decorating the floor in front of my fireplace."

Out of the corner of her eye, she could see Logan's lip twitching. "That sounds kind of nasty, Darin. I think I'd back off if I were you."

"That promise wasn't made exclusively to Darin."

"Maybe not, but he's the one who's going to have to defend himself from both sides in about thirty seconds, if he doesn't back off."

What started in a reasonable and slightly amused voice had become decidedly serious by the end of that statement. Honor clenched her teeth to keep herself from screaming. If she'd been human, she probably would have screamed a split second later when Darin obeyed orders by removing his hands from her desk, but then ruined the moment of sanity by swinging around and launching himself straight for Logan's throat.

The force of Darin's attack pushed Logan back through the door of the office and down the front steps of the small cabin that housed it. The two figures landed on the ground in the snow-covered front yard, teeth snapping and hands clawing. The flakes barely had time to settle before Darin made the stupidest decision of his life and howled a challenge at a man who was not only stronger and faster than him, but also a hell of a lot smarter. As evidenced by the fact that Darin had attacked him to begin with.

Instead of screaming, Honor roared and leaped out of her chair and over her desk to launch herself after the two combatants. By the time she found herself in the yard with them, she could already see blood—though she couldn't be sure whose it was—and the sounds of vicious growls and snarls seemed to echo in the air around them. If she'd had a water hose, she'd have turned it on the two of them, but as it was, all she could do was stand on the sidelines and recite every curse she'd ever heard and a few new ones she had just made up herself. Necessity being the mother of invention and all.

She heard the sound of Max thundering out-side right behind her and braced herself for impact just before he skidded to a halt at her side.

"Holy shit! They're totally throwing down! Right here!"

"This is not WWE, Max." She figured if she clenched her jaw any harder her teeth would shatter, but hey, she could still get the words out. "And I'm going to kill one of them if they don't cut this out in the next ten seconds."

"Gotcha. One. Two. Three—"

Honor howled then for herself—not a happy sound—and leaped for the struggling figures. She landed on top of Darin's back and tried to yank the two men apart. When she couldn't do that, she sank her teeth deep into Darin's side and tugged. That at least got his attention. He snarled something obscene, but mostly unintelligible, and back-handed her across the face with casual force. A human might have been killed by the power of the blow snapping her fragile little neck, but Honor was neither human nor fragile. All the smack did to her was piss her off. Royally.

Rearing back, she let the reins of her beast slip just a little and felt a set of razor-sharp claws springing from the tips of her fingers. Sturdy as metal and sharp as glass, they ripped through Darin's muscular flesh like a jackhammer through tissue paper, leaving deep, bloody furrows be-hind them. Darin jerked and screamed in pain, momentarily losing his concentration and giving

Logan the advantage. The Silverback didn't even hesitate. He grabbed Darin by the throat, lifted him off the ground and threw him into a tree forty feet away from where he stood.

She turned on him with a growl and snapped her teeth in his direction. "My fight. *Mine*."

Logan's hand shot out, wrapping around Honor's neck this time. But instead of squeezing and lifting, it curled around the back of her neck and yanked her forward until her breasts flattened against his chest. He stared down at her with glowing golden eyes and growled possessively.

"Mine."

Logan saw the way his statement sent Honor's temper into overdrive, but he really didn't give a shit. This was his mate, and every hour that passed brought her closer and closer to the peak of her heat and to ovulation. The changes in her scent maddened him, and after searching for her—unsuccessfully—for hours the day before, he didn't intend to let her get away.

And if she thought that he would just stand aside while she was verbally abused and physically threatened by another male? Well, she wasn't half as intelligent as she'd led him to believe.

Out of the corner of his eye, he saw the lanky young man who'd rushed out of Honor's office behind them hurrying to the now unconscious Darin. If the youth had looked to be tending to the fallen challenger, Logan would have stopped him, but all he did was grab the moron by the ankles and begin dragging him away from the small cabin out of which Honor reportedly ran her father's business. Dismissing them from his mind, he shifted the struggling burden in his arms and growled in pleasure at the way her squirming rubbed all her softest parts against his most appreciative ones.

"Let. Me. Go!" Honor herself sounded less appreciative. "Hands off, Fang."

"No." He ignored her fighting, except that he grabbed her flailing hands in one of his and pinned them behind her back. Then he began backing her up toward the cabin they'd just left, his hips bumping against hers as they walked. "Told you. Mine."

She snarled. "Told you! No!"

He didn't intend to take that for an answer. He could smell the heat rolling off her in heady waves, making his heart race and his cock stand at attention. If he didn't have her soon, he'd explode. In more ways than one.

Ignoring her demands, he continued backing her to the cabin, one step at a time. He almost had her there, too, and was already imagining the things he would do to her once he had her bent over her daddy's desk, when she got sneaky. Going suddenly limp, as in falling completely boneless in his arms like dead weight, she forced him to hesitate and look down at her to see what had happened.

That split second of inattention nearly cost him all his grand plans for fathering cubs with this woman. As soon as his hold loosened a fraction, she brought her knee up hard between his legs. She might have damaged him permanently if he had moved a fraction of a second slower. As it was, he ended up with a baseball-sized bruise high on his thigh and a howling bundle of rage and frustration in his arms.

She yanked so hard at the arms he had pinned behind her that he started to fear she'd break her own wrist struggling to get away from him. He shifted his grip to take one hand in each of his, and she fought even harder. She threw herself bodily against him, disrupting his balance until the two of them went crashing to the ground not three feet from the cabin steps. Snarling like a she-wolf guarding her den, Honor launched another attack, surprising Logan. He had thought she must be nearly done. She went for his eyes with her curving claws, but she got a shoulder instead, tearing several wide strips through his thick hide. She threw herself forward, trying to get her teeth around his throat, but found herself flat on her back instead.

Logan pinned her carefully, making sure not to use too much of his weight and strength against her, but she made his gentlemanly behavior nearly impossible. She fought like a cornered badger, only meaner. She was going for his eyes yet again when he finally got fed up and flipped her over onto her stomach where it would be harder for her to reach his vital areas. He covered her from behind, weighing her down, but it still didn't deter her. She began to buck like a Brahma bull at a rodeo, nearly unseating him twice.

The third time she did manage it. She bucked and twisted so hard and fast that Logan lost his balance and fell, tumbling off to the side of her. Luckily he managed to keep his hold on her arm, or she'd have been part of the ether before he could so much as sneeze. Still, she writhed like a snake and managed to get to her hands and knees and crawl for the cabin before he fell on her again.

She'd gotten as far as the second step when he took her down, draping himself over her back like a blanket and pressing her stomach against the rough, wooden boards of the steps. She growled something obscene and tried to claw her way out from under him, but he held firm. One deep breath told him she was fighting herself just as hard as she fought him. He could smell the sharp, spicy sting of her arousal perfuming the air around them, made even more intense by her rapidly approaching heat. Just sniffing her made his mouth water, not to mention what it did to the fit of his jeans.

For all that she refused to admit it, Honor felt the attraction between them as deeply as he did. He knew that if he reached between her legs just then, he would find her warm and wet and dripping with the honey that he had drawn from her.

The idea made his mouth water, and he licked his lips.

"You ran away from me this morning, Honor love. I don't think I'm going to let you get away again. This is too important to let that happen." He leaned down and let his tongue tease the shell of her ear. "You smell much too good to let that happen."

"Not . . . your . . . decision . . . *bastard*."   She panted the words out, as if she had trouble drawing breath, but considering he had her pinned beneath his considerable bulk, anything was possible. "Let go."

He shook his head and nuzzled through the thick curls of her hair to get to the skin beneath. He drew her in, savoring that spicy fragrance and ignoring what it did to his self-control. Who needed self-control?

With that in mind, he shifted his weight slightly and slipped his free hand beneath her body to the spot where her T-shirt had ridden up to expose the soft skin of her belly. He felt her flinch when he touched her, heard her gasp when his finger circled her navel before dipping inside. Her hips bucked against him, but this time it had more to do with reaction than with any attempt to get him off her. Things were looking up, but that still didn't mean he had any intention of testing it by letting her go just yet.

He caught her hands in his and drew them up over her head, stretching her out beneath him like a picnic blanket, and pinned them there. The position made her T-shirt draw up even farther, and Logan rumbled his approval at the extra inches of bare skin it exposed. She felt smooth and soft and hot to his touch, and in the cool winter air, he would bet that anyone looking at them from a distance would see steam coming off them in waves. Of course, it wouldn't have stopped him if the entire Lupine population of North America had been watching. This woman was his mate, and he intended to have her. Now.

When he unfastened her jeans, she gave a growl of protest, but when his hand slid between her legs to her dripping core, all she could do was moan. His fingers parted her slick folds and stroked delicately, searching for every nuance of her reaction—the tightening of muscles, the faint trembling, the quiet hitch in her breathing. Sometimes those acute Lupine senses came in very handy indeed.

"Hands. Off." She growled the threat, but the words lacked a certain authenticity. Her scent told him how his presence affected her.

Logan's fingers slid a fraction deeper and teased small circles around her opening, drawing even more moisture from her body. Damn, but she was responsive. It made his mouth water almost as much as her scent did.

"Somehow I'm not convinced that's what you really want, honey." He leaned forward and nipped at her earlobe, savoring her small intake of breath. "Are you sure you don't want something more like this?"

His hand shifted and two long fingers slid inside her, filling and stretching her eager body. She felt tight and hot and incredible around his fingers, and he moaned, nearly drowning out the soft sound of her cries. He could imagine few things more perfect in this world than the feel of her slick pussy closing around his cock and milking him to completion. And if he didn't get his mind off that memory right now, he'd be "completing" right there in his jeans.

Quickly withdrawing his hand from between her legs, he used it to shove her jeans down until they tangled around her ankles. She growled a protest, but his urgency drove him, and he didn't bother to pause to let her kick them off. Instead, he ripped her burgundy satin panties into shreds, not even taking time to appreciate the smooth, silky feel of the material or the contrast of the rich color against her fair skin. All he cared about was getting inside her, and the panties were in his way, so they had to be destroyed. It was that simple.

Logan threw away the scraps of fabric and reached for his own jeans, racing to get them out of the way before he died of a critical buildup of sperm. The top button defied him, refusing to slip from its hole, and he snarled in frustration. He released her hands so he could use both to tackle the issue, but the second she shifted and braced them beneath her as if to push herself up and drag herself away from him, his hands slammed back over hers. Irritated, he growled, a low, dark warning.

Honor growled right back. Shifting her weight, she braced her hands on one stair and her knees on another. The jeans still around her ankles and lower legs forced her to keep her thighs pressed together, but it made no difference. Pushing herself into place, she dropped to her elbows in front and thrust her bottom out behind her, raising her hips and curving her back until she had presented herself to him like an offering.

Logan froze in place. He recognized the mating stance for what it was, but he hadn't been expecting it. For all the lust he could smell on her skin, he'd thought Honor meant to play the reluctant mate to the bitter end, and now here she was, presenting herself to him like a lusciously unwrapped birthday gift. For a few seconds all he could do was stare. Then she reached back and drew her hair forward over her shoulder and out of the way, turning to look back at him. She invited him with a look, and when she raised an eyebrow and canted her hips a fraction higher, he gave in to his instincts and covered her.

Honor fought fiercely, but in the end she was overpowered. Not by Logan, but by her own fierce desire. She needed to feel him inside her again and damn the consequences. She had done enough fighting against her instincts lately, enough self-denial, enough of what was good for the pack instead of what was good for her, and she was done. This time, this one time, she would take what she needed and damn the consequences.

If she was lucky, maybe he'd fuck her to death, and she wouldn't be around to face any consequences.

By the time she decided this, though, and made him a clear offer, it was evident he barely remembered what to do with her. How quickly they forget. Drawing her hair over her shoulder, she put a little wriggle in her hips and looked back at him with one brow raised, as if to ask how much clearer she had to make it.

Not much.

He fell on her like a starving man on a feast table, with the same greed and the same touch of fear that the bounty before him was only an illusion and would fade away if he hesitated even a moment longer.

She heard his rough growl of hunger and approval, then felt his large hands gripping her hips, holding her in place while he positioned himself at her entrance. She felt him savoring that moment of quivering anticipation before sliding home with one deep, forceful thrust.

Honor threw her head back and screamed. He drove into her, the momentum of his body carrying him hard and high inside her. He parted her body and made a place for himself in her heat. Her internal muscles quaked and shivered and protested, but in the end they softened, letting him force his way inside. He repaid the kindness by stroking every nerve ending she possessed with his flared head and thick shaft. He reached deep inside her, to the heart of her, and paused there before drawing back for another assault.

She whimpered and dropped her head to the cold, wooden step. The sensations threatened to overwhelm her, so intense she could barely draw breath. The denim around her ankles forced her to keep her legs pressed together, and that made her channel tighter, forcing it to clamp down hard around him and milk him from the very first. She wondered what it felt like to Logan, if it could possibly feel as amazing to him as it did to her. Her entire body seemed on fire, shaking and twisting like a flame as he rode her hard there on the steps to her father's office.

She felt his fingers bite deeply into her hips, then he shifted, falling forward on top of her, his chest pressed tightly against her back, his hands coming down to pin hers to the rough wood. His hips continued to thrust against hers, his cock working a hard, regular rhythm inside her. She shivered wildly and the tremor passed from her flesh to his, making him growl softly right into her ear.

"More." His voice touched her like another hand, and abruptly Honor found that she wanted to give him more.

Dropping her chest to the steps, she drew her

knees in until the tops of her thighs were digging
into the front of one of the stairs and lifted her
hips higher. The change in position shifted his
cock inside her, sliding him a fraction deeper
when she'd thought that he already filled her to
overflowing. Now she could feel him so deeply,
she thought her heart might explode.

Logan rumbled his approval and increased
the speed and force of his thrusts. In her position,
Honor had given up all of her leverage and now
all she could do was kneel before her mate and
take him, however hard and fast and deep he
wanted to go. The knowledge of her position sent
another shiver through her—one of delight—and
she could have laughed at how positively unalpha
she was in this moment. She couldn't have cared
less. She'd have cheerfully agreed to be omega at
that point if it meant this man would never stop
mating her.

Whimpering with the impact of his thrusts,
wanting to give him everything he needed, Honor
reached up behind her, hesitated a moment, then
swept her hair to the side and pulled it taut, exposing her back and the nape of her neck to the
Silverback beta. She felt him freeze, hesitating as
he stayed buried deep inside her. Then her ears
rang with his roar as he nudged ever deeper inside her and claimed the right she had given him.
His teeth sank deep into the tender exposed nape
of her neck, definitely deep enough to leave a

mark. That was the point. Honor had given this man permission to mark her as his mate, and she would deal with the consequences later.

Right now, she operated on pure instinct, and her instincts told her she would never do anything more right than what she did in this moment.

She felt the breaking of her skin, the warm, slow trickle of blood from the wound, and it made her clench around him. His shaft leaped inside her, as excited as he was by the dark eroticism of the moment. She felt the tightly coiled tension inside her begin to break, and all she could do was brace herself for the wave.

It nearly dragged her under; the force of it caught her so strongly. She threw back her head and howled to the skies as she came and came and came beneath him. The climax seemed endless and painfully intense, shaking the foundations of her world. She felt him tense and explode as well, pulled along not by the force of her pleasure, but by the sweetly tight contractions of her body around his. He echoed her howl, the sound muffled against her neck, and poured himself into her body, quivering in ecstasy.

The world slowed and blurred and the only stable point in the swirling riot became the place where his teeth joined to her flesh, making them one in a way even him buried inside her hadn't been able to accomplish. As the tension of arousal and climax began to fade, they remained locked together, shivering with the faint ripples of after-shock. She bowed her head, feeling with acute awareness that faint trickle of blood against her skin, and she shivered again. This was joining, in the truest Lupine sense of the word. Logan had become her mate, and she had become his.

And what fresh kind of hell had she just sentenced herself to?

Ten

She still hadn't figured that out an hour later, when they were separated, cleaned, and clothed, and sitting in her father's office, eyeing each other warily. Well, her gaze remained wary. Logan's had gone all wicked and focused again as he stared intently at her neck, waiting for her to turn her head so he could admire his handiwork.

Silence stretched between them for several long moments. Logan looked too self-satisfied to speak, and Honor wasn't quite sure what to say. Were there rules of etiquette for handling this type of situation? Did Emily Post have a chapter on Post-coital Small Talk for the Modern Werewolf? If she didn't, she really should.

Honor shifted in her seat and tried to ignore the raw, liquid feeling between her legs. As hard as he'd just taken her, she ought to be screaming at him to never lay another hand on her as long as he lived, and here she was trying to keep him from noticing how damned horny she still felt. Was *that* in Emily Post?

"You can relax, you know." His drawling tone sounded sleepy and rough and sexy in the small cabin. Honor couldn't suppress a shiver of reaction. "I'll give you a couple of hours before I attack you again. I'm not entirely uncivilized."

She drew a deep breath. "See . . . about that 'again' thing . . ."

He raised an eyebrow and settled into a deeper slouch. "You surely don't intend to tell me, your mate, that I can't touch you again, do you? You couldn't be quite that foolish, honey. Tell me."

She scowled. "You know, I really hate those casual endearments. Ones like 'honey.' It always makes me wonder if you just can't remember my name."

"Oh, I remember it. It just don't think 'Honor' is something I can hear myself yelling out in a heated moment. It would be like yelling 'Mother Teresa' or something."

She rolled her eyes. "Now that's just nasty."

"That's what I thought. So you have two choices. You can have 'honey,' or you can have 'Nora.' Up to you."

"Those are my only choices?"

He shrugged. "They are if 'Honor' is your only name."

She grumbled and crossed her arms over her chest.

Logan cupped his hand to his ear and cocked his head to the side. "Sorry, what was that? I couldn't quite catch it."

"Honor Strength." She bit it out like a particularly vile curse and then glared, as if it were his fault. It was actually her father's, but if she could have a few minutes to think, she'd find a way to make it Logan's fault. She'd put it on his tab.

He blinked. "Right. Those are your only choices."

She opened her mouth to protest, then caught herself and shook her head. "And that is so not important right now. We have other things we need to discuss at the moment."

"Not if those discussions are anything like the one you were about to start where you tell me I can't touch my own mate anymore."

"Do you honestly think that what we just did has changed anything?"

"I honestly do," he snapped, eyes flashing gold. "I think it's changed your status from my potential mate to my actual mate. You're mine now, Honor, and don't try to say anything different, because you gave yourself to me. If you're feeling forgetful, try touching the back of your neck. It might jog your memory."

Honor tried not to flinch at the vicious sarcasm of that remark. As if she needed to touch the mating mark to remember it was there. She damned well couldn't forget it, and she damned well couldn't stop calling herself ten kinds of fool for giving in to the instinct that had prompted her to let him put it there. She could chalk it up to the heat of the moment, or to her own heat, which was getting harder to control with every passing moment, but blaming either of those things wouldn't change the fact that she'd allowed him to mark her. Just like it wouldn't change the fact that the question still hanging over their heads remained a choice between true or false. A hot fuck and a mating mark hadn't miraculously opened door number three.

Goddess, how she wished that it had, though. The wolf inside her had already begun to pace and whine in grief. It wanted to return the mating, to mark Logan as hers as surely and as visibly as she'd been marked by him. It wanted them to do whatever they had to, to run off to the woods, live in a cave, and get down to the serious business of making love and pups and a future together. Her human brain, though, knew that was impossible. She still had a pack to lead, or to die trying. Having a mate made not one iota of difference to that fact.

She steeled her expression and erected a wall around her cracking heart, all while the sounds of her wolf's howl of despair echoed in her mind.

"I haven't forgotten anything," she told him, keeping her voice even and emotionless. She had practiced that a lot lately. "I haven't forgotten your mark, just like I haven't forgotten that I haven't marked you in turn, or that I have no plans to do so. I also haven't forgotten that I have a pack to run, and that you have a decision to make. Mate or no mate."

His lip curled as he glared at her. "You insult me if you think that being my mate doesn't mean that I would do anything and everything in my power to ensure your safety and your happiness. Damn you for thinking that poorly of me."

"Oh, so you've made your decision, then?" Her tone taunted him, the impulse to share a little of her own pain impossible to deny. "You've suddenly developed a burning desire to go from being the second most powerful wolf in one of the most powerful packs in the country to being my hunky piece of arm candy? Terrific. You can start by taking off your shirt. If I'm going to keep you as my little boy toy, I'll want everyone to see exactly what you're good for."

He crossed the desk in a single leap, spinning her chair to face him and bracing his hands on the arms, surrounding her with a looming shroud of furious, feral male. Honor choked back a gasp, but she couldn't control the way her heartbeat took off like a scared rabbit in the face of a hunting wolf. For the first time in her life, she understood what it meant to be prey.

"Don't push me, little alpha." The words came out like a spray of heated gravel, dark and rough and potentially damaging. "If I go over the edge, I'll take you with me."

"And where will we go, Hunter, hm? Straight to hell?" Her fight-or-flight response had broken days ago. She had only one reaction left to threats now, the one that made her lip curl and her chin lift and her gaze lock defiantly with his. "I got here last week. Welcome to the neighborhood."

For a long moment he continued to stare at her, and she watched as his eyes shifted until all traces of brown disappeared behind the glow of liquid gold. Part of her was hypnotized by the visible signs of his internal battle, recognizing his struggle for control in his changing eyes and the sound of the fabric of the chair ripping where his claws lengthened and sliced into the cloth-covered arms.

With a howl he tore his gaze from hers and jerked away, throwing his head back and howling at the ceiling, the sound echoing with fury and frustration in the small room. Hairs rose on her arms and the back of her neck, the skin there tingling and throbbing where his teeth had cut into flesh. Her throat clenched as she bit back the cry welling in her own chest. Her wolf would always respond to his this way. She knew it, and that made it even more important that she make sure she crushed any illusions he had of a future they could share. She needed him gone so she could mourn for their lost chances and learn to live with the pain of losing her mate, not to death, but to circumstance, whose deceptive blade cut even deeper.

Honor watched, bleeding inside, while her mate—the mate she could never claim—struggled for control. She saw his skin ripple as the magic of the change moved through him, saw his muscles tense and clench as he fought to hold on to his human form. She saw him grimace and watched his canine teeth lengthen and sharpen into vicious fangs. She saw fur begin to sprout from his cheeks and throat, and saw the minute he lost the battle against his wolf.

His head jerked to the side, golden wolf's eyes pinning her to her seat, and the warning ripped from his throat even as his face began to stretch toward the shape of a muzzle.

"This isn't over," he growled, the words barely intelligible as he lost the ability to speak as a man. As he surrendered his manhood to the magic in his blood. "You . . . mine. Mate. Ever."

Then the Logan shape was gone and a huge, dark wolf snarled at her once, spun toward the door, and disappeared into the woods, the tip of his tail flying behind him.

Honor had no idea how long she sat there, staring out the door, waiting for the blood from her heart to puddle on the floor beneath her chair. Of course, it never did, because all of her wounds were internal, metaphorical, the kind that couldn't kill her, that could only make her wish she were dead.

She wasn't, though. Honor Tate still lived, still ran the White Paw Clan, and still had to deal with the fact that no matter what her heart or her mind or her gut wanted for her future, the only future she had was the same one she'd been staring in the face for the last week: she would rule, she would lead, and she would lock her protesting psyche away behind a wall of solid steel so thick, not even a werewolf could make a dent in it.

She would go on.

Soon. Just as soon as she could find the will for it.

And so she sat in her chair and stared out into the woods where Logan had disappeared. She didn't notice the time passing, or the afternoon shadows lengthening. She didn't notice her stomach rumbling with hunger when she missed her second meal of the day, and she didn't notice the cold that invaded the cabin through the open door, not even when her breath swirled around her head in a visible cloud of steam. She didn't notice any of it until two figures stepped into the doorway and cut off her sight line.

Honor blinked. It took a moment for the change to register, for her sluggish mind to claw its way out of the numbing hole of depression and start working again. She didn't want to think; there was too great a chance that thoughts would lead to more feelings, and more feelings only meant more pain.

She frowned. "What are you doing here?"

"At the moment? Freezing our tails off, same as you." Her uncle Hamish stepped into the cabin, followed by another of the pack elders. Barney Andrews drew the door closed behind them. "Pete's sake, Honor, if you want to just give money to the electric company, wouldn't it be easier to write a damned check? Be a hell of a lot more comfortable. It's so damned cold in here, I don't even want to take my jacket off."

"Maybe she was trying to let in some fresh air." Barney took a deep breath and eyed Honor with speculation. "I'd say she definitely let in something."

Honor turned to glare at the old man, baring her teeth.

"Down, girl," Hamish advised, settling into a chair facing her desk and leaning back to study her. "Doesn't do you any good to snap at a man for pointing out the obvious. We're all pack here. It's not like you can hide the smell of a new mating."

"If that's what you came here to talk about, you can turn around and walk right out the door again."

Her uncle ignored the snarl. "It's not, but it does have a thing or two to say to the matter."

"Exactly what matter is that?"

"The one you can't afford to not be thinking about, missy. You know, a little matter about how there's a Howl scheduled for the day after tomorrow, one that could just decide not only whether you continue to lead this pack, but whether or not you continue to live. Ring any bells?"

Her mouth tightened, but she kept silent. It was that or say something she would likely regret. She'd done enough of that for a while now.

"It's a serious matter," Barney threw in, taking

the other chair and fixing Honor with a gaze she felt certain he meant to be sobering. She found it more irritating. "One that was complicated enough before you threw caution to the wind and decided to mate with a wolf who isn't even a member of this pack."

That made Honor want to laugh. Yeah, as if she had "decided" anything about this fiasco. The only decision she could remember making since the day her father died was what it would take for her to be able to look herself in the mirror when she dragged her ass out of bed every morning. And just look at how well that one had worked out for her.

"Now's not the time for casting blame." Hamish frowned at the other man, and Barney subsided. Elder he might be, but Barney had always ranked below Hamish in the pack; he knew when to shut up.

"Oh, why the hell not?" Honor asked with a snort. "Sounds like just what I need to top off my day."

"It's not the time for self-pity, either. We've got plans to make, and important things to consider before the pack gathers."

Honor sighed. "What's to consider, Uncle Hamish? The pack will meet. I'll claim the title of alpha. One or more of the stupider males in the pack will challenge me. Either I'll win, or I'll die. The pack will hunt together, and life will go on. You know, for everyone who's not dead. I don't see much room for negotiation there, unless you've thought of a way to force the Silverback to decide in my favor once I've won the challenges."

"It's not the challenges that I think you need to be worried about, sweetheart. There're some stories flying around the pack this afternoon that say those males who were thinking of challenging you have changed their minds."

"Well, isn't that good news?" Honor asked, ignoring the uneasy feeling gathering at the base of her spine. "No challenges means my place as alpha is uncontested. That will have to count for something with the Silverback. It shows the pack has confidence in me."

Barney snorted. "They aren't giving up on the challenges because they're behind you, little girl. They just think it would be more fun to fuck you than to kill you."

Hamish's big hand flew before Honor could blink, catching the other man square on the jaw. "I told you that as an elder, you had a right to consult with the alpha on the matter, Andrews, not that you could flap your damned jaw like the idiot you are."

Barney winced and cradled his bruised chin, but he kept his mouth shut. He also lowered his gaze at the other man's rumbled warning.

Honor didn't intervene, but she did hold up a hand and fix her relative with a hard stare. "What is he talking about, Uncle Ham?"

Hamish sighed. "I might not like the way he

blurted it out, Honor, but I can't pretend that his words weren't the truth. The males who've been planning to give you trouble at the Howl haven't backed down from their plans, they've just shifted gears. Instead of challenging you for your place as alpha, they think they're going to call for an Alpha Mating Rite."

"What the hell is an Alpha Mating Rite?" Her mind went blank for a moment, and Honor had to search her memory to make sense of what she was hearing. It didn't register at first, so it took a few seconds to dredge up a vague recollection of an obscure point of Lupine tradition. When she made the connection, she felt her heart stutter in shock. "You've got to be kidding me. Isn't that when—"

She broke off, unable to complete the thought.

"It's when an unmated female tries to take her place as alpha of the pack," Hamish declared flatly. "Any males who question her ability to lead can call for either an Alpha Challenge, or an Alpha Mating Rite. If it's the first option, the female has to fight her male challengers to the death; if she loses, the male who defeats her takes her place as alpha. If it's the second, she has to fight until either the males are dead, or she loses; and if she loses, the winner gets to mate her and then he takes his place at her side as a second alpha. Now you have a female stuck spending her life with a male who already tried to kill her once and doesn't have much of a reason to treat her as anything other than a whipping post, plus you have a pack with two alphas. History tells us that lasts just long enough to break the pack apart, but not so long that one of the alphas doesn't end up dead after all."

Honor swallowed against rising bile. "But that no longer applies to me," she reasoned, fists clenching. "I have a mate. You know that. You scented the bond as soon as you walked in here."

Her uncle shook his head. "What I scented was that a male had put his mark on you. The Silverback male. That's not a full mate bond, and the males making trouble aren't going to accept it. First off, because there's no indication in the scent he left behind that you marked him back. And second, because Logan Hunter isn't a member of this pack. Only a member can mate a female alpha. He'd have to petition to join the pack before your bond would be recognized, and if you think the morons gunning for you are gonna let that happen at this point in the game, you're out of your pretty, stubborn head. They'd kill him to keep that from happening."

"Logan could take on any male in this pack and win, even in his human form. With his hands tied behind his back."

"What? You think they're gonna come at him head-on? One at a time?" Hamish snorted. "Sweetheart, I don't know what fairy tales you've been reading these days, but fair play has no part in games like this, not when an alpha position is part of the stakes. They'd take him together, if they thought that was the only way. Or better yet, they'd just put a bullet in him. No fuss, no muss. Then he's out of the way, and the female alpha is still unmated. Only now, she's too damned shook up to think straight. Makes her more vulnerable, easier to take down."

The words struck like strands of a whip, cutting through her already pessimistic view of the future and leaving nothing but bleak, ragged shards. She struggled to breathe.

"They can't do that," she choked out, her throat threatening to close on a mix of anxiety and mindless fury. "I am *alpha* here. I won't allow it."

Hamish leaned forward in his seat. "I think you need to pay attention to some very important points, sweetheart. Ones that I came out here to remind you of. You've been acting like taking over for your daddy was a guaranteed home run. Sure, a couple of idiots tried to give you trouble, but the first one was too young and too dumb to pose a real threat, the second one underestimated you from the start, and Paul . . . well, he just didn't have his heart in it. That boy's been half in love with you for three quarters of his life. If you hadn't taken his hand, he'd've gnawed it off himself when he realized he'd hurt you. But from here on out, things are different.

"First off, you need to wrap your mind around the idea that this Howl is not going to be some sort of rubber-stamp act where the only thing standing between you and making this job as alpha permanent is a few words from you and a round of applause from the crowd. A lot of the members of this pack respect you, sweetheart, but there are a few bad apples in every barrel, and the ones in yours are just crawling with worms. They *are* ready to kill or rape you if that's what it takes to put you in your place.

"And second, you obviously need to brush up on your knowledge of Lupine traditions, or none of this would be coming as a surprise." He shook his head at her. "You made this pack a good beta, Honor, and I doubt anyone telling the truth would be saying any different, but a female beta who's the daughter of a strong, dominant alpha is a hell of a lot different from a female alpha who half the pack can remember seeing in diapers. Even those who respect you, those who like you, they might still have doubts about your ability to lead. You ought to know that Lupines are never wild about change, kid. Progressive thinking isn't one of our strengths. You should remember that an unmated female alpha has never gone over well with our kind."

Honor swore. "What did you really come here to say, then? That I should just give up and step aside and make way for a man to come forward and do my job for me? If that's what you've been trying to tell me, uncle, just go ahead and say it. I'm a big girl. I can take it."

Hamish swore right back. "It doesn't really

sound like you can, Honor Strength. What part of what I've said sounded to you like I'd rather have some hotheaded, loudmouthed asshole for an alpha than you? Was it the part where I called them morons? Or later, where I compared them to wormy apples? Hell, girl, I'm on your side, but I'm trying to tell you, you need to open your eyes and see what's coming for you. I know your daddy taught you never to walk into a challenge circle unprepared, but you've been walking around here like you've already won all the battles. Did you really think you could get away with it being that easy? That someone wouldn't dig up all our oldest and ugliest traditions, no matter how you—or the rest of the pack, for that matter—really feel about them? Admittedly, the Alpha Mating Rite isn't the prettiest of our legacies, but it exists, and I guarantee you it's going to come up at this Howl."

Not the prettiest of our legacies.

Now that was an understatement to end all understatements. As proud as Honor might be of her heritage at the best of times, the Mating Rite did not qualify as the best of times. It qualified as one of those times when it sucked to be a female in a culture where masculine traits like strength and speed and stubborn stupidity were valued above everything else. It qualified as something out of her worst nightmares.

"It's archaic," she felt compelled to point out, but the protest sounded weak even to her own ears. She knew her uncle was telling her the truth, and she knew she had no hope in hell of preventing the future he'd just described. "No one in their right mind could think we should still be carrying on a tradition of condoned rape in this day and age."

"I hear that the Silverback Clan ran a mate hunt just last year," Barney threw in, careful to keep his gaze from meeting those of the others. "The alpha and a bunch of other prime males chose mates that day, by running them down in Central Park and fucking them where they caught them. And these were city wolves. It might seem archaic when we talk about it, but I bet that when the males carried their mates out of the woods over their shoulders, it just seemed real."

Honor shivered. Her arms wrapped around herself as if warding off the cold, but she still hadn't noticed the ambient temperature. This chill came from the inside.

"This is the modern world," she said. "Our females are allowed rights equal to those of the males in the pack. They get to vote on issues where the opinion of the pack is weighed. We educate them alongside the males. They live in a world outside their homes, have lives and careers of their own. They're treated as equal members of our culture. And yet you say that when a female alpha calls a Howl to assume her rightful place at the head of the pack, that pack will refuse to grant her their obedience unless she has a mate to protect her in case she turns out to be too weak? That's just frickin' asinine!"

"It's the truth," Hamish said.

She pushed out of her chair to pace the length of the small room. She hated to be still when she needed to think. She had to pace and prowl and roam around. Lupines always thought best on their feet. "I don't agree. I think that things are changing all around us, and it's time this pack kept pace with the world we live in. We need to change, especially when this is the alternative some of our males come up with. We can't keep clinging to the old ways like this, especially when the old ways are so entirely repulsive. I won't let it happen."

"You won't have a choice."

She stopped and met that assessment with a fierce glare, fists clenched on her hips, chin lifted high in the air. "I'm the alpha here, and I lead the pack. When I make a decision, it stands. If I say there will be no Mating Rite, there will be no Mating Rite."

"If you say there will be no Mating Rite, there will be a riot," Barney spat out.

Honor turned on the old man, prepared to rip him a new one, but her uncle moved slightly to the side, drawing her attention away.

"It's not like you to kill the messenger, sweetheart," Hamish said. "Don't start picking fights with the man for speaking the truth. Saying no won't change anything. The pack's been working itself into a state since Ethan died. They've had too much time to be uncertain by now. You've been challenged repeatedly, and you may have won those battles, but everyone knows the war isn't over. They know this Howl is big, and having the Silverback sniffing around and asking questions about you and the pack is only ratcheting up the tension. Everyone knows tomorrow night isn't going to end without blood spilled, but most of them don't want to see you dead. They're hoping—*I'm* hoping—that you aren't that stupid, but they won't accept a decree from you that flies in the face of thousands of years of Lupine history and custom. Once you've established yourself, maybe, but not now. Now, you need to play the hand you'll be dealt."

"So what is it that you want me to do, uncle?" she demanded. "Go along with this stupid, bass-ackwards tradition and let myself be raped? Because I can't do it. I'd sooner step aside and let the Silverback Clan name Bozo the Clown the alpha of this pack."

"And you see? That's why you need to start thinking this thing through."

"What are you talking about?"

"About the fact that the male sent here by the Silverback Clan is now a great big variable in an already complicated equation." Hamish braced his elbows on his spread knees and clasped his hands together between them. "Setting aside the fact that he's already marked you for a minute, it hasn't helped shut any mouths that Graham Winters felt it necessary to send one of his men here to judge your fitness to lead. It made some folks in the pack who had never questioned you taking over wonder if there might be something to the question."

Honor swore. "I knew I should have kicked his sorry ass out of my territory before he had time to shut his damned car door."

Her uncle raised a brow. "Right. Either way, it's too late for that now. The cat's out of the bag. Having him here has only made the Mating Rite more likely. You aren't the only one who finds the thought of it hard to swallow, but having the Silverback question you will make it go down easier for quite a few of them. What really throws a wrench in the works is finding out that he's marked you for his mate. That's a hell of a thing to have happen right now."

"You already told me it wouldn't be any help. Since I haven't marked him back, and he can't put forward a claim to stop the mating hunt, what the hell good does he do me?"

"None. What he does for you doesn't have a damn trace of good about it. He makes things worse."

At that, something snapped in Honor's chest. She threw back her head and laughed, loudly. She felt like a camel hauling straw when that one last blade drifted down onto her back, and the picture of herself as a were-camel only made her laugh harder. As did the look Barney Andrews threw her way. The man couldn't have appeared more horrified if she'd stripped off her clothes and decided to dance a tarantella on top of her daddy's desk.

That thought set her off again.

By the time she had to stop or quit breathing altogether, she was wiping tears from her eyes and clutching her aching belly.

"Goddess' sake, Ham, she's lost her damned mind," Barney hissed, as if Honor couldn't hear him, standing as she was less than five feet away from him. "Not that it doesn't make the question of her fitness to lead a lot easier to answer, but what the hell are we supposed to do now?"

"Whew." Honor blew out a deep breath and grabbed ahold of herself. The elder might be looking at her funny, but she recognized the laughter for what it was—a release from the vibrating knot of tension that had been winding tighter and tighter inside of her for days. Hell, maybe even years. "Don't fit me for a straitjacket just yet, Barney. I haven't gone off the deep end. Not yet anyway. But you've got to admit, at this point saying things have just gotten worse is like saying that when a man's wife steals his truck to leave him, not only does she run over his dog, she mails him back the bill to get the fender fixed."

That comparison didn't seem to reassure him.

Shrugging, she turned back to her uncle. "Okay,

Uncle Ham. Lay it on me. What's the bottom line about Hunter's impact on the situation? I won't even question that he makes things worse, but what did you mean by it?"

Hamish nodded, looking unfazed by her outburst. Hell, the man had known her since her first breath; he'd seen her act crazier.

"Logan Hunter doesn't just undermine your claim to be alpha," he said, holding her gaze with his own, his age and her affection for him making it possible. "I said before that the males who want to move against you at the Howl, they won't recognize him as your mate, not with the mark unreturned and him being the beta of another pack, but that doesn't mean Hunter won't want to stake his claim." He pushed his upper body back up straight. "Now, I spoke to the boy, so I don't think he's dumb enough or mean enough to try to join in the rite, even if our males would let him, but he's not going to just stand aside and let anyone try to hurt you, either. So my guess is, when the rite is declared and the first male steps up to challenge you, Hunter is going to try to take him down."

Closing her eyes, Honor let her head fall back and sighed. Now she could see where this was going—straight to hell, just like everything else in her life. "And when he does that, it will set off all the other males. There really will be a riot. Anyone who doesn't like me—or who just doesn't like having an outsider interfering in pack business—is going to try to kill Logan. When the whole thing is over, I'm left with either half a pack, with the rest lying dead at the Silverback's feet, or a dead Silverback and the beginnings of a war with the most powerful Lupine pack in the eastern United States."

"That about sums it up."

Honor was silent for a moment, just letting the irony of it all sink in. Here she stood, a female who didn't even want to be alpha, faced with a situation that redefined the idea of a no-win scenario. She felt like she was trapped in an episode of *Star Trek*. She had no good choices, and no matter what choice she made, someone was going to die. It seemed like it would be a hell of a lot easier if that someone were her, but her stubborn pride wouldn't allow it.

Finally, she blew out a breath and opened her eyes.

"So, what do you suggest I do?" she asked, her mouth twisting into a wry curve. "If I shift and start running now, I could be halfway to the Canadian border before moonrise on Saturday."

Hamish returned the expression. "You'd never get that far. If the pack didn't track you down, that mate of yours would."

She shook her head. "We both know he can't be my mate, uncle. There's no way it can work. When this is over, if either one of us is still alive, we'll be going our separate ways. I can't leave the pack, and he can't take orders from anyone but his own alpha. That's just the way it is."

"One step at a time, sweetheart. First, figure out a way to get through the weekend, then worry about your love life."

"Right. Survival. Check." She paused for several long seconds. "Any idea how to make that happen?"

"Not at the moment, but you've got forty-five hours left to figure it out."

"Forty-five hours? Sure. Piece of cake."

Or not.

Eleven

Logan left Honor alone in her office and ran. He entered the woods in a blind fury, his heart pounding in his ears, rage burning through his veins like poison. He paid no attention to the snow that crunched icily under the callused pads of his feet, or to the scent of more snow coming in on the ozone-sharpened breeze. None of it mattered, and none of it could penetrate the red haze that fogged his mind and kept him operating on pure instinct, the instinct to run or to kill. Preferably both.

He ran for hours, zigzagging through the dense New England woods, letting his sense of smell inform him whenever he got close to the edges of the White Paw Clan's territory. The first time the scent hit him, it only increased his fury. He should have smelled his mate at those borders, because the edge of a Lupine territory was always scent-marked by the alpha of the pack. Instead, all Logan could smell was an unfamiliar dominant male who must have been Honor's father. The fact that his mate's position was still too tenuous for her to go out and mark her own lands made him seethe inside, but gradually, as he expended the adrenaline that drove his rage, he began to take comfort in the lingering traces of her scent he picked up here and there around the forest. Honor might not have scented her borders quite yet, but that didn't mean she hadn't left her mark on this territory. She had become part of the land here, just as it had become part of her.

Shortly after sunset, the last of the driving anger burned up in the relentless pounding of his paws against the earth, and Logan collapsed, panting, under a towering pine tree. The dry needles piled beneath it crunched under his weight, exposed where the thick forest cover had shielded the ground from the last light snowfall. Ears back, tongue lolling, Logan took a moment to catch his breath and let the sounds and scents of the forest soothe and calm him.

He had needed that run. Badly. The tension of the last couple of days had piled on top of his already deep sense of restlessness and discontent until he'd come within inches of losing control completely and going on the kind of rampage that made humans write stories about mindless, bloodthirsty werewolves who could only be stopped by the impact of a silver bullet. Logan had always wondered where that thing about the silver had come from. As far as he knew, if you put any kind of a bullet into the dead center of something coming at you, it was pretty much done. Choice of metal really just boiled down to semantics.

Now, with night closing in on the forest, Logan reluctantly began to pad back toward the Tate house and a set of dry clothes. Goddess knew what had happened to the ones he'd been wearing earlier. They had most likely been shredded during his shift, but he needed to shift back to his human form and work through a few things. The humans might be off base with that "mindless beast" crap, but it was easier to think wearing skin as opposed to fur. When the fur was on, the accompanying instincts could get in the way and cloud his thinking.

He was guessing he'd need every human brain cell he could muster to find a way out of the mess he and his mate now found themselves in.

Thinking about his mate—or, more specifically, thinking of Honor as his mate—sent a surge of primitive satisfaction jolting through him, enough of one that he almost wore a smile when he shifted back after slipping through the dog door located off the kitchen in the main house. No one seemed to be around, so he padded naked up to his room and took the time for a quick rinse-off in the shower before dressing in fresh clothes.

Finding his mate was about the only bright spot he could come up with in an otherwise totally FUBARed situation. If he'd ever seen a mess that was fucked up beyond all recognition, this was it. Logan had finally found the woman of his dreams, the one fate had destined that he would live happily with for the rest of his life, and who did she turn out to be? A potentially outclassed female wannabe alpha of a pack that appeared to have needed a serious makeover well before she had been forced to take over.

Yeah. Fun times.

The morning he had spent talking to the members of the White Paw pack had opened his eyes to a few things he hadn't expected. From everything Graham had told him before he left for Connecticut, Logan had painted a picture of Ethan Tate as an old-school alpha, the kind who ran a tight pack, who knew all of his wolves and commanded if not their love and devotion, then certainly their respect. The stories he had heard hadn't mentioned any uneasy rumblings coming from this small, somewhat remote clan, so he—and Graham, he was certain—had assumed that this pack ran just as smoothly and seamlessly as the Silverbacks. You know, discounting for insane cousins who attempted to incite coup d'états.

That wasn't quite what he had found. The stories Logan had heard from the pack members he had spoken to implied that Ethan Tate had earned more fear from his pack than he had respect. No one had ever thought to make a move against him, but their restraint stemmed from the certainty that even the smallest rebellion earned a death sentence under Tate's harsh rule. No one complained because no one wanted to end up with a permanent limp or the kind of scar that even a Lupine metabolism couldn't heal, not because they didn't have things to complain about. Bringing a grievance to the alpha had long been seen as a quick road to retribution. If a member of the pack hoped for anything like actual help with a problem, they went to the beta.

They went to Honor.

Honor—his mate—he had learned, had been the one who really kept the White Paws running. She made sure the families with sick babies got seen by a doctor, even when neither parent had a job that offered health insurance. She organized hunts during the lean months of winter and had instituted the twice-weekly communal meals as part of her efforts to make sure no one in the pack had to truly go hungry. When the nearby lumber mill, the pack's largest employer for generations, had closed, she had set up van pools to take pack members to the Native-American casino forty miles outside pack territory, because that had been the only place hiring new workers. The reason the White Paw Clan had not died out a decade ago, Logan had learned, was because of Honor.

The knowledge should have made his job easier. Hearing all those stories told him that Honor already possessed one of the most important qualities of a pack alpha—a fierce and unyielding determination to protect her pack and to do whatever she could to ensure their survival. If being alpha were all about organization and people skills, ingenuity and hard work, he would confirm Honor in the position without so much as a blink of hesitation—but being alpha meant more.

The alpha was the strongest wolf in the pack. Period, end of sentence. Sure, strength came in a lot of forms, from moral strength to emotional resilience to sheer dogged determination, but not one of those qualities was enough to take down an opponent who was bigger, stronger, faster, and more experienced. Honor was probably the best beta her pack could have had; she had kept order, maintained the peace, and had done what she could to ensure that no one in her charge had suffered unduly under the thumb of what sounded like an increasingly unstable alpha. The problem was that if Honor had been meant for the alpha position, she already would have taken it. Knowing what her father's tyranny cost her and the rest of the pack, a natural-born alpha would have challenged and overthrown an aging and increasingly infirm leader. If that had happened, none of this would be in question. An alpha who took her title by force wasn't one anyone questioned, not even Graham. If Honor had overthrown her father, Logan would never have come.

Wasn't that just a boot in the ass, he acknowledged silently as he left the house and headed for a small group of cabins Honor's cousin Joey had told him about shortly after his arrival. If Honor had been born to be alpha, he never would have met her, but because he had met her, he had to find a way to fix her pack—one where, as far as he could see, there was no one who fit the requirements of the position. Somehow, no matter what decision he came to, he knew he'd be screwed.

Pushing the worries aside for the moment, Logan focused on the path to the cabins. According to Joey, the cluster served as a sort of community center for the Lupines who lived on the White Paw land. There were almost always people there, he'd heard, and if you wanted to learn the latest gossip or locate someone in a hurry, it was the place to go. At the moment, what he wanted was to deal with a certain outstanding issue left over from this afternoon. It involved a very stupid Lupine who was lucky Logan had been more interested in claiming his mate the last time they'd met than in claiming his pound of flesh.

Make that ten pounds, he thought, snarling. Inflation and all.

If he couldn't solve the alpha problem tonight, at least he could solve the problem of exactly how badly he wanted to knock out a few of Darin Major's teeth.

A group of teenagers talking and tussling around a barrel fire in front of the house stopped what they were doing when he approached, and the women chattering away on the front porch fell silent. He ignored the scrutiny and prepared to ask his question when the door to the cabin opened and the young man who'd dragged Darin Major away earlier walked outside.

Max was exactly the Lupine Logan had hoped to see. The kid had kept his head during the fight back at the office, even though he still had some growing up to do before Logan could comfortably call him much more than a pup. He looked like a college kid, but he smelled like he'd turn into a powerful wolf one day. He had the makings of a beta, or maybe even an alpha, once he'd finished maturing. Either way, he could definitely prove useful at the moment.

"Max." At Logan's deep rumble, the women all followed his gaze and turned curiously toward the young man still poised in the doorway. "I'd like to talk to you, please."

Max hesitated, and one of the women on the porch shot Logan a suspicious glare. "He's busy. And he doesn't have to go anywhere he doesn't want to."

Logan didn't bother to acknowledge the rudeness.

Max quickly brushed the protective woman away. "It's all right, Cindy. Hunter's cool. I'll be back later on." He jogged down the porch steps to join Logan in the yard, shoving his hands into his pockets and hunching his shoulders as he looked up at the much larger man. "What's up?"

Logan jerked his head away from the house and steered them onto the path leading back to Honor's house. They didn't go far, but Logan wanted privacy, and with the full moon barely two days away, there was plenty of light to see by, even under the cover of the trees. "I wanted to ask you a question."

Max's eyes widened. "Dude, I swear there's nothing going on between us. Honor is like a big sister to me. I mean, sure she's beautiful and all, but I would never—"

One look at the kid's earnest and slightly panicked expression, and Logan burst out laughing. He laughed so long and hard that he had to stop walking to bend over and catch his breath. It was a good thing they were already in the thick of the trees and out of sight, or it could have gotten really embarrassing. As it was, it took him a good minute or two to calm down. By the time he could stand up straight and look Max in the eyes, the younger man had his arms crossed over his chest and a truly irritated expression on his face.

"It's not that funny a concept," Max snapped. "Sure, she's a few years older than me, but I'm not exactly repulsive, you know. I've had more than a couple of older women find me very appealing over the last few years, if you know what I mean."

Logan sobered abruptly and scowled at the young man. "Watch it, kid. Believe me when I tell you, it's better for you if I find the whole thing funny, okay?"

Max smiled sheepishly and let his arms drop back to his sides. "Right. So, then . . . um, if it's not about Honor, what did you want to talk to me about?"

Logan's eyes narrowed, his jaw set, and his mouth curved into a smile that probably would have scared women and small children. It certainly made Max's eyes widen in the silvery moonlight. "Darin Major. Where is he?"

"Dude, I swear, he's okay. I dragged him back to his cabin and got him into bed. He had a knot the size of a golf ball on the back of his head, but his head is harder than most tree trunks. He probably slept it off and was as good and as obnoxious as new when he woke up. I haven't seen him tonight, but it wouldn't surprise me if that was because he decided to stay in and sulk. He always was a sore loser."

"Where is his cabin? I'd like to talk to him."

Again. Apparently Logan hadn't made things quite clear to the man at their first meeting, and now he had to add in the advice that touching Honor had recently become a very unhealthy move.

"Um, yeah. So, um . . . d'you really think that's such a good idea? I mean, him being a member of Honor's pack, and you looking like you want to kill him and all? 'Cause I can see her giving you all sorts of noise over it if you, like, ripped out his spleen or something."

"Where is he?"

"All right, fine. It's your lecture. Just don't say I didn't warn you. Darin's place isn't far from the big house. This way. I'll show you."

Shaking his head, Max turned and led Logan

to a fork in the path and then east for a while until they came to the old logging road that ran through much of the property. They walked another quarter of a mile or so, past a couple of the small cabins Honor's father had rented to members of his pack, until Max stopped in front of one of the buildings and pointed.

"That one's Darin's. I gotta tell you, though, the headache he's gotta have after he woke up is going to look like a stubbed toe compared to the one Honor's gonna give you when she finds out you came out here and hassled him some more. And if you rip him open or something, then she's going to get really steamed."

Logan turned to his companion and asked very, very quietly, "Are you telling me what to do, Maxwell?"

Max jerked back and raised his hands, palms out in the universal gesture for "don't hurt me." He shook his head. "Dude, maybe you need to get a pair of glasses or something, 'cause do I look that stupid to you? I'm just offering a little friendly advice, is all, and I'm even done with that. See you later."

The young man turned and loped off down the forest path, still shaking his head. Logan watched until Max faded from sight before he put his hand on the railing and began to climb the front steps of Darin's cabin. He paused to knock at the front door and a flash of movement from inside caught his attention through one of the windows.

There were no lights on in the small building and the reflection of the moon on the glass made it difficult to see anything, but he could have sworn he'd seen something.

He stared for a few moments, then raised his hand and knocked again. Getting no answer, he reached for the knob and let himself in. One distinct advantage to this place over Manhattan, he thought as he stepped inside, was that here no one bothered to lock their doors.

The cabin lay quiet and empty. And surprisingly clean for an uneducated man who lived alone and seemed to have been raised in the Stone Age. Somehow Logan couldn't picture Darin doing his own laundry or washing his own dishes or even just picking up after himself. Maybe he paid a local female to come in and do it for him. The jerk probably pinched her ass and called her "baby" while she did it, too.

He couldn't keep his lip from curling as he made his way through the darkened house. Logan might be an old-fashioned kind of guy—he believed in opening a woman's door for her, paying for their dates, and always treating her with respect—but he had no patience for those who called themselves "men" and yet treated women like objects or emotionless dolls. Logan himself was possessive, but he always remembered that the women he felt possessive toward had their own thoughts and feelings and opinions and brains, and that sometimes their brains reached more intelligent conclusions than his own did. He'd seen the way Darin had tried to treat Honor, and he hadn't liked it.

It wasn't just that Honor had become his mate, it was that she deserved better simply because she was a better person than Darin. Hell, Logan suspected she was a better person than him. Still, even cats didn't deserve the lack of respect Darin had shown to Honor. And so, Logan thought it might be like a gift to the world at large if someone taught the flaming idiot a thing or two about manners. Luckily, Logan believed he just might be able to work that into his schedule.

He moved quietly down the cabin's short hall to the master bedroom. He could tell where Darin spent most of his time by the scents permeating the small building, and since he wasn't in the stinking recliner in front of the battered television, Logan thought it a pretty good bet that the next strongest pool of scent would be the man's bedroom.

The door swung open with a minimal squeak, but from what Logan could see, it could have made the sound of a dying antelope without doing much damage. The figure stretched out on the rumpled excuse for a bed remained solidly unconscious, slack-jawed and drooling. An unmistakable haze of cheap whiskey hovered over him like a poison-gas cloud.

And this slob thought he had what it took to be alpha of a Lupine pack.

Logan felt his lip curl in distaste and decided to make use of his visit here for something. If he couldn't take his frustration out on Darin's motionless body, he might as well accomplish something worthwhile.

As places to snoop went, the small cabin left much to be desired. As he could have predicted, the refrigerator didn't hold much more than half a case of beer and an opened Styrofoam tray of ground beef, beginning to turn gray at the edges. The thought of meat made Logan's stomach rumble. The couple of rabbits he'd munched on in the forest that afternoon had long since worked off, but he promised himself he'd get dinner up at the house when he finished here. Closing the door, he turned away and kept searching. The cabinets were all but bare, but again, neatly tended and relatively dust free.

The small living room looked tidy, for all of its shabby furniture. Someone must come in to dust fairly regularly, because the coating of powdery dirt he'd expected to see didn't seem to be there. The *TV Guide* and remote had been stacked neatly on a battered end table beside the easy chair, along with a coaster and a half-empty tin of peanuts. The presence of a beer coaster settled it. No way was the man who lived here worried about water rings on the cheap wood. This cabin definitely saw the presence of a woman more often than he supposed Darin the Dapper could manage to get lucky at the local bar.

Making his way back into the bedroom, Logan glanced wistfully at the still unconscious object of his frustrated anger and sighed. He turned back to searching and had checked under the bed and in all the dresser drawers before he actually found something interesting in the man's closet. Women's clothing.

Judging by the sizes—all 6 petites—Darin didn't have a guilty little secret, nor a desire to be a certain kind of lumberjack. There was no way the man could fit his beer-bellied bulk into those dresses. But the fact that they hung in his closet to begin with shot Logan's theory about an occasional housekeeper totally out of the water. This was no maid who endured the games of slap and tickle in exchange for a measly paycheck. This was a relationship, or at least evidence of one.

He felt his lip curl as he closed the closet door. What poor woman could be desperate enough for company that she chose to settle for the charms of Dull-Witted Darin?

Just as the door closed sufficiently to reveal the window that had been blocked by the open panels, Logan caught a glimpse of the dull, sandy-gray fur and bushy tail of a wolf disappearing into the woods behind the cabin. The last he had heard, there were no native wolf populations in Connecticut, and what he had seen had definitely not been a coyote, which meant a shifted Lupine had been lurking outside of the cabin while Logan snooped. Clearly, someone had been spying on the spy. Logan wondered if that might have been the flash of movement he'd seen through the window when he'd been standing on the front porch. It was possible a Lupine could have been in the house and let itself out through the back when Logan entered. Then it would have been a simple thing to shift in the woods or behind the house in order to keep an eye on what the stranger was up to.

Logan would have done the same. It was only smart. He'd been through more introductions since arriving in Connecticut than he'd done in most of the last five years, and he still hadn't met every member of the White Paw Clan. Those he had met had all been introduced in human form. The best way to remain anonymous to him would be to take wolf form. It was hard enough to keep a hundred new faces straight, let alone a hundred furry muzzles. These days, all but the most traditionally minded Lupines considered human form to be the politest one for introductions. It cut down on the need for immediate dominance challenges and therefore on the likelihood of bloodshed. So a Lupine in wolf's clothing, so to speak, would be the perfect way to conceal his or her identity.

Instinct told Logan it was a "she," not a "he." The wolf he'd spotted fleeing had been too small for an adult male, but not gawky enough for an adolescent. He felt fairly certain he'd seen a female. Maybe even the "she" who at least occasionally shared Darin's cabin. The intriguing question, then, became who would Darin be that intimate with if he still had feelings for Honor like the ones he'd expressed in her office earlier? If those qualified as feelings, anyway, and not just a bad case of testosterone poisoning, combined with the pain of thwarted ambition.

Logan stared out the bedroom window for another minute, but the wolf did not reappear, and the night was beginning to grow colder. It had been a long day, made longer by the exhausting run he'd put himself through earlier. He needed to get back to the house and find something to eat, maybe call Graham with an update. Then he'd work on his plan to keep his mate as his mate and figure out how to give the pack she was determined to protect the alpha it needed. Whether that alpha was Honor herself, he still hadn't decided. Coming up with a workable solution wouldn't be the easiest thing he'd ever done, but if that was what it took to ease his mate's worries and lift the burden of holding together a collapsing pack, then it had just become the sum total of Logan's ambition. Graham would just have to deal with the fallout.

He closed Darin's front door behind him and started off down the old logging road toward the main house. He'd even gone a good few strides when the truth kicked him in the chest and he had to pause to catch his breath.

All of the time that Logan had been savoring the idea of having Honor for his mate, he had never once considered that putting her best interests above those of the Silverback Clan meant that he was no longer really acting as Graham's beta. Instead, he had begun thinking and planning as though—whether Honor assumed her position as alpha of the White Paw Clan or not—she would be staying here in Connecticut, and that wasn't exactly the place that Logan had always called home. Logan lived in Manhattan, with the Silverback Clan. Where he was beta, a position he had grown to chafe under more and more with every passing year.

Well, shit.

As adaptable and urbane as Logan liked to consider himself, he still had a bit of the basic Lupine dislike for change lurking in his soul, way down there where he could mostly pretend it didn't actually exist. Right now, he had to stop pretending. He did hate change. He hated it fiercely and unrestrainedly. If he could, he would turn back the clock to the days when he and Graham were a team, when the position of alpha in the Silverback Clan was about tradition, and Logan had been able to pretend that Graham only held the title because his father had held it before him, and his father before that; that it would have belonged to Logan if he had been born a Winters instead of a Hunter. These days, he found that harder and harder to remember, his own need for dominance wearing away at the contentment he had always found in working side by side with the man he considered a brother.

If he could, Logan would go back to the time before Missy, when women had been women—fun and beautiful and delicious, but for the most part interchangeable. Before he'd smelled her scent and seen her mate pinning her to the floor of their home. Before he'd seen and smelled the changes pregnancy made in the female body, and smelled the scent of fresh milk on a woman's skin. Damn it, things had been so much easier before any of this had happened.

Logan threw back his head and howled at the injustice of it all. If he could, he would go back in time and change things that way, make things the way they were before those feelings of dissatisfaction had begun gnawing at his insides. But he couldn't go back, and only now did he finally begin to realize it. The only thing he could do was to go forward.

At least forward had its advantages. Forward meant Honor—a very distinct advantage, especially during her heat when she smelled so good he could get drunk on her scent alone, but it also meant Connecticut, and leaving behind his friends and his pack. It meant going from beta to Sol, the mate of the Luna, with no distinct position in the pack but the one he had by her side. He swore again, his hands clenching into fists.

He'd been having a hard enough time lately

dealing with being beta, being second to the leader of the most powerful pack in the eastern U.S. Could he honestly deal with being Sol of the pack with fewer members than the club where he worked? With having to defer not only to the alpha, but to his own mate on every decision that had to be made? Would he be okay with that because the rewards were so great, or would it eventually make him resentful and bitter, strangling the love he had for his woman?

Double shit.

Shit with a side order of fuck, no less.

It all became very plain to him, as if written out before him in black-and-white. He had a choice to make. He could have Honor, or he could have his pride. Now he just had to decide: which of the two things he loved most in the world could he most easily live without?

Twelve

There was no rest for the wicked, nor apparently, for the werewolf needing to come up with a plan to save her own life, let alone the pack that apparently wanted to see her mated or dead. On Thursday night, Honor collapsed into her bed, mental and emotional exhaustion sending her spiraling immediately into sleep. Too bad it wasn't a restful one. Plagued by dreams in which she found herself covered in the blood of those she considered family, or standing over the bloodied body of her mate, the night proved short and restless. When a fist pounded on the door just before dawn, it came almost as a relief.

"What is it?" she demanded hoarsely, sitting up and pushing a tangle of hair out of her eyes.

"We've got a fence down." Max's voice was easy to recognize, even through the thick panels of wood. "Moody's cows are tramping through the gap to the northeast."

Honor cursed.

While most Lupines much preferred the taste and entertainment value of wild game, when the spirit of a hunt was on them, they occasionally forgot to exercise their better judgment if confronted by the easy pickings of a domestic dairy cow. It kept the farmers happy to know that the "timber wolf" and "red wolf" populations on the supposed wildlife sanctuary next door to them stayed safely contained behind a stout ten-foot-high wooden fence.

Well, the fence had started out ten feet high and stout. As Honor stood looking down on it twenty minutes after the summons came, it resembled firewood waiting to be stacked. Someone had done a number on it.

Trouble had come, she heard, when said stout, ten-foot wooden fence wandered directly into the path of a bunch of rowdy teenagers who had decided to do a little cow-tipping and four-wheel mudding to entertain themselves. Their truck had spun out of control on the dirt road—barely more than a path, really—that bordered the fence line, and slammed sideways into the fence, which was already twenty years old and in need of repair. It had collapsed under the strain, and forty of the neighboring cows had stampeded through the opening, enlarging it quite a bit in the process.

"I smell you and a few of the others," Honor said to Max, who stood close behind her, "but I'm giving you credit for being too smart for this shit. Inside the car, were the kids ours?"

If they had been, none of them would be driving for a while. Hell, none of them would be conscious for a while. Not after the smacks she planned to deliver upside their fool heads.

"No, it was a bunch of townies. Human kids. Tom Sergeant got a whiff of them when they peeled onto the main road trying to get home. He saw the damage to their truck. Definitely not ours."

For which both Honor and the teenaged population of the pack could be grateful. The teenagers, because their asses would remain unbeaten, and Honor, because that was at least one thing she wouldn't have to add to her already overcrowded plate. Although at this point, she probably wouldn't even notice one more crisis. It could just get in line behind the others, and she'd deal with it in turn.

Hey, maybe that was a point in favor of *not* surviving tomorrow night. If she died during the challenges, someone else got to deal with all this shit. The prospect sounded almost appealing.

"All right." She sighed, rolling up her sleeves both figuratively and literally. "Let's get the cows back to Moody first. Get Henry and Jay on that. Animals are usually okay with them. You can help me sort through all this crap to see if there's anything we can salvage. We need at least half a dozen usable posts. Then someone needs to go to town to the feed store and pick up some razor wire. It will have to do until I can order new material for a permanent replacement.

"Let's get to work."

It meant a lot of sweaty hours, clearing up all the broken timber and debris of the accident. Thankfully none of the kids had been hurt and the truck had been operational enough to limp back to town under its own steam, so she didn't have to deal with the headache of injured humans or irate parents blaming her for their progeny's stupidity. It all just came down to cleanup and repair. Until she could get the materials to replace that section of the barricade, they had to make do with what they had on hand. On the farmer's side of the old fence, she and a handful of the pack dug temporary postholes and hammered in posts made up of scraps of the former fence. Then they'd strung and stapled razor wire to keep the cattle in their field.

Keeping curious Lupines out of said field would prove to be a sight more challenging.

The only effective barrier against wandering werewolves was a fence at least as high and strong as the one the truck had taken down, and that just wasn't going to happen without time and the proper materials. Actually, even a fence that tall did more to soothe the farmers than it did to actually contain the Lupines. An adult werewolf could easily clear the ten-foot barrier with room to spare. But it did generally serve to make one think twice about leaving the pack's territory, and that was its primary job.

This time, since she couldn't rely on that job

being done by wood and post, she would have to be a little more resourceful.

Wiping a dirt-streaked forearm across her brow, Honor stood in front of the temporary barrier and waved Max forward. The kid had proved to be a lot of help that morning. "Send everyone home and make sure no one like Moody wanders by." And by "like Moody" she meant human. "I need to finish this off."

Max nodded, quickly catching on to her plan. "You got it, boss. Just give me a second."

Honor waited until she could scent that her workers had turned and headed back toward the pack's main buildings, then she slipped deeper into the tree line. Stripping quickly in the cold air, she shifted into her wolf form. Then she walked along the perimeter of the patchwork-fenced area and marked the whole thing with her scent.

On the one hand, the smell of a mature female close to heat might end up drawing more males than it repelled, but the smell of an alpha was the important part of the equation. If she marked the barrier and therefore the field beyond as her private territory, then any members of the pack would know she meant, "This is mine. Stay away and don't touch." It would have to do until she could order wood and permanent posts for the new fence.

Shifting quickly back, she dressed and looked at her watch. It was nearly noon.

"Come back up to the house with me," she said to Max. "Least I can do is feed you for helping out here. Joey can make you a sandwich, or something."

"Uh, thanks, but no thanks, boss." Max shook his head. "No offense, but I don't think your cousin likes me very much. I'm sure my mom's got food at home. I'll grab something at her place."

Honor sighed. "Don't take it personally, Max. These days, Joey doesn't seem to like anyone, really. Maybe my dad's death hit her harder than she expected. He was kind of her last link to her own father. I barely remember Uncle Joe, but I do know he and Dad were a lot alike."

Still, Max accepted the offer of a lift back to his mother's cabin, and Honor swung the pickup in that direction before heading back to her own house. She climbed out of the truck slightly sore and extremely grubby, dreaming of nothing more than a nice hot shower. All thoughts of the upcoming Howl had been pushed to the back of her mind and locked away, at least for another few minutes. When she was clean, she'd think about that again. Maybe when she was clean, it wouldn't seem like such an insurmountable obstacle. She just didn't have the bandwidth for it yet. She barely had the bandwidth for a shower and lunch.

She climbed the stairs to the second floor, moving more like a ninety-year-old woman than a twenty-four-year-old Lupine, but she just felt battered. She knew enough to realize that at least half the sore muscles had less to do with wrestling barbed wire than with wrestling a male Lupine yesterday afternoon, but she didn't mind those aches nearly as much. She knew very well they'd be gone within a couple more hours, and for now she almost savored the reminder . . . especially since she knew better than anyone that it might have been the last time she'd ever make love with the wolf who had mated her.

Honor shivered and found herself weaving a little as she padded down the hall to her bedroom. Her mental and emotional exhaustion just kept deepening, and while the end might be in sight—with the Howl coming up tomorrow—the type of end it had the potential to become made it look less like the light at the end of the tunnel and more like the oncoming train.

Who knew things would work out like this? she wondered as she turned on the shower and stripped while the water warmed. When she'd complained that this wasn't a good time to find her mate, she hadn't realized what a fine mate he would be, or how irresistible she would find him. She'd thought all those old pack legends about one perfect mate for each Lupine had been hogwash—romantic, but useless. And yet here she was, finding herself drawn to one man and one man only, not even able to picture touching another as long as she lived. She'd even found herself holding her breath at times while she and the five male members of her pack had been working on the fence.

Their scents had been offensive to her, something she'd never experienced with any other Lupine who bathed. It was just weird.

She almost smiled as she stepped under the shower spray. Having a mate might have turned out to be very interesting, she decided. Provided, of course, that she could have kept him.

The stinging hot needles of water pounded down over her, rinsing away the worst of the debris and splinters and mud splatters. When she felt the nastiest grime sluice away, she reached for a washcloth and her soap and began lathering her skin. She lathered and rinsed twice, but the need to scrub off her skin had not reappeared since the day she'd bitten off Paul's hand. It boggled her mind that the incident had happened only a couple of days ago. So much seemed to have happened since her father's death. She felt as if she'd lived an extra lifetime in that one week.

She shampooed and rinsed her hair, leaving the conditioner in while she washed her face with a moisturizing cleanser. Being a werewolf didn't excuse a girl from a skin-preserving regimen. When she was clean and rinsed, she stepped out of the shower and wrapped herself in an enormous towel, using a smaller one to twist into a turban around her hair. She still had to moisturize, or all that nice clean skin of hers would end up dry and chalky before her hair even dried.

She nearly laughed at herself as she spread the milky cream into her legs. She'd always been a bit too much of a girly girl for a Lupine beta, not to mention an alpha. That might have been part of the reason why it took so long for her father to start paying her any attention. Before she'd begun fighting challenges, she'd been too busy playing with her dolls, and then later painting pretty pictures and decorating the dollhouse her nanny bought her to interest a man who lived and breathed the eternal combat of strength. What use did he have for a pretty little girl who preferred to make things rather than destroy them? Not much, as she'd found out.

As Honor had grown, she had developed into the sort of daughter her father could love, a woman who could challenge a grown male and win, who could bench-press a small bus and bite a hole through a sheet of stainless steel. She'd had to give up all of her more feminine hobbies and traits to please the man who refused to be pleased. The only thing of her own she had kept was her pottery, and it was the only area of her life where she truly felt at home and at peace. She didn't feel it when playing alpha or beta, when managing the business or ordering people around. So why was she still doing those things, and why was she planning to fight for the right to continue doing them for the rest of her life?

The answer came easily, but not prettily. Pride. She was too much her father's daughter in that one respect, too bloody proud to admit she'd been wrong her whole life in struggling to make someone else happy by doing things that made her miserable. How dumb did that make her?

Sighing, Honor unwrapped the towel from her head and combed through the mass of curls. She squeezed out all the excess water she could, then left it to dry naturally. Leaving her other towel on the floor in front of the sink for Joey to get later, she turned and padded silently back into her bedroom.

She stood in front of her closet for a long time, just staring blindly at the contents. It seemed like such an effort to reach in and grab a pair of jeans, a snug thermal pullover, a practical button-down shirt. And, sheesh, lacing up a pair of boots . . . ? Just the thought of it exhausted her.

Hm, so maybe this was what burnout felt like? Too bad she couldn't afford the luxury.

A force of will had her tugging out an outfit and pulling it on. Whether any part of it matched any other, she neither knew nor cared. She was covered. As long as the law was satisfied, so was she.

Honor made her way down the stairs conscious of the silence surrounding her. The big house felt empty. She couldn't sense her cousin moving around on one of her cleaning rampages, and her nose told her that her mate was nowhere within these walls. In fact, she smelled no one until she stepped into the kitchen at the same moment that her uncle came in through the back door.

He took one look at her and headed to the coffeepot. Pouring two steaming mugs, he handed one to her and raised the other to his lips.

Honor accepted it and opened the refrigerator for the cream.

"Heard you had a busy morning," Hamish remarked.

Honor recapped the cream, put it away, and dropped a spoonful of sugar into her mug. A quick stir later, she sipped, nearly sighing with pleasure. Any morning that started without coffee made her want to cry. She hadn't taken the time for a cup earlier. Now her day could really begin.

"Some kids from town came out here joyriding last night and took down a section of fence," she said. "Max found it when he was out for a run and came to tell me about it. It took a few hours to get the cows back where they belonged and rig up something to keep them there until we can replace the fence. Of course, trying to dig postholes was bad enough today. It's going to be a real bitch in a couple of weeks after the materials come in and the ground has had a chance to freeze even more solid."

"Gotta do what you gotta do."

"Ain't that the truth."

Hamish eyed her. "So why are you standing around here, then?"

Honor blinked. "Excuse me?"

"Don't you have a few other things on your plate right about now?"

"I thought I'd finish my coffee first, but sure, Uncle Hamish. Just as soon as I'm done I'll wave my sparkly magic wand and go fix everything. Thanks for the reminder."

He chuckled, apparently unfazed by the dark look and rude gesture she threw in his direction. "Sweetheart, the day I see you wave a sparkly magic wand is the day I go vegetarian. I wasn't criticizing. Fact is, I was suggesting that you need to get away and clear your head. The Howl is tomorrow night. If you waste today taking care of a thousand little chores that won't spell the end of the world if they get missed, you won't be doing yourself any favors. If you want to come up with a plan, you need to get away from the pack and do some thinking. If it were me, I'd hightail it so deep into the woods, the squirrels couldn't find me, and then I'd do some thinking."

Honor deflated like a popped balloon. "I've been doing nothing but think for a week now," she admitted, "and so far it hasn't gotten me anywhere but right back to where I started. I don't know if I *can* figure this thing out, Uncle Ham. I'm not even sure I've got the energy to keep trying. Tomorrow night, half my pack is going to try to kill me, and the other half is going to be urging them on, and I don't have a damned single idea about how I'm going to stop them."

Hamish stepped forward and wrapped Honor in a hug, the kind of big, encompassing, comforting squeeze she hadn't felt in a long, long time. "That's why you need to get away, Honor. I have faith in you, little girl, and I have faith that you're going to figure out a way to beat this, but even if you come up with a plan worthy of Machiavelli,

Sun Tzu, and the Duke of Wellington all rolled into one, it's not going to do you any good if you drop from exhaustion before you can put it into action. You need rest, you need quiet, and you need the pack to stay the hell away from you for twenty-four hours. You hear me?"

Honor snorted against his chest, but hugged him back briefly and fiercely. "I hear you, old man, and I appreciate the advice. Now are you going to be the one to tell the pack that I ran away from home when they come up here or to the office looking for me?"

"It would serve them right if that was exactly what I told them. Don't worry about it, sweetheart. I'll make sure Max and Joey know. Between the three of us, I'm sure we can put out enough DO NOT DISTURB signs to give you a nice little vacation. Now get out of here."

Leaving her empty coffee cup in the sink, Honor took a deep breath and gave her uncle a small smile, the first one in days that felt like she meant it. Hell, maybe even in months.

"Thanks, Uncle Hamish. I really do appreciate this."

Before he could finish telling her to shut up and scoot, Honor was out the back door and halfway into the woods. She knew exactly where she'd go for her little meditation, too. At the far southwestern edge of the pack's territory, one arm of their miniature lake jutted out into the neighbor's property, but behind that was an isolated little strip of land with an old shack that her father had never bothered to tear down. He didn't think anyone would want a cabin out that far, and he'd likely been right, but for Honor it was a little piece of heaven. She'd worked in secret for an entire summer when she was sixteen making sure the roof didn't leak, the walls were sound, the chimney drew, and the little hideaway held a stock of blankets and first-aid supplies. Every few months, she also replenished it with firewood and bottled water. None of the pack ever went near it, something she could verify by scent, and it was the only place in the clan's territory where Honor ever felt like she could be herself. Maybe there, her head would clear enough for her to think.

Her stomach rumbled, reminding Honor that she'd missed breakfast, and she'd just walked away from a giant refrigerator filled with lunch possibilities. She never left food at the cabin, since attracting wildlife wouldn't help keep the place clean and sound, so there was nothing there for her to eat, but she didn't care. As soon as she got there, she planned to strip off her clothes and go for a nice long run. There would be plenty of game near the shack to satisfy her hunger, but what would really be satisfied was her soul. It might be nice to remember what that felt like.

Thirteen

Logan found himself storming up to his bedroom on Friday evening in a piss-poor mood. Again. It seemed like he'd suffered from piss-poor moods just about every hour that he'd spent among the White Paw Clan, so it didn't surprise him that he had another one currently digging a pickaxe into the headache brewing behind his eyes.

It didn't help his mood that he'd seen neither hide nor hair of his erstwhile mate since their altercation yesterday afternoon. Last night, of course, he'd spent half the night roaming around the forest taking his aggression out on bunny rabbits, but Honor had been gone from the house before he woke up in the morning, and he hadn't run into her even once during the day. His hours furthering his education about the state of the pack had provided him with neither any reassurance as to their state of general organizational health, nor a single mate sighting. He'd wondered if she was deliberately avoiding him, but when he'd asked casually about her, none of the other pack members seemed to have spotted her, either. He heard all about her early-morning foray into fence-building, but she hadn't turned up all afternoon. He'd even gone back to her office, only to find the small cabin dark and empty. No fresh tracks led up to the door, either. It was as if his mate had vanished.

He could have tried to follow her scent trail, he supposed, but he didn't know how much good that was likely to do him. Honor's scent spread across most of the territory her pack held. As acting alpha, she had reason to go almost everywhere, so even the freshest bits of her scent could lead him in circles for hours. He had better things to do than chase his tail at the moment. Like ditching yet another phone call from his own persistent alpha.

Graham had called five times that day already, and it was only just after five P.M. Apparently becoming a mate and a father hadn't taught the other male very much about patience, or about other Lupines not jumping every time he walked into a room or pushed the buttons on a phone. Logan, however, had nothing to say to him at the moment, so he let the call go once more to voice mail.

What was he supposed to tell Graham, anyway?

Oh, yeah, buddy, everything's great. I've pretty much decided that while Honor has the intelligence, the drive, and the character to be alpha, she would never be able to whip this pack into shape the way it needs. Not after her father left it in such a shitstorm-shape of a mess.

Who should take her place? Well, none of these numbnuts, that's for sure. There's one kid who'll probably make a decent beta in a few more years, you know, after he graduates from college and gets his damned hormones under control, but there aren't any alphas around here, that's for sure. As far as that goes, Honor stands head and shoulders above the lot of them.

What should you do? At this point, I'm not sure just setting fire to this whole territory wouldn't be the smartest move you could make. The problems facing this pack will take years to sort out, and that's provided you can find an alpha strong enough to take over, and charismatic enough to do it without making the entire pack hate his guts.

Oh, and by the way, I've discovered that Honor is my mate, so no one is allowed to kill her, okay? Okay.

Right. That would go over well, he was sure.

Logan needed a plan, not just one that would give him something to tell Graham, but one that would provide some sort of acceptable resolution to the matter of providing a permanent alpha for the White Paw Clan. Not to mention that it had to take care of all that and still manage to keep his mate alive and by his side. So, you know, no pressure.

He had been driving himself crazy trying to figure all of this out. Every time he thought he might be on to something, some complication would smack him in the face and force him to start over again. Like, he could just remove Honor from the situation. She was his mate now, so it would be perfectly in keeping with tradition if she left with him and moved to New York to join the Silverbacks—except that Logan knew he'd have to drag her away from her ancestral pack kicking and screaming, and he'd likely wake up missing his testicles the first time he let down his guard around her afterward. But maybe having a mate would take care of all that restlessness and discontent he'd been feeling before he left Manhattan. Maybe once Honor was with him, he could go back to being a beta and liking it. Provided she let him live.

Then he considered backing her claim as alpha—because she was, though he hated to admit it, the best of some bad choices—and helping her to defeat any challenges from within the pack. The problem there was that when the fur stopped flying, Logan would find himself as nothing more than his mate's Sol, with no power to institute any of the changes he knew the pack would need to survive. Sure, he could suggest them to her privately, work behind the scenes to try to guide her into doing what was necessary, but Logan was not a behind-the-scenes sort of man. He was too used to doing what needed to be done and worrying about the consequences later. Plus, he knew already that his mate wouldn't take kindly to the feeling of being manipulated and second-guessed, which could very well happen. If she began to think he was trying to rule the pack through her, it could end up ruining their relationship and still not fixing the pack.

Then there was the idea that the two of them could run away to join the circus and let the goddess-damned White Paw Clan just go fuck itself. At the moment, that last prospect appealed the most to him, but he figured his mate might have something to say against it. She was, after all, a stubborn little thing, and she had a lot more than he did invested in seeing this pack live on in perpetuity. He doubted he'd ever be able to convince her to abandon it.

The question remained, then, where did they go from here?

Logan contemplated that as he stripped off his shirt and prepared to go down to dinner. If his mate wasn't waiting for him in the dining room, or at the very least in the eat-in kitchen, he *would* go out looking for her. Better to dress warmly now than to waste time changing clothes later.

A sharp *ta-ta-tap* at the bedroom window caught his attention.

Frowning, he looked over at the dark glass. His room was located at the back of the house on the second floor, and Logan couldn't imagine it being invaded from the outside. Sure, werewolves could jump that high if they wanted to, but there would be nothing to land on with the

window closed, and anyway, he couldn't picture
even his nosy questions having pissed anyone off
enough for them to try attacking him. So where
had the sound come from?

He crossed to the window, noting that the
trees around the house were trimmed, and none
of them stood near enough to the house for their
branches to be tapping. Maybe he'd just imagined the sound.

Ta-tap. Ta-ta-tap.

It came agan.

Curious, Logan unlocked the window and
pushed up the sash. He leaned out and looked
around, at first seeing nothing. Then a cold splat
of snow hit his cheek, followed closely by a small,
stinging pebble, and he lowered his glance to the
ground near the tree line. There, he spotted a small
gray wolf with fur ranging from silver-white to
dark, sooty charcoal standing and watching him.
While he watched, the wolf turned her tail toward
him and scratched her back paws on the ground
with a hard, stiff-legged motion, tossing a small
shower of snow, dirt, and pebbles up toward his
window.

This time he ducked.

The wolf turned back to him, her tongue lolling out the side of her muzzle as if she laughed at
him, and her ears pricked forward to indicate
that all her attention focused on him. Her dark
eyes shone in the moonlight, and the expression
in them made identifying her easy.

Mouth beginning to curve into a smile, Logan leaned forward and rested one arm on the windowsill. "What is it, Lassie? What are you trying to tell me, girl? Is Timmy caught in the well?"

His mate responded with a sharp yip followed by a low growl. Apparently, she didn't find him all that funny. The wolf threw her head back and gave a short, sharp howl, the sound carrying clearly on the cold night air and raising the hair on the back of Logan's neck. His mate was lonely, and she wanted him with her. She didn't have to ask twice.

He sprinted down the stairs wearing only his jeans and stripped those off in the mudroom just inside the back door. He didn't particularly care if Honor's cousin got a glimpse of his bare ass, but luckily, he didn't run into her. Shifting, he launched himself through the flap on the dog door straight toward the spot where he'd just seen his mate. As soon as she spotted him, she turned tail and ran.

Logan didn't mind. Wolves loved to play chase, and he could sense his mate's laughter as she led him deeper into the forest and away from the areas where other members of the pack could be expected to congregate. If she wanted to get him alone, Logan was all for it.

When he pounced on her in a small clearing south of the meeting hall, he knew she had let him catch her. She yipped breathlessly and rolled around with him on the thick blanket of snow for a dizzying minute before she twisted as quick

as an otter and sprinted back into the trees. His
mate led him on a merry chase through miles of
empty forest, and Logan felt his heart swell with
joy and exuberance. This was a gift his mate gave
to him, a time that wiped away all of the worries
that had been weighing each of them down,
when they could just enjoy each other, and the
strength of the bond growing between them.

They played that way for more than an hour,
running and chasing and catching and escaping
from each other in the peaceful woods. When they
grew hungry, they stalked and flushed an enormous wild turkey from a small thicket and shared
the kill. Logan nosed all the tastiest bits toward
his mate, not even worrying about whether or not
he looked like a scene from *Lady and the Tramp*.
After all, no one was around to see.

After dinner, Honor lured him into a game of
hide-and-seek—more like hide-and-pounce, actually, since her tactic seemed to be to sneak off for
high ground, then leap out at him the minute he
got within range. Logan didn't mind. Oh, he'd
snarl at her, but she'd just laugh and dance away
and look for a new hiding place.

They had left the main house less than an hour
after sunset, with Honor leading the way gradually
to the southwest. Instinct and the height of the
moon he could glimpse occasionally through the
trees told Logan it must now be close to mid-
night. He didn't know about his playful mate,
but his energy had begun to flag. After the last

couple of restless nights—not to mention the stress that dogged his every waking moment—he knew the adrenaline of playing furry games with Honor wouldn't be able to carry him much further. He needed to take a breather.

Just about the time when he was ready to abandon the games and begin looking for a secure place to rest, Logan followed his mate through a gap in the trees and into another small clearing. This one sat right on the lake, more like a postage-stamp-sized beach than a bare spot in the forest. Nestled up against the tree line he could see a tiny, one-room building clearly illuminated in the moonlight that glinted off the water and reflected in the glass of a single visible window. It had a brick chimney rising from the roof at the back, a tiny overhang above a single step, and a single door leading into darkness. The door stood slightly ajar, and the place appeared empty, but Logan still felt a surge of alarm when his mate dashed inside and disappeared. Immediately he launched himself after her, crossing the threshold on the heels of the fleet female before him.

The shack appeared just as small on the inside as it had from the outside. The chimney he'd spotted a minute ago led down to a large, open hearth that took up almost the entire back wall. To the right of the door a dry sink and a couple of built-in cabinets lined up beneath the window he'd noticed in his initial summary, and to the left, someone appeared to have built a platform bunk with storage underneath. It looked a bit larger than a single bed, but nowhere near as comfortable as the spacious king-sized one that he'd spotted previously in Honor's bedroom. That didn't stop his mate, though. She leaped up onto the mattress, surprising him when no dust cloud rose up around her. Come to think of it, he didn't notice any other signs of neglect in the little cabin, either. No cobwebs hung in the corners, and the combination of moonlight streaming through the window and his own keen night vision told him the bin in the far corner held enough firewood for at least a full night's heat. Without his fur, he might appreciate that a bit more.

Nothing else appeared to occupy the cabin. No shapes lurked in the corner, and his nose detected nothing but the sweet, musky smell of his mate. Before the scent could give him ideas, however, he turned back to find his mate completing a final circle and settling down amid a nest of blankets. She glanced at him and yawned, her pink tongue curling lazily, then tucked her muzzle up against her thigh and draped her tail daintily over the tip of her nose.

She looked adorable, like a little stuffed animal, and when she began to blink drowsily, Logan gave up the fight. Nosing the door closed, he waited for the latch to click, then padded the few short steps to the bedside. A quick gathering of muscles had him springing lightly up beside Honor and turning three circles of his own. Instinct, after all, was instinct.

With a mighty yawn and a low snort, Logan made a place for himself in the cloth nest, curling his larger body around Honor's smaller form and tucking his muzzle affectionately against hers. One last sigh, deep and heartfelt, and he allowed himself to drift into sleep, his mate curled contentedly at his side.

Honor awoke some time later, lying still as memories of the night slowly began to seep back into her consciousness. Her body felt pleasantly tired, as if she'd recently finished a good workout, and for the first time in days, her mind appeared pleasantly blank. She was aware of some kind of dark cloud pushing on the edge of her consciousness, but she ignored it, pushing it aside. She didn't want darkness right now, only this sweet, sleepy contentment that drifted along on the easy rhythm of her mate's breathing.

She lay still for a while longer, but eventually, the sharp chill of the cabin began to nag at her. Sure, in her current form her fur and her mate's shared body heat would keep her from freezing even if the temperature dropped another ten degrees, but the advantage of being a Lupine and not an ordinary wolf was opposable thumbs.

Well, opposable thumbs and matches.

Moving carefully so as not to disturb Logan,

Honor slipped from the bed to stand on the cold wooden floor. On the callused pads of her paws the planks felt icy enough, but on the tender soles of her human feet, they made her curse softly. Wrapping her arms around herself to conserve every bit of body heat she could, she crossed quickly to the fireplace and struck a match to the pile of tinder and kindling she always left waiting for her next visit. When she left the shack, her last task would be to lay the beginnings of another fire for next time. It never hurt to be over-prepared.

It took only seconds for the fire to catch, and within another ten minutes, she was adding real logs to the merrily crackling flames. Soon, the inside of the shack began to grow warmer, the benefit of her careful attention to the soundness of the structure and the building's tiny footprint. A twelve-by-twelve room didn't take much to heat.

The heat of the fire felt amazing on her bare skin, and Honor turned slowly to expose every inch of her body to the flames. When she stopped with her back to the hearth, her gaze fixed on the sight of Logan stretching his furry limbs and slipping seamlessly back into his skin, still sound asleep. The shift came in response to the change in temperature, Honor knew. The warmth was much more appealing to the man than the wolf, and frankly, she wasn't about to complain, not when the resulting view turned out to be so appealing to her.

She stood there for a long moment, savoring the warmth of the fire and watching the rise and fall of Logan's chest as he slept peacefully before her. He should have looked softer, she thought. More innocent and less dangerous, but that wasn't the case. He still looked huge and strong and lethal, even in sleep. His muscles still bunched and rippled when he breathed, and occasionally his arms or legs would flex as he dreamed unknown dreams. She smiled and stepped silently forward, two long steps the only requirement to bring her to his side. She reached out to touch him, her fingers settling light as a feather on his shoulder.

She hesitated for a moment, watching his face intently in the moonlight, not yet wanting to wake him. She did want to wake him eventually—already the hunger built again inside her—just not yet.

His breathing remained smooth and even, though, and Honor grew bolder. Her hand settled on him more fully, her palm tingling with the heat of his skin. It stroked down across his collarbone and over his chest, marveling at the sculpted muscles she found. She leaned down, needing now to taste him, and pressed her mouth against the skin at the base of his throat. She laved her tongue against him and felt his heartbeat in her mouth, then drew at the flesh until it reddened from the suction.

Her hands slid slowly over his chest, savoring

every texture, from smooth skin to rough hair. She felt him stir and lifted her head briefly, but his eyes remained closed and his breathing even so she lowered her mouth back to his skin and continued to explore.

She drew a moan from him when her thumbs found his tight, flat nipples and circled them with teasing pressure. She smiled against the center of his chest where her tongue drew intricate patterns on his warm skin. She let her thumbs and fingers and mouth play over his chest for long minutes before she decided to begin easing him from his dreams.

Climbing up onto the pallet beside him, she settled on her stomach with her head even with his chest and her breasts pressed up against his belly. She let her hands glide down over his chest and rib cage to his stomach, nails ever so slightly scraping his skin. He inhaled deeply, and Honor waited for his chest to expand fully before she laid her mouth over his nipple and drew deeply on the little disc.

Logan groaned, loud and deep, and his body flexed beneath her. Honor moved her mouth in a slick trail across the center of his chest until it could close around the other nipple, her tongue teasing the taut skin. Raising her eyes until she could see his face, limned silver and gold in the combination of moon- and firelight, she watched very carefully as her teeth closed around the point of his nipple and bit down gently. She knew the moment the sweet-sharp sensation registered in his sleep-charged brain, because his eyes flew open and his hands shot up to grab her and pull her closer.

But Honor had been watching him and she was not so easily caught.

She shimmied out of his sleep-slowed grip and pushed herself farther down the bed, licking a trail across his belly and hip until she could blow streams of hot, moist breath across his urgent arousal.

His cock stood eager and fully erect, straining against his belly in anticipation of her touch. But she didn't touch it. Instead, she braced her hands on either side of his hips and set her tongue against the base for a long, slow lick to the top. Logan's entire body tensed and then shuddered and he growled his pleasure, his hips lifting clear up off the mattress in search of the wet heat of her mouth. She eluded him, not yet ready to end her teasing. She loved the response she drew from him, loved this chance she had to explore him, now when he was too sleepy and aroused to take control as he had the other times they had made love.

She continued to lick him like a Popsicle, not taking him inside her mouth, just tasting his cock with the flat of her tongue from base to tip, over and over, while he panted for breath. Finally, when he got enough air to groan her name in a nearly unintelligible rumble, she took pity on him and closed her mouth around the head of his cock, taking him deep inside.

He roared as if he'd just won a battle, and she felt his hands fisting in her hair, looking for something to hold onto in the midst of the mind-blowing pleasure. Honor shared that pleasure. She loved the taste and feel of him, stretching her jaws, pressing against her tongue, filling her senses with the salty-sweet taste of him.

She hummed her enjoyment and he groaned again. If she could have smiled with her mouth full she would have, but instead, she pulled back, drawing on his cock with firm suction. When she held just the head between her lips, her tongue stroked the sensitive bundle of nerves just under the crown, and she listened to him fight for air. The sounds and flavors of his arousal incited her own, until she could feel her own moisture slicking the insides of her thighs with sweet cream.

She drew him back inside, lips sliding down the length of his shaft until she could feel the head of him butting against the back of her throat. Then she pulled back again, drawing deeply and establishing a rhythm that made him throw back his head, dig his heels into the rough mattress, and chant her name like a mantra.

"Honey. Honey. Oh, shit . . . that's so good . . . God. A little more, honey. Just a little more . . . I know you can do it . . . shit . . . oh, yeah . . . that's a good girl . . ."

She glowed under his praise, working harder

to please him, to tear those incredibly erotic words from his lips, the ones that made her pussy slicker and more needy with every passing second. The ache no longer mattered to her, though. All she wanted was to hear those words, to feel his fists clenching in her hair, or his shaking hands release her to pull her long, damp hair to the side until he could watch her mouth moving over his cock.

She whimpered her own arousal and worked him faster, but he'd already reached his breaking point. Grabbing her under the arms, he pulled her up his body until they pressed hip to hip, then he reached down to pry her legs apart.

"Now," he ordered, his voice all dark gravel and need. "Ride me, honey. Want in you. My love. My mate."

She moaned and obeyed. Her legs parted around his hips, and she pressed herself into a sitting position, straddling his lap. He wouldn't let her tease him, though. Before she could even think, he had his hand between their bodies, guiding his cock to her dripping entrance, while his other hand gripped the flare of her hip and pushed her down to meet his upward thrust.

He sliced through her, pushing deep on that first stroke, but he satisfied neither of them. Suddenly both hands were on her hips and he forced her inexorably down, his cock surging high and hard inside her, filling every last corner and leaving her stretched and aching.

Breathless and nearly sobbing above him, Honor watched his face smooth from a fierce scowl to a look of complete ecstasy as he found his home again inside her body. He paused for barely a minute before the urgency was on him again and he began thrusting hard and rhythmically within her. Honor met him, thrust for thrust, taking all he had to give and returning eagerly for more. They moved together as if they were two parts of the same machine, fitting perfectly together and working in tandem at their appointed task.

They struggled together for their pleasure, but it felt like more than that. They moved and slid and strained against each other, but it seemed like a cooperative thing. She shifted her hips to let him slide a fraction deeper. He changed the angle of his thrust until he could reach the sweet bundle of nerves inside her and make her shiver with joy.

She braced her hands on his chest to keep herself steady, and he cradled her hips between his hands to be sure she didn't fall away. They had become one. His pleasure was hers, her pleasure was his. The burst of ecstasy they shared at the end of the journey left them both breathless and aching and sure that the only way to stay sane in the future was to never be farther apart than the touch of the other's loving hand.

Fourteen

Logan woke again, though this time not nearly as pleasantly as last time, when he felt Honor slip from the bed. For a minute he lay still, imagining she had just gone to add more wood to the fire, but he never heard the clunk of wood on wood or the crackle of renewed flames. Instead, he heard a rustle of cloth and the unmistakable click of the cabin door opening. When he heard it shutting, he frowned and threw off the blanket that covered him.

The night air bit at his bare ass as he stood and glanced around the cabin. He knew he had heard her putting on clothes—which was weird, considering they had both entered the building in wolf form and neither had been carrying a duffel bag—but no sweater or conveniently sized pair of jeans appeared for him. Instead, he yanked the door open and stalked outside buck naked. It wasn't the first time he'd found himself bare assed, and the Goddess knew it wouldn't be the last. Right now, the important thing was finding out where his mate had run off to.

And why.

It almost surprised him when he spotted her immediately, standing at the edge of the lake, her head tilted back, dark eyes fixed on the heavy, silver orb of the moon. It hung low in the sky, indicating the hours were transitioning from late to early. It was tomorrow now, the day he knew both of them had been dreading.

Stepping up behind Honor, he wrapped his arms around her and lowered his chin to the top of her head. "Looks like it will be morning soon."

"Sunrise in another hour or two," she agreed, not turning to look at him. Her eyes remained fixed on the moon.

Logan felt his mouth quirk. "This is the part of the movie where we wax all rhapsodic and romantic in the moonlight, isn't it?"

Honor snorted. "Right, because there's so much romance in this situation. I don't know if you've noticed, but we're not in a movie. No one is going to yell 'Cut!' and tell us to break for lunch. And definitely not during the final climactic battle sequence."

He tried not to stiffen. "You're picturing a final climactic battle sequence?"

"Aren't you?"

"I've been hoping it wouldn't come to that."

"And I've been hoping for a pony and a big brass band. Luckily, I'm used to disappointment."

Logan leaned back and grasped her shoulders, easing her around to face him. "I'm not going to let anything happen to you, Honor."

"You're not going to have a choice."

He wanted to shake her, but he retained enough restraint to control himself. They hadn't been talking for long. "You're my mate. No matter what happens at tonight's Howl, I will do whatever it takes to protect you. There's not even a question about that, so just let it go."

She sighed deeply. "See, that's the problem. Well, two of them, really."

He waited for an explanation.

"I was hoping to persuade you to leave at dawn. I know it sounds kind of melodramatic, but it really would be for the best."

"Okay, let's pretend that was ever a remote possibility. Why would you want me to go?"

Honor stepped to the side, and Logan reluctantly released her. He kept his eye on her, though, turning as she moved away from the water and stuffed her hands into the front pockets of her jeans. The motion drew her shoulders up around her ears, and he watched as she forced them back down.

"You know the situation I'm in," she finally said, stopping in a clear ray of moonlight. "I won't give up this pack. I won't give up *on* this pack, but no one seems real inclined to just step aside and let me claim it as alpha. It's funny, when I think about it, that if I'd just been born with a dick, none of this would be happening. You"— she glanced at him—"would never have even come here."

"I also wouldn't be your mate," he pointed out dryly.

"True." She shrugged. "For all it really matters."

Logan felt a stab of anger, laced with something else, something uneasy. "Are you saying it doesn't matter to you that we're mated?"

"I'm saying it doesn't matter to the pack," she corrected. "At least, it won't tonight, and that's when it counts."

Logan frowned, letting that phrasing tumble around for a moment. It tugged at something, something tucked away in the back of his mind. Something that took that trace of unease and stretched it into real worry. He watched her while he thought, saw her expression reflect a mix of emotions: worry, anger, resignation, determination. Fear. Disgust.

And it hit him.

Felt like it literally hit him, like a kick to the solar plexus, nearly knocking the wind out of him.

"You think they're going to call for an Alpha Mating Rite."

Her mouth twisted. "I'm sure of it."

Logan struggled for breath. Fury and fear threatened to rip it away again. Other males would try to hurt her, to touch her. To take her from him. And he would be powerless to stop it.

"You think they won't recognize us as being mated. Why?" His mind raced. "Because you haven't marked me? Well, fang up, sweetheart, and let's get this done."

"It wouldn't make any difference. Sure, they'll point to that, but even if I did mark you, it wouldn't matter. You're not a member of the pack, and I'm claiming to be alpha. Only a pack member can mate a female alpha; you know that. It keeps rogues from being able to come in and seize control of a pack too easily. You know, because we females are clearly too weak to hold them off."

She sneered at that. Logan wanted to howl.

He struggled for control, fought to concentrate on the chill in the air, the rustle of the tree branches, the scent of the lake, the sound of pine needles snapping in the woods. Anything that would take his mind off the killing rage that threatened to consume him.

"And because I'm not a member of the pack, I won't be allowed to join the challenge for you."

"Of course not. You know the rules. They'd take you down if you tried. Or if they were afraid they couldn't, they'd just shoot you and save themselves some trouble."

Logan cursed. "But I suppose you're just going to walk into that situation, even knowing what's going to happen. You're going to walk into that and just let them have at it."

"What the hell else am I supposed to do?" she demanded, her calm demeanor cracking around the edges. "What choice do I have?"

"How about you can *not* set yourself up to be raped or killed? Have you thought about that?"

"Of course I have. I'm not an idiot. Trust me when I tell you they're going to kill me. I'll *make* them kill me, because I am dead serious when I say I will die before I'd ever let one of those sleazeballs fuck me."

The tips of his fingers began to tingle, and Logan had to fight back his need to claw something into shreds. "Are you listening to yourself? Did you hear what I just heard? You are not going to die tonight. I will not allow that to happen."

"For the Moon's sake, Logan, you're the one not listening to me. You. Don't. Have. A. Choice. This is over. There's nothing you can do. This is what's going to happen tonight. The pack will gather, I'll call the Howl, and one or more of the idiot males in my pack—who, by the way, couldn't lead a marching band, let alone my pack—will call for an Alpha Mating Rite, and I will kill any one of them who touches me. End of story."

Logan snarled viciously.

"Hey, maybe neither of us has enough faith, huh? Maybe I'll win the challenges, and it will be those sick bastards who die, not me."

He saw the way her lips twisted on that thought, and he knew she realized the truth, just as he did. If there was just one challenger, Honor could defeat him. Maybe even two. But if there were any more than that, or if two or more of them worked together to take her down, thinking they couldn't fight it out among themselves after she was defeated, Honor was doomed. As fierce as she was, as strong as she was, she was still a female. Nature just hadn't gifted her with the same musculature. In the end, a male Lupine would always be more powerful.

It took a moment to gain enough control so that he could manage speech. Even so, his jaw was clenched so tight, he couldn't be sure his lips even moved. Only the breeze blowing in off the lake kept him from spontaneously combusting.

"Why?" he demanded. "Why are you doing this? You have choices, Honor. You can walk away from this. You can leave, and make a life for yourself somewhere else."

Somewhere like Manhattan, he thought, but he didn't say it.

She almost smiled at him. "You know that's not true, and if you don't, you should. I can't just walk away. This is my pack. As sick and twisted and screwed up as it's turning out to be, it's still my pack. I know I've basically just told you that the job you came here to do is irrelevant, but if you're half as smart as I think you are—as I *know* you are—then you've already realized that there's no one in this pack who could lead it better than I can. Hell, there's no one else here who could lead it, not in the long term. If you named one of the males here as alpha, he'd lead the pack straight to hell. Within three years, maybe five if he's lucky, the White Paw Clan would be dead."

Of course he knew that. Hadn't he thought the very same thing himself? "Someone else could take over. I'd find someone."

"What? You mean you'd bring in an outsider? No way, and if you tried, I'd go after you myself." She stopped him when he tried to protest, speaking quietly over the rustling of branches. "No, Logan. I won't let it happen. I'm sure there are packless alphas out there who would be happy to take over our territory, and I'm sure there may even be some who could do it and even strengthen the pack, but they wouldn't be White Paw. Would some outsider know that the name White Paw comes from the founder of the pack, Stephen Tate, who settled here in 1687? Sure, he could find that stuff out, but would he bother?

"Would a stranger bother to find out that little Evie Stanton isn't named after her aunt Eva, like everyone assumes, but after her great-grandfather Evelyn Bright, who moved here from England after World War II because he discovered his mate was an American nurse stationed in Dover? More important than that, would he care?"

Logan opened his mouth to answer, but he never got the chance. The words were ripped right out of his mouth. By the force of the bullet that pierced his chest.

Honor screamed.

She couldn't help it. It was a stupid, dangerous, girly, childish reaction, but it escaped her

throat before she realized what was happening.
She saw the hideous bloom of red on her mate's
chest and the sound came out completely against
her will. It was instinct.

As was her next action, which was to leap forward and carry both her mate and herself to the
ground in case the shooter was still out there.
Draping herself across Logan's body, she turned
her head into the breeze and inhaled deeply. She
smelled pine and snow, lake water and soil,
the smoke of the dying fire inside the shack, but
she couldn't scent any enemies. Neither human
nor wolf scents drifted to her on the breeze, but
that didn't mean the trees were shooting at them;
it just meant that whoever had pulled the trigger
knew enough about his quarry that he'd made
very sure to stay downwind where Honor and
Logan wouldn't be able to detect him.

And that pointed to another Lupine.

Of course it did, Honor reasoned. Who else
would be shooting at them? She ruled out the
idea of a misguided hunter immediately. The pack
hadn't been troubled by those in years. The locals
knew enough about the "wildlife sanctuary" on
Tate land, and about the Tate family's rigorous
enforcement of the hunting ban on their property,
that hunters had given up prowling these woods
decades ago. Hunters didn't wander onto pack
lands, but pack members roamed it deliberately.

Besides, it wasn't like Honor didn't know that
certain members of her pack already had plans to

get her out of the way, and she didn't imagine Logan was much more popular with that contingent. If one of the males killed her and then Logan didn't support the usurper's claim to the position, he could bring the force of the Silverback Clan into play. Not even the world's biggest moron would wish that on himself.

No, the shooter had been pack. Honor was certain of it.

Her gaze scanned the tree line, searching for any sign of movement, but she found nothing. She strained her ears, but heard the same. That was when she realized that the occasional rustle and snap of twigs she had heard during her conversation with Logan hadn't come from branches moving in the breeze, or moles and other nocturnal critters moving in the forest; it had been the shooter making those small noises. The lack of a suspicious scent had lulled both her and Logan into a false sense of security.

As if responding to her thoughts, Logan groaned beneath her, and Honor cursed. Her mate had been shot, and she could smell the rich, metallic scent of his blood mixing with the earth as he lay still on the cold ground. Damn it! She needed to get him to shelter and see how bad the injury was. That meant going into the shack, which meant potentially exposing them to more gunfire.

Honor didn't have a choice.

She wasted a precious few seconds doing another aural and visual sweep of the surrounding woods. That plus several intense inhalations yielded nothing. If the shooter still lurked out there in the darkness, Honor couldn't tell. Time to move Logan inside.

Planning every move in her head beforehand let Honor follow through on her thoughts with maximum efficiency. She rolled off his body in the direction of the woods so that when she moved into a crouch, she kept her body between her mate and any lingering danger. It took every ounce of her considerably enhanced Lupine strength to lift the two-hundred-odd pounds of dead weight and maneuver him across the short distance to the shack. She did it at a dead run—well, a dead stagger, really—half laying and half dropping him onto the bed with a grunt. Her ears rang a little from the strain, but she knew she hadn't heard any further shots from the woods.

Maybe that was a good sign.

It took a second to light the hurricane lamp she kept on the cabinet, and one more to catch her breath, but she did that while she peered down at Logan's gunshot wound.

The bullet had pierced his chest just below his collarbone, tearing a hole in his shoulder, but missing his heart. Honor almost wept in relief when she realized he was still breathing, but she could see that he'd lost a lot of blood.

The shot had come from behind Honor, meaning the bullet had entered Logan from the front and left a gaping hole, but she'd watched enough television to know that exit wounds were generally more serious than entry wounds. She needed to roll him over and look at his back.

The bullet had left his shoulder almost directly across from where it had entered. She had no idea what that meant forensically with regard to the shooter, but she did know that at least there had been no vital organs, like the heart or lungs, directly in its path. That meant she needed to be most worried about blood vessels and blood loss.

Hands trembling, she pulled the sheet off the mattress and tore it into sections. She immediately folded one section into a thick pad and pressed it to the exit wound. She knelt next to him and used her body weight to apply pressure. That elicited a groan, but Logan didn't wake.

Honor really wished he would wake up.

Lupines had amazing healing powers. Things like minor cuts and bruises lasted barely more than minutes for them. Uncomplicated broken bones? A few hours. Some of it was probably linked to their freakishly rapid metabolisms. It stood to reason that they burned through fuel so fast because their bodies were constantly repairing and replacing cells. A good dose of magic likely helped the process as well, which was why Honor would be a lot less worried if Logan were conscious.

Something in the shifting process hated injury. An injury sustained in one form could be rapidly improved simply by shifting into another. Honor had always theorized that the magic tried to create a perfect version of the shifter at every change, so when the shifter was injured in one form, the magic tried to erase the injury during the transition to the other. It wasn't a perfect system. Serious injuries took more changes to heal, and some injuries could be made worse; for instance, a badly broken bone had to be straightened into the correct position, or there was a chance it would heal but remain deformed. Honor had never seen a Lupine heal a bullet wound, but she'd be very glad to see it now.

Until he came back to consciousness, though, Logan would retain his human shape. While shifters could and did occasionally shift in their sleep, unconsciousness caused by injury or illness worked differently. The trauma somehow cut off access to the part of the mind used in the shift, so the unconscious Lupine couldn't even be triggered by a large group shifting around him, or by a powerful alpha, as could sometimes otherwise happen. The wolf was trapped until the man woke.

Honor kept the pressure on the wound for ten minutes, counting silently in her head to distract herself until it was time to check for bleeding. It had slowed, but it took another ten minutes before it seemed to have stopped completely. She took a deep breath as she set the cloth aside and moved the lamp closer so she could examine the wound.

It looked angry, of course, dark and meaty and

just plain wrong. She could see the path carved by the bullet and the inflamed tissue surrounding it. Bits of metal appeared buried amid torn flesh, along with small pale flecks that she realized after a moment must be shards of bone carried along on the bullet's way through the body. It must not have missed the collarbone as completely as she had thought.

Cursing, Honor rose to grab the first-aid kit out of the cabinet beside the dry sink. Usually, she used it for removing splinters or bandaging up a cut that had gone particularly deep. Once, she'd even used the tape inside to make a splint for a young duckling with a broken wing, but she'd never really imagined she'd need it for a medical emergency. How often did werewolves have those?

She placed it on the bed beside Logan's hip and popped it open. Inside, she found a ton of useless Band-Aids, some totally inadequate alcohol wipes, and some individual human-dose packages of aspirin. As if that would help even if all he'd done was stub a toe. Thankfully, she also found a small, but unopened, bottle of hydrogen peroxide, a roll of gauze, surgical tape, thick absorbent pads, and a package containing a sterile pair of disposable plastic tweezers.

Honor took a deep breath, tore open the package, and adjusted the lamp once again, turning up the wick for a brighter light. Then she leaned forward and began to meticulously pick debris from her mate's open wound.

The work was slow and tedious, but necessary. While Lupine immune systems could do amazing things to fight off infection, leaving the metal and bone fragments in the wound would cause them to remain in place after he shifted and the wound closed. Shifter bodies hated foreign objects. The fragments would be pushed slowly to the surface through the healing tissue, both delaying the final healing process and causing pain until they finally broke the surface and could be removed. Better to deal with them now.

The wound had already begun to heal at the surface, necessitating that Honor occasionally dig and reopen an area to get at the shards of bone and bullet. She gritted her teeth every time she did it, praying she wasn't really hurting her mate. Not that she would mind the occasional moan or curse. The fact that he'd gone completely silent worried her more than if he'd woken up and tried to fight her off. She almost wished he would.

When she had removed all the material she could see, Honor slipped the tweezers back into their package and tossed the whole thing in the trash. She doused the wound in peroxide and used gauze and tape to fashion a bandage which she placed on top of another absorbent pad, just in case there was more bleeding. Then she turned her mate back over, cleaned the entrance wound with peroxide, and bandaged that as well.

By the time she sat back on her heels and

stretched to relieve some of the tension and sore-
ness in her back, she realized that the lamp had
ceased being necessary a long time ago. Judging by
the light pouring into the shack through the single
window, it had to be mid-morning at least. With
no other trouble since that single gunshot, she
imagined the shooter hadn't stuck around to assess
the damage.

On the one hand, the fact that the shooter fled
meant there was likely no imminent danger to
either herself or Logan. If the shooter had meant
to stay and finish them off, he could have done so
a hundred times over by now. On the other hand,
if he had fled immediately after pulling the trigger, the trail the shooter had left would be cold.
Honor could still follow it, of course—with her
nose, hiding it would be close to impossible—
but the time lapse would make it a bit more challenging.

Her feet itched to move. She wanted nothing
more than to spring into action. The urge to head
straight into the forest in the direction the bullet
had come from made her literally vibrate with
suppressed energy, but she couldn't do it. Just because she suspected the shooter had disappeared
didn't mean she felt anywhere near comfortable
leaving Logan alone. Not while he remained unconscious. Until he could shift and begin speed-
ing his own healing process, it was too big a risk
for her to go anywhere.

She knew she could summon help if she just

threw back her head and howled, but could she take the risk? Her cry would draw the attention of any Lupine within hearing range, but who knew what that would mean? Would the shooter return to finish the job? Would one of the males gunning for Honor's position in the pack hear and come first? It would be easy out here for them to take advantage of the opportunity to get rid of both her and the wounded Silverback interloper.

Right now, about the only people in the pack that Honor would trust to help her out of this situation were her uncle and Max. Joey would be useless in a crisis situation; she was too girly and squeamish to cope. Uncle Hamish loved her and had supported her from the beginning, and Max was a good kid, loyal to the pack, which to him meant the Tates, Honor included. Too bad there was no way to get to either of them without attracting the wrong kind of attention. Honor couldn't bring herself to leave Logan even for a few minutes, and it would take longer than that to find Hamish or Max. They could be anywhere in the territory. Logan would be too vulnerable without her.

And she was too vulnerable to keep standing out here in the open.

With a growl, Honor spun around and returned to the shack. Being cooped up inside while her wolf howled for action didn't exactly top her list of pleasant ways to spend the day, but at least she'd be able to keep a close eye on Logan. Within the cramped confines of the single room, there wasn't anything else to do.

Honor climbed onto the edge of the bed, careful not to disturb Logan. She wanted him awake, but causing pain wasn't how she wanted to see that happen. Resting one hand on his uninjured shoulder, she leaned back against the wall of the shack and prepared to wait.

Fifteen

The earsplitting screech of a barn owl jerked Honor out of a fitful doze. Boredom and stress had combined to weigh down her eyelids, and she'd found herself catnapping all afternoon. Every time she woke, her gaze flew straight to her mate, but Logan never stirred. For the last few hours, she had gradually begun shifting her mental state from concerned to slightly frantic. He should be awake by now.

The owl screeched again, the second call finally penetrating through Honor's haze of preoccupation. Owls didn't screech during the middle of the afternoon. They were nocturnal, sleeping during the day and not waking until dusk.

A panicked glance at the window had her leaping from the bed and swearing. While she'd been dozing, the day had slipped away. Dusk had fallen over the forest, and in minutes, the moon would begin to rise. As soon as it topped the trees, the Howl would begin. And if Honor wasn't there, she'd be labeled a rogue and a coward. The entire pack would hunt her down. She had to get to the stone yard. Fast.

But what could she do about Logan? Damn it, leaving him would be a risk, but she couldn't see any other choice. If she stayed, eventually the pack would find them, and then they'd both be in danger; if she left him here, at least the shack would provide some cover, and hopefully the Howl would keep the pack occupied and away from him.

She didn't really have a choice. She would just have to pray that if she didn't make it back to him, he would wake up before someone else found him.

With one last look at her injured mate, Honor exited the shack, stripped off her clothes, and shifted. Her gray form glinted briefly in the dying light, then bolted into the shadows of the tree trunks, and disappeared.

Honor reached the stone yard during that brief slice of darkness when the sun had fully set, but the moon had not yet risen from behind the cover of the trees. Still, her keen night vision allowed her to clearly see the figures, mostly remaining in their human forms, that milled around the clearing, waiting for the Howl to begin.

Howls held Lupine packs together. A Howl was a time to celebrate milestones, like births and matings, a chance to hunt together and revel in the magic that ran through every Lupine's blood, and the moment when power passed from hand to hand. All formal challenges for rank were settled at a Howl, whether the combatants ranked at the bottom of the pack or the top. At Howls, alphas were made, and no able-bodied member of the White Paw Clan would be likely to miss one.

Especially not this one.

Pausing at the edge of the trees to catch her breath—and to muster her courage—Honor sent up a brief prayer to the Moon Goddess who had breathed life into the first of her kind.

Silver Lady, she thought, closing her eyes and feeling the power of the rising full moon, *give me the strength to lead my pack into the future; but if I cannot, then give me the dignity to die in the attempt. And above all, please protect my mate from harm. No matter what my fate is, he deserves better than to be punished for my failings.*

As if in response, the first sliver of the pale moon rose above the dark expanse of the forest, but Honor knew better than to take that as a sign. The moon might be beautiful, but she could also be cold. One never knew which face she would decide to show.

The Lupines already in their furry forms yipped in excitement, and more of the ones still in skin began to remove their clothing. Using their distraction to add to her cover, Honor began to move toward the far side of the stone yard where the stump of an enormous ancient oak had served as a podium for generations of White Paw alphas. Tonight she would take her place on that platform; only the moon knew how long she would keep it.

She hugged the tree line, sticking to the shadows, as she circled closer. It wasn't so much that she feared what would happen if she were seen, as that she wanted to take every opportunity to survey the scene and arm herself with a good grasp on the assembled wolves. Most of them meant her no direct harm, but those who did needed to be watched.

A group of males loitering near the path from the main house caught her attention right away. She could make out the faces of Pete Scott and Greg Carpenter easily enough, but a third man stood with his back to her, and it wasn't until he took a step to his right that she spotted a fourth figure leaning arrogantly against a tree trunk. Darin Major—who apparently hadn't given up his ambitions, in spite of his close acquaintance with her mate's canine teeth—had his arms folded across his chest and an attitude of macho arrogance clinging to him like stale sweat.

Her lip curled involuntarily.

She had no doubt about her ability to defeat each one of those males in an honest challenge. As strong as they might be, she was no weakling, plus she had speed and agility on her side. Then there was the fact that not one of them had ever fought a real challenge before. The scuffles that had gained them their places in the pack as they reached adulthood had amounted to little more than a bullying of weaker males or showy wrestling matches that had more in common with pay-per-view cable than real battles for dominance. Honor should know; she had fought three real challenges just this week. She had won those, and she could win these.

Well, she could have, if any of the males had been inclined to fight fair. One at a time, none of them posed a challenge, but if they banded together, or demanded that she fight them in quick succession, she knew they would wear her down. They had strength in numbers, but Honor was on her own.

She looked away as she approached the oak stump. She could see her uncle and Max standing in front of it, almost as if they were saving her place. The thought almost made her smile. At least she knew she had two pack members on her side. Two was better than none.

Probably.

A flicker of movement drew her eyes to the far side of the stump, about halfway between it and the trees on the east side of the clearing. Joey stood there, slightly apart from a small group of females, some of the women she usually hung out with.

Okay, so maybe Honor had more than two pack members on her side. She didn't think any of the females would try to kill her tonight, either. None of them believed she was strong enough to defeat Honor Tate. But more than that, Honor couldn't imagine any of them being dumb enough to want to run the pack. Most of them realized what rough shape they were in, and they'd rather let someone else clean up the mess.

She didn't blame a single one of them.

As she moved around behind the stump and paused, Honor took a moment to say her good-byes. Even if she survived the coming battle—and she was too much of a pragmatist to plan on that—she realized that life as she knew it was ending. Either she would die on this ceremonial ground, or she could emerge the alpha of the White Paw Clan. At that point it would be too late to wish things were different, that her life were different, that someone else would take responsibility. Once Honor became the alpha, there would be no looking back.

She waited for a moment, until she heard the crackling sound that signaled the huge bonfire had been lit in the fire pit she'd been working on the morning after Logan's arrival. She took that as her cue.

Drawing in a single slow, deep breath, Honor closed her eyes and let the magic flow through her. When she opened them again, it was to step forward and climb atop the remains of the oak tree.

All talking stopped when the first Lupine spotted her. Honor knew she would be hard to miss. Not only was she standing in the spot reserved for the alpha of the White Paw, she was standing before her pack, tall and bare, her pale skin glowing in the light of the swiftly rising moon and the leaping, flickering flames. The nudity was the least of her concerns. Before long, the entire pack would be naked, because clothing never fared well during a shift. Being naked was natural for a Lupine; being a female alpha was not.

Well, fuck that, Honor thought as she lifted her chin and opened her mouth to speak.

"Brothers and sisters." She spoke clearly, lifting her voice to be heard even at the far edges of the stone yard. She was done with hiding, done with being doubted. She was alpha now, and her pack would listen. "Tonight we gather beneath the moon to mourn the passing of our leader. Ethan Tate led this pack with strength and courage for nearly four decades and for that we honor him. Raise your voices for our fallen brother!"

Throwing back her head, Honor opened her mouth and let her wolf sound the call. Sharp and mournful, her howl rose into the clear night sky, followed soon after by another, then another, then another, until the entire pack sang a Lupine dirge in memory of her father.

When the last note died, Honor opened her eyes and let the golden light of her beast shine out over the pack, reflecting the bright glow of the bonfire.

"And now," she said, her voice low and rumbling as if a growl struggled somewhere in her chest to be released, "let us do as Ethan Tate would do and move our pack forward into the future."

She paused for a second and caught her uncle's

eye, drawing deeply of his supportive strength. Max, too, watched her with calm dedication. She could do this, Honor told herself. She had to do this, because there was no one else.

"I, Honor Tate, the last surviving member of the alpha bloodline of the White Paw Clan, take for myself the place of alpha. This title is mine. This pack is mine. This territory is mine. Let anyone who would protest come forward and feel my wrath."

That, as the stories would one day say, was when all hell broke loose.

Logan fought in silence, struggling with all his strength against an enormous weight that pressed him down into a dark, suffocating fog. His limbs felt like granite and moving them even the slightest bit took every ounce of his strength. Something pinned him down, but he knew, he *knew* that he couldn't stay here. He knew something was wrong, something that he had to fix, to stop, to make right. Logan needed to wake, and he needed to do it now.

Consciousness returned on a rush of magic, not the kind that tickled just beneath his skin in the split second before his change, but that kind that rushed forth from a hundred Lupine throats, all raised to the sky in a flurry of song. A pack was calling. It wasn't precisely his pack, but it felt almost the same. It felt like they were calling out for something; it felt like they were calling him.

He sat up like a coiled-spring snake bursting from a can of nuts. Adrenaline coursed through his system, making his heart pump hard and fast and leaving him gasping. He felt as if he'd been underwater for too long, and now he sucked air frantically into oxygen-starved lungs. Wide-eyed, he took in his surroundings—the rough, bare walls, the spartan bunk, the moonlight shining in through the single window. For a moment, he felt panic rising. He had no idea where he was. Then Honor's face appeared in his mind, and the memories came rushing back.

Racing through the woods. Honor leading him to the cabin. Waking up to the mind-blowing sensation of her mouth on his flesh. Mating. Their argument. The gunshot.

His right hand flew to his injured left shoulder, feeling the rough texture of gauze beneath his fingertips. Clearly, his mate had stayed with him long enough to bandage his wound, so where was she now? Why had she left? Had she gone for help? That seemed a bit like overkill, given that she would know he'd begin recovering quickly the minute he woke enough to shift.

The still night air shattered under the impact of a Lupine battle cry, at least three—maybe four— males joining together to howl out their intent to kill. What followed was the most bone-chilling sound Logan had ever heard. A single female howled back, her call a lonely symphony of rage and violence and farewell.

Before the last note had sounded, a huge dark shape flung itself through the door of the cabin and into the woods, leaving behind nothing but a splintered panel of wood and a bloodstained bandage, glowing white and black in the silvery light of the moon.

Astonishment failed to overtake Honor when her four challengers stepped forward. Each man wore an identical expression of smirking arrogance, and each one stared at some point south of her face when they stopped a few feet in front of the oak stump to issue their challenge. They had their backs to the fire, but that didn't keep Honor from reading their expressions.

"I protest your claim, little girl." Darin spoke first, typically. He was neither the strongest, nor the most dominant male in his little group, but that didn't stop him from having the biggest mouth. "But I've got in mind to feel something a whole lot more interesting than your wrath, baby."

His leer would have been comical if it hadn't made Honor long so desperately for a shower. She said nothing, letting her curled lip and rumbling growl speak for her.

"I protest." Greg Carpenter stepped forward next, followed closely by Richard Maloni, the man whose face she hadn't seen earlier.

"Me, too," Maloni added eloquently.

"I protest, bitch." Peter Scott managed to combine his own leer with what Honor guessed was supposed to be a sneer. The mating of the two expressions ended up looking something like what she pictured on the faces of first-trimester pregnant women who'd been force-fed rancid sauerkraut, then taken for a rough-weather sailing trip.

"Your protests have been acknowledged," Hamish said, stepping up onto the stump beside his niece. It was the responsibility of the pack elders to ensure that any challenges were heard and settled according to pack law. "As this is an alpha challenge presented to a female claimant, you have the right to a choice of methods. You may select either—"

"We claim the option of the Alpha Mating Rite." Darin looked at Hamish and grinned with taunting menace. "Don't waste our time, old man. We're ready to get down to business. We got bitches to fuck."

"I hope you don't mind the cold," Honor snarled, "because you'll have to kill me and hump my corpse, Major. I wouldn't let you near me any other way."

Darin spat something vicious, but it was drowned out by the growls and barks of the other males. The crowd at the edges of the stone yard had gone eerily silent as the pack awaited the outcome of the challenges.

"Save your energy for the challenge circle," Hamish snapped. "You all know the parameters of the challenge. An Alpha Mating Rite has been

called. Having failed to win the unanimous support of the pack, the unmated female claimant
must now accept her strongest male challenger as
her mate. There will be no quarter given. If the
female is defeated while more than one challenger
still stands, the remaining males fight to the surrender or to the death for the right to mate her.

"Do you all understand?"

"I understand that your ass is mine, little girl,"
Darin threatened, licking his chops as he stared
at her exposed breasts.

"You'll be dead before you touch it."

Hamish extended his hand high overhead
and raised his voice to be heard over the growing
chorus of growls and snarls. "Let the Mating Rite
begin!"

His hand dropped, the male challengers surged
forward, uttering battle cries, and Honor flung
herself into the fray with a fierce howl, shifting in
the air like a molten gray nightmare.

Sixteen

The wolves jolted together in midair, two feral shapes made of claws and fangs and fury. The male, a dull, sandy-blond color, outweighed the female by at least thirty pounds, but she drew first blood, sinking her teeth into the meat of his side before they even hit the ground. The blond wolf screamed in pain and anger, landing in a crouch to snarl at his smaller opponent. She licked her chops, then made a loud hacking, gagging noise, as if she had tasted something that turned her stomach.

The male howled and surged forward. The female danced out of his reach and flicked her tail in disdain.

Honor had identified Darin as her attacker immediately. Even if she hadn't seen his wolf form a hundred times during her life, she would have recognized his stupidity. He had never learned to control his temper, which was one of the reasons she had known she could easily defeat him. When he was angry, what few brain cells he possessed began to shut off like a light switch. He wouldn't be the one to bring her down.

Quickly, she chanced a look at the other three. All had shifted and begun to spread out, clearly looking to surround her. She knew they would use Darin's impulsive assault to their advantage, letting him distract her and wear her down until they got themselves into position to attack her from behind. It was sneaky and something less than honorable, but it was a time-honored hunting technique among wolf packs. And it would probably prove to be effective, unless Honor found a way to counter it.

She knew her strengths and weaknesses. She would never match the males for size or power, but she was quick and agile and could move in ways they simply couldn't. Her best bet would be to stay out of reach and slip under their guard when the opportunity presented itself.

And, of course, to thin the pack.

A single glance had told her that Carpenter was the weakest link. He might have enough brains not to have gone for her immediately like Darin, but he was smaller than the other three, and younger. Inexperienced. He'd never had to fight for his life before. It was an advantage Honor could exploit.

She waited for Darin's next rush, held her ground until she could all but feel his breath in her face, then twisted to the side and launched herself at Carpenter's unguarded flank.

He never saw her coming. Her jaws opened,

teeth flashing white and deadly, and closed on his near hind leg, slicing through his hamstring and effectively hobbling him. That made one less wolf who could sneak up on her. If he stayed down, he'd heal eventually. He'd probably limp, but he'd heal.

Carpenter was made of stronger stuff than she had reckoned, though. Instead of immediately crumpling to the ground, he howled in pain, but then shifted his weight to his opposite leg and lunged for her.

She felt the graze of his fangs against her shoulder, felt the shock of pain as he opened a slice in her side, and yelped as she threw herself to the side. When he turned to come at her again, though, she was ready. He made the mistake so many men made and headed for her straight-on. Honor braced herself, then dropped into a crouch just before impact and threw back her head. Her jaws clamped around his throat and pulled using his own momentum against him. He was dead before he hit the ground.

A part of Honor mourned. The alpha in her hated to lose even a single member of her pack, but he hadn't left her a choice. In this moment, it came down to life or death, because Honor would sooner die than allow herself to be condemned to rape and a life mated to her rapist. No female on earth deserved that.

Maloni hit her next. He slammed into her like

a professional wrestler, knocking her to the earth and attempting to pin her beneath him. Allowing him to do so would doom her.

Honor squirmed like a freshly caught eel and managed to swing her back end free, giving herself the advantage of leverage. She shook hard and fast, while her rear paws dug into the earth and provided her with something solid to work against. The shaking kept Maloni from getting a good grip on the back of her neck, and bracing her back end meant that the minute he drew back to change his angle of attack, she was able to thrust herself to the side, out of his grasp.

He didn't let go easily, however. He lashed out with a large paw and caught her on the side of the head.

For a minute, her ear rang on that side, and she stumbled, temporarily off balance. Her eye stung, and when she shook her head, a drop of blood clouded her vision. Maloni's claws had been out. Honor might as well have engraved an invitation to the others.

Scott sprang forward, growling and snapping, a blur of motion and showy threats. He darted in, then retreated; danced to the side, and leaped forward again. He was trying to herd her. Honor knew what that meant.

She gathered her legs beneath her and jumped, carrying herself over Scott's head just as she felt the rush of energy attacking from the rear.

Darin missed, his howl of rage echoing through

the clearing, but Honor had bigger things to worry about. She had reduced her number of attackers from four to three, which was good for her, but she'd been clumsy, and she'd let herself be injured. Neither the slash on her shoulder or the claw mark on the side of her face was serious, but every wound weakened her, something she couldn't afford while she remained outnumbered.

She had to be careful.

She knew her chances of living through this weren't great, but she'd be damned if she didn't take at least one more of them with her.

Logan had known what that sound meant the instant he heard it. He'd slept the day away while his mate's pack prepared to slaughter her. The Howl had begun.

He raced through the forest at top speed, ignoring the insistent pain in his left shoulder. He knew he couldn't cover ground as fast as he normally did, but he also knew the wound would already have begun to heal the minute he shifted. Now, it just had to hold up and help him reach his mate.

The sounds drifting toward him from the direction of the stone yard only served to confirm what that first group of howls had told him; the males had called for an Alpha Mating Rite. Honor currently faced at least three males intent on beating her into submission, raping her, and holding her captive for the rest of her life.

Logan would burn down this entire forest before he allowed that to happen.

He didn't know these woods as well as a native, but the sounds of the battle currently being waged in the stone yard allowed him to ignore the trails and paths he occasionally crossed and move through the trees straight toward the ruckus. He didn't have to waste time trying to remember the way, because the sound of his mate fighting for her life guided him like a satellite readout exactly where he needed to go.

He knew he was getting close to the stone yard not just from the volume of the battle sounds, but because he could begin to see the glow of firelight illuminating the space between the tree trunks. When he could finally see into the clearing of the ceremonial meeting place, his instincts urged him not to hesitate. His wolf smelled blood, some of it his mate's blood, and it wanted death.

The man inside him, however, hauled hard on the reins of his self-control and urged him to assess the situation. The scent of Honor's blood nearly disappeared under a much larger volume belonging to someone else. His mate might be injured, but it didn't smell like it was serious. Someone else smelled like he was dead.

A surge of pride rushed through him, and Logan paused, hidden in the underbrush, to catch his breath. He could see into the clearing from here, and while tree trunks and branches obscured some of the view, he could make out enough to know that the situation looked just as he'd feared. His mate was surrounded by three much larger males and was holding them off like a modern-day Boadicea.

Then she maneuvered to the side and he caught a glimpse of the bloody wound on her shoulder. His control nearly snapped like a cheap pencil. Only the sight of a bloody lump of fur and flesh lying still a few feet away from her kept him sane. He hoped that was the asshole who had dared to lay a finger on Logan's mate. That made four initial challengers, and Honor had already killed one.

That's my girl.

His girl circled her attackers warily. She tried to keep all of them in sight, but with three against one, it was too easy for them to split up and divide her focus. While he watched, the gray one began to harry her, like a terrier with a rat, distracting her from the blond wolf behind her, who was preparing to pounce.

Before he could move, Honor detected the trap and sprang forward, which the gray wolf had not been expecting. She soared over his head, evading the blond's attack and making him howl with rage. He and a wolf with dark, sooty fur converged on her like buzzards.

Logan had seen enough.

Damn the rules and damn tradition and damn the male chauvinists who had made them. That was Logan's mate, and he would not stand by and watch her be destroyed.

He burst through the trees in a dark blur of motion, headed straight toward the closest of Honor's challengers, the gray male she'd left behind, confused. Logan had the element of surprise on his side, and within a fraction of a second, he also had the back of the gray wolf's neck between his teeth. Biting down powerfully and shaking like a wet dog, he broke the male's neck with a snap and an echoing growl.

There went the element of surprise.

Actually, it accomplished one more thing; it drew the attention of every single Lupine in the clearing, including Honor's two attackers. She used their distraction to dodge their concerted attack and put some distance between them.

Logan moved immediately to her side and nuzzled her gently. She answered his whine with a quick swipe of her tongue. She had bled, but her wounds weren't serious. She would be fine.

But the battle wasn't over.

A few feet away, the blond wolf began to twitch and grunt, a prelude to him rising on his back legs, growing four and a half feet, and taking the shape of the wolf-man of Hollywood legend. He had shifted into his were form, one that provided him with the basic, guttural power of speech.

"Violator!" the werewolf roared, his voice broken and rasping and unnatural to all but a

Lupine ear. "No one but a challenger may enter the battle. Who is this interloper?"

Behind the blond, the other male began to shift as well, taking on the towering seven-foot muscularity of a mature werewolf. Logan responded to the threatening gesture in kind. The bullet wound in his shoulder protested loudly, but he ignored it.

"She is my mate," he snarled, the words hard to form with his face still bearing a pointed muzzle not designed for speech. "Touch her again and die."

The darker male leaned forward and sniffed. "Silverback! You are no part of this pack. You have no rights here. Leave, or you will be slaughtered like a common trespasser."

At his side, Honor shifted as well. Maybe she had been feeling left out? Now they all wore their were forms.

"If you attempt to harm my mate, I will tear out your throat, just like I tore out little Greggie's," she growled, her lip curling in contempt. "What's wrong, Richard? Are you not such a big, bad wolf when the odds even out?"

The four of them faced off for a long, tense moment, waiting to see who would make the first move, but it was Hamish's voice that broke the silence.

"Richard Maloni is correct," the elder called out from his place atop the oak stump platform. "Only a member of the pack may participate in the Alpha Mating Rite. You have no authority here, Logan Hunter. You must step aside and allow the Rite to continue."

Logan turned on Hamish with a howl of rage. "I won't stand by while another male attempts to claim my mate. She is mine!"

Shocked whispers began to rumble through the assembled pack members. Until that moment, they had remained still and silent while they watched the battle rage.

"As beta of the Silverback Clan, you should know that only a member of the pack in question can claim an unmated female alpha."

"Then I renounce my ties to the Silverback alpha and petition for entry into the White Paw Clan."

"He can't do that," Richard said, his rumbling were voice managing something like triumph. "No lone wolves can join the pack until the matter of the alpha has been settled."

Honor gave a low growl. "Then let's settle it," she said, and took the dark male werewolf to the ground.

Chaos erupted.

The pack, seemingly jolted awake by the news that Honor had mated the inquisitive intruder from the Silverback Clan, now exploded in a cacophony of screams, shouts, and howls, none of which penetrated the fury clouding Honor's mind. Fighting for her life had been one thing, but now that her mate's life had been threatened—for the second time in twenty-four hours—Honor knew that threat had to die, and die quickly.

Her move had caught Maloni totally off guard. The battle had stopped for the discussion as if someone had hit the pause button, but he knew the rules just as well as Honor did—there were no breaks in a Mating Rite. Her attack might have been sneaky, but it was in no way illegal. Maloni should have kept his guard up.

She knew the surprise wouldn't keep him down for long, so she had to make this fast. Even while she was moving through the air, she was lifting her legs so that she impacted him first with her heels against his chest. At the same time, she bent forward and grasped his head between her hands. Using his own momentum against him, she twisted her upper body hard to the side just before they hit the ground. She rolled away just after the sound of the second neck of the night snapping in two filled the clearing.

Honor staggered a little as she got to her feet. She had taken out the third challenger, but she had landed on her injured shoulder, tearing open what the shift to her were form had begun to heal and nearly wrenching the joint out of its socket. She was nearing the end of her strength, but only one challenger remained, and her mate had entered the fray and vowed to protect her. Maybe she really would live through the night.

She knew that Logan would do everything he could to protect her, no matter what the rules of the Mating Rite said. When he had claimed her as his mate, he had made a commitment to her, she realized, and he would honor that before everything else. If he had to tear her pack down to its foundations, he would do it in order to keep her safe. And Logan could do it, too. He was the strongest Lupine that Honor had ever met.

While the pack shifted and murmured around the edge of the clearing, Honor drew her shoulders back and began making her way to her mate's side. She had started out this night determined to become alpha of the White Paw Clan, but it had just occurred to her that maybe she could become something even better, provided her mate agreed with her plan.

"Cheater!" Darin's whining accusation interrupted her train of thought. "She attacked another wolf during his weakest moment. She had no honor! I demand an Alpha Challenge, here and now!"

Oh, come on, Honor thought. Was this guy serious?

Hamish shook his head. "You already called for an Alpha Mating Rite, Darin Major. You cannot have both. You can either finish what you have started, or you can show your belly to the female and acknowledge her as your alpha."

"Actually, I believe that's my decision," a new voice said as a tall male figure stepped out of the forest and into the glow of the bonfire light. He had thick, dark hair, a frankly impressive physique, and absolutely no clothes on. The last bit was what marked him as Lupine.

Or a nudist, but in this neck of the woods in the middle of the winter, which sounded more likely?

"Graham!"

Logan said the name as if he'd just been punched in the stomach, which was about how Honor felt when she realized that the stranger in their midst was none other than the alpha of the Silverback Clan.

Logan quickly shifted back into his human form, and Honor followed suit. Into her birthday suit.

"What are you doing here?" Logan asked.

Graham Winters looked at his beta and curled his lip. "Three days. Three days of unreturned phone calls and unanswered voice mails, and you ask me what I'm doing here? I'm checking to make sure you're not dead, you son of a bitch!" The alpha paused and peered at Logan's shoulder. "Is that a fucking gunshot wound?"

"Well, yeah, but it's getting better. A few more shifts, and I bet you won't even notice it."

Hamish cleared his throat. "Graham Winters," he said, making certain his voice carried around the clearing. "Normally you would be welcomed to our territory by the alpha of the White Paw Clan, but I'm afraid you've caught us while that matter was being decided."

"Is that right?" Graham continued to stare at Logan. "And here I thought that who should be alpha of this pack was what I had sent my beta to Connecticut to decide."

"The right to be alpha is decided by a show of strength," Darin interjected, reclaiming the attention of those who had frankly forgotten about him. "I've challenged Honor Tate to fight me for that right."

"And I already explained to you, boy, that you can't issue an Alpha Challenge after you already chose to invoke the Alpha Mating Rite. It's one or the other." Hamish scowled down at the whiny werewolf. "Either finish the Mating Rite battle, or acknowledge Honor as your alpha."

"And this is where you came in," Honor pointed out.

"This is also where I said that as alpha over this entire region, I am actually the one who decides who will be alpha," Graham said, clearly forcing the words out through clenched teeth. "I'm just waiting for my beta to inform me of his decision in that matter."

"No, I demand the challenge!"

Fed up at last, Honor threw her hands in the air and rounded on the repetitive troublemaker. "You just don't get it, do you, Darin? The battle is over, but no one has officially won. Graham Winters is the overalpha of our pack, and he's going to install the next White Paw alpha. If you don't like it, feel free to leave, but if you don't shut up about the damned challenge, I'd be happy to prove to you exactly why that next alpha is not going to be you. Understand?"

Darin surprised all of them, maybe even including himself, by throwing himself straight at Honor.

It wasn't a fair fight, and unlike Honor's earlier surprise attack, was completely against the rules. In human form, Honor lacked the weapons to fight back.

So Logan did it for her.

Shifting just the fingers of his right hand, Logan reached out and drew his claws in a bloody line across the werewolf's abdomen. It was an impressive move, since only the most powerful alpha Lupines had the ability to selectively shift like that. If she hadn't been busy shifting into her own were form, Honor might have taken a moment to stare in awe.

Darin spun away from the blow that had given Honor just enough time to level the playing field. Acting on pure instinct, she turned into his spin and used her own claws to open up the large arteries in his neck. He bled out into the slushy remains of the challenge circle.

"No! I won't have it!"

The shrill cry took Honor by surprise, but not nearly as much as the small form of the woman who launched herself into the circle toward Logan, shifting as she went.

By the time she landed atop him, Joey Tate

wore her were form, which was nearly six feet as opposed to her normal five feet three inches. Her body had bulked up with muscle and wore a covering of sandy-gray fur. Her face had elongated into a muzzle full of razor-sharp teeth; the claws at the ends of her fingers sliced cleanly through Logan's skin and into the muscle beneath. He howled in shock, but it was Honor who howled in rage.

Immediately she leaped for her cousin's back, tearing her off the form of her fallen mate and wrestling the other female to the floor. Joey fought back fiercely, her usually dull green eyes glowing with the fire of madness. She squirmed like a serpent, wriggling out of Honor's grasp and launching herself once again at Logan.

Honor roared in anger and grabbed her cousin by the ankle, her claws biting deep into the furry limb and drawing enough blood to mat the hair with sticky red fluid. Joey yelped in pain, but she didn't turn away from her target. She lunged, and if Honor hadn't pulled her up short by the grip on her ankle, she would have sunk her sharp teeth deeply into Logan's human throat.

Dragging Joey away, Honor threw her several feet across the clearing and leaped atop her, securing the smaller Lupine's hands beside her head, her powerful body pinning the woman's legs as well. Joey might have been spurred on by some rage of her own, but she was really no match for an alpha female, and Honor held her easily.

A moment later, she found herself holding thin air as Joey shifted back into her human form and slipped out of her cousin's grip to curl up in a fetal position and sob piteously.

"Not supposed to be this way," she moaned, tugging at her disheveled hair and rocking back and forth. "Darin. Darin should be alpha. Then I'm Luna. I get to make the rules and that slut of a cousin gets to do what I tell her to do. That's what's supposed to happen."

Stunned to her toes, Honor fell back onto her haunches, shifting as she went. She landed buck naked in the trampled slush, her bottom making an embarrassing squish on impact. She was too busy trying to fit the fragments of her reality back together to notice.

"Joey, what are you saying?" she asked. "Are you telling me that you and Darin conspired to take over the pack? What were you going to do? Were you planning to have him challenge me? Because I don't know if you were watching what just happened here, but what Darin actually did was challenge for the chance to be my mate."

"NO!" Joey screamed and launched herself at Honor. "No! Darin loves me! Not everyone in the world loves you better than me! Some of them love me better. Darin loves me better. He does!"

Honor just shook her head as Logan plucked Joey out of the air inches from her throat and pinned her hands behind her back. "She's out of her mind."

"Yeah, I'd say that's a safe bet." Graham watched as Joey dissolved again into tears, collapsing bonelessly in Logan's firm grip.

"Here, give her to me," Hamish said gruffly. He stripped off his shirt and quickly fashioned a rope to bind the woman's wrists.

"I can't believe we didn't see it before." Honor shook her head and let Logan help her to her feet. "I lived in the same house with her. How could I not have realized she was insane?"

"Because you don't remember her mother." The look on Hamish's face spoke of regret and resignation. "Marie was just the same. Sweet as pie one minute, and coming at you with a carving knife the next. When I first heard that Joseph was dead, I honestly thought that she had snapped and killed him. It took five minutes for it to sink in that it had been an accident that killed them both."

Honor frowned at him. "And you never bothered to tell me about this? Uncle Ham, this pack is my responsibility. I deserved to know if there was a danger they needed to be protected from."

"I'm sorry, sweetheart, but I could never be certain about Josephine. She was better than her mama at hiding it."

Graham growled, an impatient sound that refused to be ignored. "As touching as this family moment might be, it doesn't solve the problem of what becomes of this woman. A nonchallenge attack on another Lupine with the intent to kill is a death sentence. But it seems a little cruel to do that to someone not in her right mind."

"Well, we can't just put her in an institution, can we?" Logan frowned. "It would be worse than a death sentence. I mean, one full moon, one shift, and she'd either be in a lab somewhere being vivisected, or she'd be killed outright as a monster."

"Not a human institution, no, but maybe I can talk to Rafe's mate. When Tess's grandfather snapped, the Witches' Council had to find someplace to put him. That means that there must be someplace where she can be confined to keep her from hurting anyone, but where they'd be sympathetic to what she is."

"So that's where you'll send her."

"*I* can't send her anywhere," Graham said pointedly. "It's up to the alpha of her pack to make those decisions, which means that it has now become even more important that this pack get an alpha. So for the last time, who is the rightful alpha of the White Paw Clan?"

"There's no question," Logan said, his deep voice steady and firm. "This is Honor's pack, and she is more than able to run it as she sees fit."

Honor nearly fell over sideways. What on earth was the idiot talking about?

Drawing back his shoulders, Logan met her gaze, then shifted his up over her left shoulder in a sign of respect to a dominant Lupine. "And it's

my hope that you will grant your mate the honor
of lending you any assistance you might need in
the course of your duties."

If it hadn't been for Graham's outraged roar,
Honor figured the sound of her jaw dropping
would have echoed through the forest like thun-
der. "You what?"

Logan clenched his jaw and drew a deep
breath. "I hope you will grant your mate, grant
me, the honor—"

"No, I heard you, you idiot. I meant what the
hell are you talking about? I'm not going to be
running this pack. You're going to tell the Silverback that I'm not fit to be alpha—which I'm really not, by the way . . . Okay, so I'm fit, but I've
realized I don't really *want* to be the alpha, so it's
really the same thing, isn't it? And then we're going to go back to Manhattan where you can be
beta of your own pack and I can maybe actually
get a life for the first time in forever. And then
I can concentrate on continuing to be madly in
love with you and giving you mind-blowing sex
at least twice a day." She shrugged and smiled. "I
had it all worked out."

Logan was shaking his head before she made
it to "idiot," and he didn't stop when she did.
"No. You don't understand." He met her eyes,
this time, his own golden ones soft and warm like
aged whiskey. "I have it all worked out. I'm going
to tell Graham that I'm resigning my place as his

beta and leaving the Silverback Clan. I'm going to move up to Connecticut, because this place is your home, and these folks are your family. We have to live here. You'll run the pack and I'll take care of the things you don't have the stomach to do, and we'd get to be together, being madly in love and having mind-blowing sex at least three or four times a day. It's a great plan. I had it all worked out."

"Did either of you even consider sharing either of these lamebrained plans with me?" Graham bit out.

The honk of a car horn prevented them from answering.

Honor, Logan, and Hamish—along with the entirety of the pack, Honor presumed—all turned to look for the source of the noise, but Graham just closed his eyes, tilted his head back, and groaned. A dark-colored SUV pulled to a stop along the rough trail that led down from the house, and the driver's-side door popped open to reveal a small blond woman with ample curves and a sweet expression on her pretty face.

"Well, he's obviously alive and well, Graham," the woman said, smiling at Logan. "So why didn't you come back to the house and get me?"

"Missy, why would I come back to the house to get you when I specifically told you to turn the truck around and get you and Roarke safely back to the city?"

The Silverback alpha sounded as if he'd asked this sort of question before and didn't expect to like the answer.

This time, he didn't get an answer at all. The woman just turned to Honor and smiled.

"Hello. I assume you are the new alpha of the White Paw Clan. I bring greetings from your cousins in Manhattan, the Silverback Clan. My name is Melissa Winters, but I hope you will agree to call me Missy." She offered the formal greeting, and gestured to the glowering male next to her. "Graham, of course, is my mate."

The mate in question sighed. "We were in the middle of discussing who would be alpha of this pack when you interrupted us, Missy. And by the way, where's the baby?"

"Roarke the Wreck is in the car, of course, still strapped into his car seat, and hopefully sleeping like a lamb. For a change. Now what was this about still not knowing who should be alpha?"

"I didn't say I didn't know," Graham growled, "I just said we were still discussing it."

"What is there to discuss?"

"I was just telling Graham that I would be leaving the pack and moving here to Connecticut," Logan said calmly. "I'm resigning my position as beta, because Honor is my mate, and my place is by her side. As her Sol."

Honor stared at Logan for a long minute. Her mind had been well and truly boggled. This man, this amazing man she'd fallen in love with faster than a lightning strike, was willing to give up his entire life. To make himself submissive to her for the rest of his days, just because he thought it would make her happy. The very idea made her so happy she almost cried. "But you can't do it," she told him.

Logan scowled at her. "Why not?"

"Because it would make me miserable." Honor laughed, feeling honestly happy and free for the first time in years. "I don't want to be the alpha. I never did. That's why I came up with my plan. Being beta was all well and good, but alpha is too much. It's too much responsibility. It takes too much time. It doesn't leave any of me left for the things I love doing, like running in the woods and having mind-blowing sex." She smiled and wrapped her arms around him. "My plan is much better. I leave the White Paw clan and move to Manhattan with you. It allows for me to not be alpha, you to be with your friends, and still leaves lots of time for the mind-blowing sex."

"Clearly a well-thought-out plan." Missy laughed.

Graham cleared his throat. "But I have a better one."

Heads all around the clearing turned to look at the Silverback alpha.

Missy's eyes narrowed. "I don't think they need another plan, Graham. It sounds like they have the situation all worked out."

"Not to my satisfaction," he replied. "It's not

that I dislike the spirit of Honor's plan. I just feel it fails to address a couple of key points. Namely, that the White Paw Clan would continue to lack an alpha, which I would then have to appoint. And also that if Logan has to spend one more week reporting to me—or to anyone at all, I'm pretty sure—he's going to end up hurting someone. I'd just as soon it not wind up being me."

Logan frowned. "What are you talking about? I have never been anything but loyal to you, brother. You ought to know that."

"Oh, I know it. I've never doubted it, but somewhere along the line I've lost the right to ask loyalty of you, brother." Graham held up a hand when Logan would have protested. "Shut up and listen, because if you find this news surprising, you're even dumber than I've always said you were. You've outgrown your place in the Silverback Clan, Logan Hunter. You can no longer be beta to anyone. Which is part of why your plan sucked. You're alpha, brother, and it's time you took your place at the head of a pack."

Logan shook his head. "No. I won't. I'm not challenging you, Graham. It's never going to happen, so just—"

Honor smiled and smacked Logan hard across the chest. She had a feeling she knew what was coming, and Logan was right—his idea was better. "You really are dumber than he's always said you were. Logan, shut up for a minute and listen to what the man is telling you."

Graham shot her a grin that almost made Honor understand why Missy had shackled herself to the head of an entire region of Lupines. "Thanks, Honor. As I was saying, I think my plan is the best of the three. In it, I will accept Honor's decision to step down as alpha of the White Paw Clan. I will then announce that I have chosen a new alpha for this pack by the name of Logan Hunter. Any challenges will be swiftly and, I'm sure, successfully dealt with, and Missy, and I will return to the city, where we will proceed to have mind-blowing sex."

Missy blushed, but winked at her mate. "Yeah, I think I like this plan best of all, too."

Logan finally broke into a grin, actually throwing back his head and laughing. "I only like it if Honor and I can have the mind-blowing sex, too. No way are you guys getting to have all the fun."

"Well, okay," Graham teased, "but you can't have any more mind-blowing sex than we do. You will, after all, still owe fealty to me, even if you will be an independent alpha."

Honor laughed with the others, jumping a little when a large hand tapped her on the shoulder. She turned her head to see her uncle Hamish standing behind her, grinning.

"Well?" he said, bushy eyebrows quirking. "What do you say we get the formalities out of the way?"

Logan draped his arm over his mate's shoulder. "I say, let's roll."

"With your permission, alpha?" Hamish nodded to Graham.

"By all means, elder."

Taking Honor and Logan each by the hand, Hamish led them to the center of the oak stump and stood between them facing the pack members still filling the clearing.

"Challenge has been made and answered," he said, his voice ringing with satisfaction. "The Goddess and the alpha of the region have spoken, and a new chapter has begun for the White Paw Clan. From this day forward, you will follow Logan Hunter as your alpha. This title, this pack, and this territory are his, and Honor Tate shall stand as his Luna by his side. To the White Paw."

Every single Lupine in the clearing threw back his head and howled.

Honor felt her heart expand until she wondered whether her body could hold it. Everything she had ever dreamed of, everything she had believed she would never be able to have was suddenly within her grasp. Her pack had an alpha who she knew would restore them to the strength and honor that had slipped from their grasp, and best of all, that alpha was someone named Not Her. She had a mate by her side who alternately fascinated and infuriated her, one who would stand by her side during her greatest trials and give her just enough grief to keep her on her toes. All the threats to herself and her pack had been removed, and the future had become something to anticipate with excitement rather than resignation.

Could life get any better?

When Logan turned to smile at her and lowered his mouth to hers, Honor got the answer to her question.

Oh, yes. Life could get better, and it would, with every minute spent by her mate's side.

Read on for an excerpt from
Christine Warren's next book

HEART OF STONE

Coming soon from St. Martin's Paperbacks

He had slept for so long that he had nearly forgotten what the world sounded like.

Centuries of frozen immobility had lulled him into a kind of trance, where the cares of the mortal world washed by him like the babbling of a stream, barely teasing the edges of his unconscious mind. If danger had presented itself, real danger, the kind he had been created to battle against, he knew the magic that allowed his slumber would have allowed a swift reawakening. Guardians, after all, were useless when they couldn't be relied upon to instantly counter any threat. But for hundreds upon hundreds of years, the world had buzzed along safely, a tacit reassurance that he and his brethren had done their jobs thoroughly and well. Evil had remained at bay. That had not changed.

Everything else had.

He didn't remember the day he had come to this particular place, this stone terrace poised atop a small garden, the large house to his side, and the incessant backdrop of noise, both mechanical and human. By the time he had come here, he had moved so many times and so far from his original post in the center of France that he had ceased to keep so close an eye on his whereabouts. He would know if the threat he guarded against had stirred, and nowhere in his journeys had even the faintest whiff of threat pierced his slumber. The world had rested at peace while he had rested in eternal readiness.

Now, however, something must have changed.

The fog of sleep had ebbed and flowed around him for some time now, how long he couldn't say, but lately something had cut through it. A voice. A scent. The disturbing presence of one particular human. The woman.

He couldn't remember when she had first begun to appear at the edges of his consciousness, but he would never forget the sudden rush of awareness he'd felt when she'd first laid her small hand on his stony skin. One minute he'd been dozing, and the next he'd felt life flood through him as if a bolt of lightning had struck directly into his chest.

Since that moment, he had watched her. He knew when she came near, as if she carried that electrical charge with her wherever she went, rousing him from his slumber just enough to stare through the stony film over his eyes and see her moving about his domain.

Sometimes, she would pause in front of him and gaze up into his fierce, carved features and speak of him. At least, he thought she spoke of him. She told the humans that he had come from France by way of England, purchased at an auction by a wealthy man who lived north of the city. She said he had been carved from limestone, but of course she couldn't know how he and his brethren had been made all those centuries ago. If he had noticed one thing over the years, it was that the longer he existed, the fewer humans seemed to understand the magic that permeated their world. It made them even more vulnerable than they had been when the Guardians had last faced down a threat to their continued survival.

Like lambs milling at the edge of the forest, easy prey to any creature with claws and teeth.

He couldn't recall the last time he had seen a human working magic. Being frozen in place didn't give him the opportunity to see more than a small sampling of them, and often only the young ones, but he had seen not a spark of power in any of them, not in an age.

Until tonight.

He had felt her gaze on him, a warmth that soaked into his stony skin like a beam of sunlight. She stood for a few minutes watching him, as she often did when she came into his presence, and as always, something about her pulled him from the depths into the shallower pool of his slumber. Sometimes, she spoke directly to him, much of it nonsense about the troubles of her day, but this time she said nothing.

Still, he could feel her presence, her warmth,

the soft curve of her hip as it pressed against the side of his foot, her shoulder brushing up against his lower leg. She felt so fragile, so human, that it took a moment for his sluggish mind to process that she also felt like magic.

It hummed softly, almost imperceptibly in the background all around her, like a halo of static electricity. It sparked against his stony skin wherever she touched him, and he wondered how he could have missed it all the other times she had been near him. Magic hated to be contained. Like sunlight, it would seek out the smallest crack and crevice, the thinnest barrier, and beat relentlessly against it until it inevitably found its way through.

Adrenaline rushed through him.

Invigorated, he began to struggle in earnest. Something was happening, something significant, and this human woman appeared to be the cause. He wanted to know why. His slumber should have lasted until and unless the threat he had been created to counter had stirred. Kees felt no indications that any such thing had happened, so why did he appear to be waking now? Why here? And why did this human seem to hold the key to finding the answers?

His human grew more intriguing by the minute.

And he grew closer to breaking free.

His human stirred, shifted as if to rise, and the magic coursed through him like an electric current, lighting every nerve ending with fierce en-

ergy. She was the source, and he couldn't let her
leave until he discovered how.

One moment he crouched poised on his pedes-
tal, frozen in the same position he had occupied
for more than a thousand years, and the next, he
and the human stood in unison, stretching to
their full heights, his even fuller due to the three
feet of slate beneath his talons. She rose in a
nearly silent shift of cloth, but after so long in his
fixed pose, Kees heard the crack of stone as he
lifted himself to his feet.

His human heard it, too.

He saw the exact instant the sound and movement registered. She froze in place, her back to
him, her every muscle tensing with the rush of primal awareness that signaled danger was near. He
intended her no harm, but her instincts wouldn't
know that. To them, something huge and fanged
and supernatural had just stepped into their or-
bit. Even before she turned and saw him, Kees
knew that the most basic, animal portion of her
brain would be screaming at her to run. Fight or
flight, and even the electrical and chemical im-
pulses in her brain possessed enough intelligence
to know that against him, to fight would be futile.

Her only chance for survival, her instincts
would tell her, was to run. Now.

She hesitated just a fraction too long.

With a shift and a flex of muscles long unused,
Kees gave his wings half a beat and launched
himself into the air above her head, landing easily

a few feet in front of her. For the first time he saw her face with no veil between them. Her features were soft and even, her lips bow-shaped, her eyes wide and gray with no hint of blue or green to muddle their purity. And in that moment, they stared at him in pure, frozen terror.

Lifting a hand, he stepped forward. "I won't hurt you."